THE BIRTHDAY PRESENT

London, 1890. Singer Rose Paton is confident that, with her looks, youth, and talent, she's destined for greater things. But when mysterious stranger Marcus Bennley asks her to sing at his sister's birthday party, as his present to her, she accepts for the half a guinea (more than two weeks) wages. But will the deal be quite so sweet as promised, or has Rose made a terrible mistake entangling herself with the Bennleys?

Pamela Oldfield titles available from
Severn House Large Print

Henry's Women
Summer Lightning
Jack's Shadow
Full Circle
Loving and Losing
Fateful Voyage
The Longest Road
The Fairfax Legacy
Truth Will Out

THE BIRTHDAY PRESENT

Pamela Oldfield

Severn House Large Print
London & New York

This first large print edition published 2011
in Great Britain and the USA by
SEVERN HOUSE PUBLISHERS LTD of
9-15 High Street, Sutton, Surrey, SM1 1DF.
First world regular print edition published 2009 by
Severn House Publishers Ltd., London and New York.

British Library Cataloguing in Publication Data

Oldfield, Pamela.
  The birthday present.
  1. Women singers--Fiction. 2. Tuberculosis--Patients--
  Fiction. 3. Large type books.
  I. Title
  823.9'14-dc22

  ISBN-13: 978-0-7278-7973-8

Severn House Publishers support The Forest Stewardship
Council [FSC], the leading international forest certification
organisation. All our titles that are printed on Greenpeace-
approved FSC-certified paper carry the FSC logo.

MIX
Paper from
responsible sources
FSC
www.fsc.org   FSC® C018575

Printed and bound in Great Britain by the
MPG Books Group, Bodmin, Cornwall.

One

Outside the rear door of The White Horse, just after ten p.m., a small bedraggled crowd waited to see the so-called 'stars' as they left to go home – second-rate performers who were billed as star attractions. Those waiting clutched autograph books, others not so fortunate waved the flimsy leaflets that told would-be customers how they might be entertained while they downed their choice of drinks. The performers could hardly be considered sophisticated but they some-times brightened dreary lives and some went as far as to ask for a signature.

The night air was tinged a dismal yellow as a thin, smoky mist drifted through the narrow streets of Stoke Newington and rob-bed the gas light of its power. As the nearby church clock struck the quarter the waiting group shuffled impatiently, books and pen-cils at the ready. There were three young women eager to see Harry Hampson, who advertised himself as 'the monologue man' and who was young and almost handsome.

There were also two older women, one with a husband in tow, who wanted to add the comedian's name to their collection of autographs – and there was a very young, very shabby pickpocket in boots that were too large for him. He was lurking among them, trying to look innocent but failing miserably.

At the back of these people, and slightly apart from them, was a tall, slim man of indeterminate age, with an intense expression on his face. He looked out of place and embarrassed, which he was, but he was determined to stay there until he achieved his aim. An elderly dog wandered up, the result of very mixed parentage. It sniffed enquiringly at his trouser turn-ups and he pushed it away irritably but not unkindly.

The door opened at last and the monologue man emerged to excited cries and, smiling broadly at each of the three younger women, he signed his name with the flourish he had perfected over the years.

One of the women said, 'Ooh, thanks ever so, Mr Hampson!'

Her friend said, 'My ma calls you Mr Handsome!' and was rewarded with a wink.

Not to be outdone, the third asked him if he had written the monologues himself.

''Fraid not, my dear,' he told her. 'I'm a performer, not a writer.'

They watched him stride away, his rolled umbrella held jauntily over his shoulder. Then, giggling like conspirators, they hurried away in the other direction.

The comedian came out next but he was no longer in a mood to make anyone laugh, thinking only of the hot mutton pie he would buy at the stall on his way home and the bottle of beer which waited beside the sink in his tiny attic room. He snatched up whatever was held out to him, scribbled something illegible and walked quickly away. He hadn't said a word.

The women muttered, making no attempt to hide their irritation, and followed him at a distance until at the corner their ways divided. Only the pickpocket remained. Marcus Bennley eyed him sternly. 'Don't you dare!' he warned.

'What?' The tone was full of offended innocence as he peered out from beneath the ragged brim of his greasy cap. 'I never done nothing!'

'Then hop it!'

'It's a free country!' He shrugged his thin shoulders.

At that moment a police constable appeared at the end of the road and walked stolidly towards them, his hands clasped loosely behind his back. He was a credit to the force with his helmet properly secured by its chin strap, his buttons and belt gleaming and his boots well polished.

'This tocrag bothering you, sir?' he asked when he was within speaking distance. The constable was tall, ruddy-faced and clean-shaven but not particularly brawny.

'No–o. I think he was just leaving.' Marcus gave the boy a warning glance and he took the hint and ambled away, followed by the dog which reappeared from nowhere and attached itself to him.

Now the policeman rubbed his hands together and settled for a chat. 'Weather turned a bit cooler, sir. Hardly summery, is it?' He frowned at the unhealthy air. 'Muggy, I call it. Bad for the lungs.'

'Yes. Not very pleasant, I agree.'

'Waiting for Miss Lamore, are you? She's always last.'

'Er ... Yes, I suppose I am.'

'Miss Love. That's what it means. Lamore.' He pointed to the printed poster on the door. The words 'Also starring Miss Lamore' had been added in ink. He smiled, proud of his knowledge of French.

'Then it's not spelled correctly. It should be L' a, m, o, u, r.'

'Ah!' He hesitated, then nodded. 'I thought so. Still, lovely little voice, so they say.'

'So I've heard.'

'You haven't heard her, then? Sings a few popular ballads when she can leave her father. He's in a bit of a state, so she tells me. Poor old boy. Lungs ... or it might be legs. I forget. Or both. My wife says I'll forget my own head one of these days!' He grinned. 'Mind you, my memory's all right when it

8

comes to villains. I never forget a face – leastways not a villain's face. I'm known for it. And his walk. That's another giveaway. If a known villain walked towards me with a sack over his head, I'd know him and he'd be down the nick in no time! Likewise the...'

'I'm sure that's useful in your line of work.' The polite reply failed to hide a definite hint of indifference.

'Certainly is, sir. Very useful.' Disappointed, the constable changed the subject. 'But Miss Lamore's a nice little thing. She reminds me of my wife – same blonde hair. I usually see her part of the way home. Miss Lamore, that is, not my wife. It's on my beat, you see, and this is hardly a salubrious area. Not in my nature to let a young woman wander the streets alone if I can be of help.' He tried to look modest but in the deepening gloom it was a wasted effort.

'Yes.'

'Friend of hers, are you?'

'No.'

'After her autograph?'

'Certainly not.'

The constable's eyed narrowed. 'Then why are you here, Mr...?'

'Marcus Bennley.'

'Well, Mr Bennley, it's getting late. Odd time for a gentleman like you to be wandering these back streets without a good reason.'

'It's ... private.'

9

'Private, is it? In that case...'

The door opened and 'Rosie Lamore – The Nation's Favourite' came out. From beneath the hem of her coat the pink satin frills and ribbons of her stage costume showed and the shoes that dangled from her right hand were pink satin with kitten heels and a buttoned ankle strap.

Rose glanced up and said, 'PC Stump! How are you?' She was disappointed that there were no giggling fans waiting for her autograph, but hid it behind a bright smile.

The constable beamed. 'I'm fine, Miss Lamore. And your good self?'

'I'll survive!' She looked at the man standing with the constable. 'I hope he hasn't arrested you! He'll have you banged up in no time if you've stepped over the line! You pinch a hot pie off a window sill and he'll have you!' She drew an imaginary blade across her throat, laughing so that her fair curls danced around her pretty face. She watched the stranger to make sure he was taking notice of her charms. Youth, good looks and a passable voice were all she had to offer but she hoped she had made the most of them.

PC Stump beamed, pleased to be portrayed as a tough and ruthless upholder of the law, but the man hesitated. He had an earnest face, Rose thought, reasonably nice looking with brown hair, and he wore an expensive coat and smart shoes. He smelled expensive, she thought. Probably his shaving soap. Hardly the 'stage door Johnny' type, though. There was something odd about him but she couldn't decide what it was – possibly his rather nervous manner. Starchy. Yes, that was it.

Rose told him, 'PC Stump has a wife and baby and is expecting another baby any day now.'

The constable beamed. 'I don't know how I shall take to being a father twice over.' He laughed self-consciously, then nodded towards the waiting man. 'This is Mr Bennley. He's waiting for you, Miss Lamorc. Something private, he says.'

'Really?' She smiled at Marcus. 'What is it?' When he hesitated she added, 'Do tell!'

He glanced pointedly at the constable who stood firm but Rose said, 'Would you mind walking on a bit, PC Stump? I'll catch you up in a bit.'

He rolled his eyes but gave a nod and strolled away at a leisurely pace, his hands clasped once more behind his back.

When he had gone about twenty yards she said, 'Let's get something straight right off, Mr Bentley. I'm not one of *those* girls in case you—'

'No!' His eyes widened in embarrassment. She had shocked him. 'No. Of course not! And it's Bennley, not Bentley.'

'So—o?'

Recovering quickly, he said, 'Look here,

11

I'm Marcus Bennley. I have a younger sister, Marie, who is really quite ill but she has a birthday next week and will be seventeen. I want you to sing your songs at her birthday party to cheer her up because she's not able to get out and about.' The words came out in a rush and it sounded to Rose as if he had learned it by heart.

He had a nice voice, she noticed, and he spoke like a gentleman but Rose had heard the catch in his voice. 'That's bad luck, that is,' she told him. 'About your sister, I mean. Lungs, is it?'

'Lungs? Yes.'

'London lungs they call it. All the soot from the chimneys. There's a lot of it about. Always is. My pa's not so hot. Cough, cough, coughing. Can't work. Not properly, just part-time, not to mention his wonky hip.'

'I'm sorry to hear that.'

Rose did not think that he looked very sorry but, if the truth were told, she did sometimes wonder if Pa was swinging the lead. She said, 'So you want me to come and sing to your sister? Well, I might be able to but...' She thought about it, vaguely suspicious. You heard such dreadful things, sometimes. It could be a put-up job to lure her somewhere. She wavered, longing to accept but fearful. She had never been asked to perform privately before and was unsure about it. It was either a useful step up the

12

ladder to fame ... or else the top of the slippery slope which led gullible girls down into the gutter. 'I've got other work booked, here and there...' she said uncertainly.

He took a deep breath. 'I'll pay you half a guinea and you'll have a taxi to take you there. There'll be food and drink and you'll be welcomed as my guest.'

Half a guinea! This was sounding better, she thought. All those lovely shillings! She could do a lot with half a guinea. Still, better act a bit dubious, she told herself. Mustn't seem too eager. 'Will your parents be there?' she asked primly, by way of delaying tactics.

'I doubt it. My parents divorced some years ago and—'

It was Rose's turn to be shocked. *A divorce!* Heavens above! She stared at him, trying to hide her reaction. She had never met anyone who had been divorced and this man was related to such a couple.

'And then he ... my father, died. My mother married a second time. A French man. She lives with him in France.'

'Ah!' Mother lives with a foreigner, she thought warily. You could never trust them – or so her father insisted. Although, if she were to become an international star like Marie Lloyd she would have to travel abroad. To delay her decision she asked, 'So where d'you live, Mr Bennley? I live with my pa in Albert Street, five minutes from here. My real name's Rose Paton. I call myself

13

Rosie Lamore because it sounds more glamorous. D'you think it sounds glamorous?' She put her head on one side and gave him a saucy sideways glance which she believed enhanced her undoubted charms.

He appeared unmoved, however, and by way of answer, pulled a wallet from his coat pocket, selected a small card and held it out. Hiding her frustration, Rose took it and stepped closer to the street lamp to peer at the name and address. 'Belview Road? Never heard of it!'

'It's in Kensington. The family home.' He returned the wallet to his coat pocket. 'It will be a small affair – myself, an older sister and Marie, of course. My younger brother Steven might be there.'

'What about your wife?' That, she thought, was a clever way of finding out this man's situation. If he had a wife it would be easier to trust him.

'I'm not married.'

Had she detected a hint of regret in the words, she wondered. She was finding him a rather tough nut to crack, she acknowledged, disappointed. She was accustomed to a better response to her feminine wiles but Mr Bennley seemed unaware of them. She fluttered her eyelashes. 'And all I have to do is sing and I get to eat and drink and you give me half a guinea and a ride in a taxi? Cross your heart and hope to die?'

'Exactly. Yes.'

At the corner of the road the constable waited, watching them.

'All right. I'll do it.' She tossed her hair. Why not? It was worth the risk. 'But I shall tell PC Stump where you live – just in case there's any funny business. He'll know where to find you!' She smiled to take the sting out of her words, and wondered if the policeman was jealous of their cosy little chat. PC Stump was a nice man, she thought wistfully. It was a shame he was married. Being married to a policeman would be a nice safe feeling. 'Number twenty-three Albert Street,' she reminded him. 'You'd better write it down for the taxi man. When is this – and what time?'

'Next Thursday at seven thirty. That's the 12th. I've written it on the back of the card.'

She turned the card over and when she looked up again, he was halfway down the street without so much as a 'Goodbye'!

Put out by his lack of manners she shouted 'And goodnight to you, Mr Bennley!'

He swung round. 'Oh! Yes. Sorry!' He walked on.

Mortified, she stuck out her tongue at his retreating back. 'Walk away. See if I care. Walk out of my life, why don't you! Who gives a button!' So what if he was rich and single? She didn't fancy him. A pity. She sighed.

Turning back, she saw that a young lad with a mangy dog had suddenly appeared

15

and he was grinning from ear to ear. He held up a wallet which she assumed belonged to Mr Bennley. 'Nice work if you can get it!' he said, poised for flight.

'You artful little wretch!' she cried and tried to grab him but he dodged her out-stretched hands, stuck out his tongue and clattered off down the nearest alley pursued by the dog, and both were immediately lost to sight.

Albert Street was no worse and no better than any other in the area. It was narrow and lacked the young plane trees that adorned some better class streets and the terraced houses were small and depressingly similar, each with an apology for a front garden, and no gate. The brickwork was grimed with soot from London's many chimneys and the bay windows were mostly hung with thick lace curtains to deter the curious passer-by. The window sills, however, and the front door steps were regularly scrubbed and the whitening block applied and some of the tenants took the trouble to polish the knock-ers. The door of number twenty-three was dark green but the paint was beginning to flake away and the small brass letterbox flap had not been cleaned since Rose's mother died. There was a rain-sodden mat on the step and a scraper for mud which was rarely used.

Rose arrived home and, noticing none of

the defects, let herself into the narrow hall-way. She was greeted by the familiar sound of a dripping tap in the scullery, her father's snoring and the stale smell of fried onions mixed with damp wallpaper and dust. She tossed her shoes on to a chair in the front room and found her father asleep in the ancient rocking chair in the living room – the chair that had once belonged to Annie, his wife, but which he had now claimed as his.

Alan Paton was small and thin and Annie had often compared him to a whippet. She had cast her daughter as a curly white poodle and herself as an overweight spaniel. She had been dead for nearly two years but Rose still missed her and so did Alan but somehow they muddled on without her and Rose did her best to keep her father cheer-ful. He had been forcibly retired from his job as a docker after an accident had damaged his hip and rendered him unable to perform the heavy lifting work. He had partially recovered from the accident but was now forced to earn when and where he could which currently meant a few hours each week behind the bar of The White Horse, pulling pints and earning a pittance for his efforts.

This, with his occasional win on the horses, plus the money Rose earned with her singing, and occasional ironing, was all they had to live on but she had learned frugal ways from her mother. They fancied themselves a little better off than some of their neighbours since they had rarely been forced to rely on the pawnbroker and had so far managed to keep the bailiffs at bay.

Her father's mouth was open and he was snoring and Rose let him sleep on while she searched the cupboard for something to make into a sandwich for their late supper. Slicing thin Cheddar cheese and spreading pickles, she made a pot of tea and finally woke him.

'So how'd it go, Rosie?' he asked automatically, already anticipating her usual answer – a reluctant 'Fine, Pa' followed by a few small grumbles.

'Fine, Pa.' Settling herself on the floor beside his chair she demanded, 'Guess what?'

'No idea.'

'Take a guess, Pa.'

He shook his head, still heavy with sleep. 'I give up!' and took a bite of the sandwich she had thrust into his hand.

'Take a guess!' She glared at him, determined to make the most of her dramatic news.

'You saw the man in the moon!' He chuckled at his own joke.

'Pa! You always say that!' She turned to look up at him, her eyes shining. 'This posh bloke was waiting for me outside the stage door and he's asked me to go to this posh

18

place in Kensington and sing for his sister's party because she's ill and can't get out and about. He's going to pay me half a guinea for my trouble and I can have some of the food and stuff so I'll try and smuggle something out for you.' Elated by his gasp of surprise, Rose also bit into the cheese and pickle.

'Half a guinea? You're pulling my leg, girl! No one's going to—'

'But he said he would and he gave me this.' She handed him the card. 'Marcus Bennley. That's what it says and that's his name.'

'Michael Bennley?'

'Marcus, not Michael.'

Alan had never been any good at reading and he was thoroughly confused by the small print. 'If you say so, Rosie, but I would not get your hopes up. I mean, half a guinea for a few songs and you're not even famous. You're not even nearly famous. I mean of course you're good but you only sing in a public house, not a real theatre or a music hall.'

'But I will, Pa. I'm not famous yet, I grant you, but I'm only young.'

'That's as may be but believe you me, Rosie, there's some very dodgy men around and this one luring you with money sounds fishy. You want to watch it. That's my advice.' He took another bite and chewed noisily. He was coming round from his doze and now looked marginally more alive than dead. 'Give it a bit more thought, Rosie.'

'There's nothing to think about! It's an offer of work and ... and it might get me some more private work. Don't you want me to earn a half guinea?'

'Depends how you earn it.'

She should have known, she thought irritably, half convinced by his argument. Whoever would believe that someone would promise someone like her half a guinea? That was two weeks' wages for some men. But Mr Bennley *had* promised it. She had the card to prove it. But on the other hand a man could *say* anything and not really mean it. The first real doubt slithered into her mind.

Her father said, 'Any more where that came from?' meaning the sandwich.

Rose shook her head. 'But we'll be eating cake next week, Pa!' If Mr Bennley was genuine. 'He sounds genuine. He's sending a taxi to collect me and take me to the house.'

Still unhappy about the offer, he shook his head. 'A taxi could take you anywhere, Rosie. You just watch out.'

Finishing her sandwich, she washed it down with the tea, but the harsh realities of life were beginning to depress her. Maybe her father was right and she had been taken for a mug. She knew the sort of things that went on in London. A pretty girl could be sold into slavery and smuggled out to far-off countries and never seen again. She didn't want to be one of them.

She thought back to the moment she met him. 'PC Stump was there, Pa. I mean, he wouldn't dare say all that in front of a policeman, would he, if he wasn't genuine, because if I disappeared PC Stump would remember him and he'd describe him to the detectives and they'd catch him.'

'Wouldn't do you much good, though, would it, if you was already stowed in the hold of a ship on the high seas or buried six feet under? Bit late for you then.'

Frowning, Rose tried to recall exactly what had happened outside the back door of The White Horse. The truth was, she realized with a jolt, that PC Stump had *not* heard Mr Bennley's offer because she had asked him to move on and give them some privacy. How stupid she had been! All the constable could do was describe the man and Bennley would deny everything.

Climbing to her feet, she collected her father's empty mug and took it, with her own, into the scullery to rinse them under the tap.

'You stupid girl!' she told herself crossly. It was vanity. Pure vanity, to believe that anyone thought she was worth half a guinea to dress up in a frilly little number, rouge her cheeks, redden her lips and sing a few songs. Serve her right. She had got her come-uppance! Coming to an instant decision, Rose marched back into the living room.

'That's it then, Pa. I'm not going. I don't want his money. When the taxi comes I'll send it back and say I've changed my mind ... Or you can go out and tell the taxi driver I'm ill.'

Instead of being pleased, however, Alan now regarded her doubtfully. 'Shouldn't you let him know? He'll be promising his sister this lovely surprise and then she'll be disappointed and everything.'

Rose groaned. 'What, write him a letter? Oh Lord!'

'Why not? You can write good enough and you've got the address on that bit of card. Tell you what – write that your pa won't let you go. That'll put an end to it.'

She nodded reluctantly, wishing that she had never met the wretched man and had never heard about his sick sister. 'First thing in the morning,' she promised and made her way upstairs to bed.

The first down to breakfast next morning in Victoria House in Belview Road was twenty-year-old Steven Bennley, who helped himself to eggs and bacon from the sideboard and sat in his usual seat facing the large windows and staring straight into the luxuriant leaves of the aspidistra which stood alone on a small highly polished table. He wore a loose fitting shirt tucked into his trousers and his feet were bare.

Steven pushed the food into his mouth

without enjoying it because he had matters to worry about which weighed on his spirits. He had looked forward to the thought of leaving school and becoming independent but he was now realizing that having a good time meant having money to spend. Like his brother and two sisters, he received a small income from the money his grandparents had left them, but for Steven it was proving woefully inadequate.

Halfway through his meal he was joined by his older brother Marcus who nodded in his direction but didn't speak. While he helped himself to porridge and cream Steven watched him.

'You were late back last night, Marcus,' he said at last. 'I heard you come in. Out with a young lady, were you?' He grinned.

'I was, actually. In a way.' He sat down, poured himself a cup of tea, and Steven passed the sugar bowl.

'You were?'

'Yes.'

A woman appeared in the doorway and said, 'Two pigs at the trough!' Letitia was twenty-five, two years younger than Marcus – dark-haired with a permanently anxious expression.

Marcus ignored her.

Steven scowled. 'Good morning, Letitia. Charming as ever!'

She sat down and poured herself a cup of tea but made no attempt to eat. 'Doesn't anyone want to know how the tennis match went yesterday?'

Steven put his knife and fork together and pushed his plate away. 'No we don't but I expect you'll tell us.'

Her expression changed. 'I was Bernard's partner and we won!' She glanced at Marcus.

'Well done.' He gave her a brief smile.

'Then we picnicked on their lawn – champagne, cold lobster, everything perfect. The da Silvas really know how to entertain.'

Casually Steven asked, 'Was Janetta there?'

'Yes she was. She came with her friend Jack. They seemed very close.' She turned to him. 'If you hadn't been such a boor last time, you might have been included. Then you'd have seen Janetta again. It's your own fault.'

'And if you weren't such a spiteful cat you wouldn't remind me! I got a bit tiddly, that's all.' He raked his fingers through his smooth blond hair. 'It's not a crime, for God's sake!'

Steven's handsome face was spoilt by his expression and Letitia gloated. 'I must say she looked relieved when they said you hadn't been invited. And of course you're not much good at tennis, are you? You don't take it seriously. I keep telling you it's not a game, it's a sport.'

'I can play a decent game when I'm in the mood. Not that it's a patch on cricket. That's a game with some depth requiring hand to eye coordination, not to mention team spirit and a certain style. Anyone can hit a ball over a net.'

'Except you, obviously!'

Growing tired of the exchange, Marcus said, 'I've invited someone to Marie's party. It's a surprise for her.'

They stopped sniping and stared at him. Letitia said, 'You've done *what*?'

He went on, 'She sings. Popular ballads. Rosie Lamore. That's her name.'

Steven laughed. 'L'amour as in 'love'? She sounds more like a harlot than a singer!'

'Well she's not a harlot!'

'You'd recognize one, would you, Marcus?'

Letitia's mouth tightened disapprovingly. 'Who said you could invite her, Marcus?'

'I don't see a need to ask permission. To make it simple – Rosie Lamore and her songs are my birthday present to Marie.'

There was a stunned silence.

Steven said, 'But who ... that is, how did you discover this Lamore woman?'

'I heard a man talking about her on the train last week and asked him for details. He said how good she was and lively ... and funny. "A breath of fresh air!" That's how he described her.'

'Oh my God!' Steven rolled his eyes. 'I've always thought you were a little mad but now I'm certain of it! Asking her here because of some Herbert you met on a train!'

Steven and Letitia exchanged worried

glances. Marcus closeted in the study working, busy with his stage designs, was one thing. That they understood. He was talented and he earned reasonable money with which to supplement his small income. They were used to their brother's hermit-like existence. Shy, awkward Marcus taking the initiative like this was a new phenomenon.

Steven recovered first. 'So you wrote to her – is that it?'

'No. I waited for her outside The White Horse in Stoke Newington. I asked and she said "Yes". She's very pretty and cheerful – and while we were talking a boy stole my wallet. I had to report it at the police station.'

'Ah! So that's why you were late home!' Steven felt vaguely relieved. His brother had reverted to type, he thought. Being robbed of his wallet was much more in character.

Marcus nodded.

Letitia also rallied. Too late to protest, she decided – it was a *fait accompli*. Not that she wanted to object. In fact, she wished she had thought of the idea. Marie would be delighted. She smiled grudgingly at her brother. 'Well done, Marcus!'

'Yes. Thank you.'

Steven asked how much he had lost with the theft of his wallet.

'Three pounds, eleven shillings and threepence. It doesn't matter.' Marcus shrugged.

His brother frowned. 'What do you know

about this person, Marcus? She could be anyone. She could be a fraud. I hope you haven't given her any money in advance.'

'I haven't.'

'I bet you've overpaid her!'

'That's my business.'

'I bet you've given her the fare.'

'No. I shall fetch her by taxi and I shall tell Marie she's coming because that way she will have something to look forward to as well as enjoying the actual performance.'

'How is she getting home?' Letitia asked. 'It will be late by the time the party ends. Sure to be past midnight.'

Disconcerted, it was Marcus's turn to frown. 'I hadn't thought about it,' he admitted. 'At a pinch she could sleep in the spare bedroom, couldn't she?'

'I suppose so. You'll have to ask Mrs Bray to make up the bed for her.' Letitia turned to Steven and gave him a challenging look. 'And you mustn't spoil it by getting drunk.'

'Get drunk? Me? As if I would do anything to let the side down! Let's hope *you* don't get drunk! That would be a shock for poor Bernard!'

'Don't be so ridiculous.' She rolled her eyes despairingly. 'What are you giving Marie for her birthday?'

'I ... I haven't quite made up my mind but I haven't forgotten it.' Guiltily Steven avoided her gaze.

She pounced triumphantly. 'You fibber!

You haven't done anything about it because you only ever think about yourself!'

'So? What have you done that's so wonderful?'

'I've invited four people from the tennis club because—'

'Oh no!' he cried, wrinkling his face with exaggerated dismay. 'Not that toffee-nosed set! Why bring them into it?'

Letitia flushed. Her younger brother never missed an opportunity to tease her about her aspirations. Her engagement to Bernard da Silva, whose family connections placed them a little higher on the social scale, was a source of fierce pride to her. Ignoring the jibe she went on. 'Because it mustn't be just any old party. Not just the family. Bernard is coming, naturally. He's bringing her an enormous box of chocolate violets which she adores and a bottle of champagne!' Her smile returned. 'His mother says a woman cannot drink too much champagne! It soothes the nerves and brightens the complexion.'

Steven spluttered with laughter. 'Brightens the complexion? Has she got a red nose, this da Silva woman?'

Letitia gave him a withering look. 'D'you know, Steven, I sometimes feel that you left school too early. You're twenty but so immature! So depressingly gauche. No wonder Janetta isn't interested in you. She doesn't appreciate schoolboy humour. Jack is a year

28

younger than you but much more sophisticated.' While he struggled for a suitable reply, and failed, Letitia turned back to Marcus. 'This time it has to be a real party with a special cake – Mrs Bray has made one and just has to decorate it ... And dancing – Mrs Bray's cousin is going to play for us.'

Steven frowned. 'Will Marie be able to dance? She's very weak.'

Marcus said, 'I'll carry her round – she's as light as a feather. We'll manage.'

Letitia ignored the interruption. 'Marie must have real guests. Your singer will count as a guest, Marcus, and Mrs Bray's daughter Cicely can come. Cicely's about the same age as Marie so they'll have lots in common ... and Cicely can bring a friend. Marie must have a wonderful time. Something she can always remember and ... oh!' She clasped a hand over her mouth and regarded the others unhappily, stricken by the slip. Because they all knew the doctor's verdict. Marie would have such a short time to live – such a very short time to remember anything at all.

That same day, Rose watched her father wipe his plate with what was left of his bread, and knew exactly what he would say.

He swallowed it, sat back and patted his stomach. 'That's better!'

Rose collected the plates and piled them in the sink. Sausage and mashed potatoes. Alan

29

Paton loved them. He also loved 'a bit of haddock', a meat pie, mutton stew and shepherd's pie. He didn't like anything green such as cabbage, or what he called 'fiddling things' like peas or beans. So whatever he had was accompanied by mashed potatoes. It made life easier for Rose who had no complaints about their unimaginative diet.

Sundays they followed a familiar routine – Yorkshire pudding with gravy, meat and potatoes followed by Yorkshire pudding with jam. Unless it was a special occasion when she made a rice pudding and then they took turns to scrape the dish for the crispy bits along the rim. Rosie told herself that when, if, she ever married and left him alone he could manage not to starve. The pie man would call twice a week, the fish man once, and for a few pence, the lady next door would bring him a dinner.

Not that Rose had any immediate plans to marry for the simple reason that, although she had plenty of admirers, she had set her heart on a singing career and fancied becoming a success on the London stage. This was going to take up all her energies and there would be no time for a husband or a child. Eventually, of course, she would be wooed by someone exciting and the newspapers would be fighting for details of the romance.

Her father glanced up. 'So you've written

this letter, have you? To this Michael Bennley? Best let me see it.'

'Why?' She laughed good-naturedly. 'You can't spell for toffee, Pa. You know you can't. You tell everyone that spelling's a waste of time and effort.' She ran the cold tap and rubbed at the plates with a cloth, then did the same with the cutlery, the saucepan and lastly the frying pan. 'And it's Marcus, not Michael.'

'What does it matter if you're not going?'

In fact, Rose had not written the letter and she didn't know why. Every time she thought about the lost opportunity, her mind rebelled. She wanted to go ahead but she knew her father had a point. Climbing into a taxi with a strange man was risky. And Mr Bennley was slightly odd. In a decent man that would be acceptable but in a stranger, being odd was not. It increased the chances of him being 'a wrong 'un'.

Her father had closed his eyes and was already preparing to doze off. An unlovely sight, she thought as she spread two worn blankets on the table and added a worn sheet. The irons were heating in front of the fire and it was already stifling hot in the small living room. To one side, high up, there was a water tank. There were four upright chairs and a sofa which sometimes acted as an extra bed. At the moment it supported a wooden tub full of Mrs Braithwaite's laundry – two sheets, two pillowslips,

31

a shirt, a pair of trousers, a blouse, a skirt, a pair of pyjamas, a sprigged nightdress and a wrap-around pinafore. Mrs Braithwaite lived in the end house of the terrace and her husband had a job with the railway which meant she could afford, from time to time, to have her washing ironed. It also allowed her to put on airs and graces.

Rose folded the first sheet to make ironing it easier and took up the first flat iron. As she ironed, she tried to decide what she would write to Mr Bennley and how she would spell the words.

'Dear Sir, I have chainged my mind...'

No, that was no good. She would invent a better reason.

'Dear Sir, I canot come to your sisters party because ... my father has taken a turn for the wurst...'

But she hadn't told Mr Bennley that her father was ill and he would smell a rat – not that it mattered if she was never going to see him again.

Alan Paton began to snore and Rose began to feel hard done to. Why couldn't she go to the party and earn herself half a guinea? It was unfair of Pa to expect her to give up such a chance. A party with food and drink. There might be champagne. And she looked so pretty in her costume. And they would all admire her singing and the men might wink at her. She would probably be the star of the evening and Marie would be dazzled by her.

Rose finished the first sheet and prepared the second and the idea came to her out of the blue. She would write the letter but she wouldn't actually post it and her father would never know. Rose would tell him it must have got lost in the post ... and then the taxi would arrive and her father would have to give in. She would have her costume ready, of course, and off they would go. Afterwards, when she arrived home safe and sound, she would buy her father some tobacco for his pipe and maybe a big bag of pear drops, which he loved.

Later that afternoon the letter was finished and her father made her read it out.

Rose cleared her throat.

Dear Sir, My father has been taken very poorly and I fear a chainge for the wurst. So I canot come to your party and am very sorry. Yours faithfully Miss Rosie Lamore. Pee Ess. I hope you have a lovely time.

He frowned. 'Pee Ess? What's all that?'

'I don't really know but it's when you think of something you've forgotten.'

'Well, you've done that letter a treat, Rosie. Now get off to the pillar box before it's too late.'

Dutifully she hurried off but as soon as she was out of sight of home she tore both letter and envelope into shreds and dropped them into the first dustbin she came to.

33

On her way back she was shocked to discover that her conscience was not pricking her and she thought that promising.

Half an hour after Rose had left for her Saturday night spot at The White Horse, there were three slow knocks on the door of number twenty-three Albert Street and Alan struggled to his feet and limped along the passage to open the door.

Through the letterbox a voice said, 'It's me, Baby.'

Alan nodded. He already knew who it would be – his friend Baby Price. He was small and shapeless with a large beer belly and today bulging pockets added to his ungainly bulk. Rose had often wondered how he managed to balance on his small feet. According to the laws of gravity, she thought, he should keep toppling over.

'Is Rose in?' Baby asked cautiously.

'No. She's off singing, bless her. Come on in, Baby!' said Alan. 'And scrape the mud off your shoes. Last time I got it in the ear from Rose for the mess you traipsed in.'

His visitor obeyed, then wiped his shabby shoes with exaggerated care on the worn mat before following Alan along the hall and into the living room. He lowered himself carefully on to a hard-backed chair and waited. Despite the limp, Alan then climbed on a chair to retrieve the rolled up sack which he kept hidden on top of the water tank where his daughter would never notice it.

'Got much?' Alan asked. The usual question.

Baby shook his head mournfully. His round, cherubic face and innocent blue eyes had earned him the nickname which made it hard for strangers to believe anything bad about him. Alan – his friend and erstwhile accomplice in a large number of burglaries – watched as Baby emptied his jacket pockets, setting each object on the table with an unhappy shake of his head.

'Wallet – not half bad,' he said, 'but the ruddy thing's got initials on it ... pearl earrings left behind in a pub ... a couple of silver tea spoons, don't ask...' He grinned as he produced a ring, set with a delicate opal. 'Old Chalky, remember him? This is his wife's, no less! He said she was always losing it, so now she's lost it for good! Poor cow's probably looking everywhere for the damned thing!'

Both men laughed while Baby felt in his trouser pocket and produced the last item – a silver snuff box decorated with gold leaf. 'Know that big house at the end of Elm Tree Avenue? We done it once before a few years back.'

Alan nodded, turning the box over in his hands. Of course he remembered. He remembered every job he'd ever done. 'Number thirty-one, Elm Tree Avenue ...

35

that was a piece of cake!' He smiled wistfully. He'd got in through a back window and let Baby in at the back door. No way the fat Baby could ever get through a window! They'd done well from that house – candlesticks, a miniature, several leather-bound books and a clock. In and out in less than ten minutes! They were good together, him and Baby. No doubt about that, until the missus got wind of their antics and put her foot down. Women! Not that it stopped them but it cramped their style ... and then they were nicked and that was it. Alan sighed as he ran his fingers over the carefully wrought design. A lovely snuff box. Worth a bit, that was.

Now Baby worked alone. Had to force the locks. Didn't trust anyone else. Still it was a partnership in one way. Baby did the thieving and Alan hid the stuff for him until it was safe to sell on. Hopefully, once Rose was fixed up with a bloke, Alan could get back to work.

Baby said, 'I done the place again. Reckoned they wouldn't expect a return visit!' He laughed. 'I bet that took the smile off the colonel's face!'

Colonel Brian Fossett, recently returned to civilian life after a successful career fighting on several fronts and being decorated twice for gallantry. Alan and Baby called him 'The Big Cheese'. Alan recalled the fuss the colonel had made after the first robbery and the way the police had rallied their resources because Colonel Fossett's brother was a magistrate. Not that they'd caught anyone.

Alan grinned. Exciting times! He caught Baby's eyes and the fat man shook his head.

'It's not the same without you, Al.'

'Don't I know it!' Carefully he placed the new stuff in the sack and rolled it up, climbed up and, balancing precariously on the armchair, returned it to its hiding place.

Baby slipped a couple of notes into his hand. 'There you are! Two quid.'

'Thanks.' His share was 20 per cent and he was worth it. If suspicion ever fell on Baby, which it sometimes did, the police could search his digs and find nothing incriminating. Alan trusted Baby. He had to.

'You're welcome.'

Alan would tell Rose the usual story about the win on the gee-gees. He didn't know if she believed him but she didn't ask any awkward questions so he was prepared to let sleeping dogs lie.

Baby heaved himself to his feet. 'Coming for a pint?'

'Not arf!'

'The Queen's Head?'

'Anywhere but The White bloomin' Horse!'

Two

Monday night was always dull at The White Horse but Rose fancied that those who did turn up came because they wanted to hear her sing. Basically it was a public house which wanted to be something more – something closer to the supper rooms which provided entertainment with their meals. The White Horse, however, did not serve food but did offer the occasional entertainment. This took place on a small dais situated in one corner of the room and entirely lacking in drapes, lights or any kind of decoration. Alongside it was a piano in need of tuning, and much of the so-called entertainment took place to a background of chatter and laughter from a mainly indifferent audience.

Rose, however, chose to imagine that her songs brought a little spark of gaiety and a touch of glamour to the evening. The comedian and the monologue man only appeared on Fridays, Saturdays and Bank Holidays. Rose did Mondays as well but, unlike the rest of the days, she wasn't paid for her ten-minute spot, relying on the tips she collected in her frilly pink purse as she made her round of the customers, smiling brightly, after each performance.

As she waited beside the improvised stage she held her new parasol – white silk with a pink fringe – which was intended to add atmosphere to the new song she had written. She was afraid to sing some of the better known songs from the music hall because she feared the comparisons the audience might make. Instead she wrote her own songs and dreamed up a tune to go with each new ditty. The latest was entitled 'Keep Away The Freckles'.

Keep away the freckles, darlings,
Keep them right away!
Use your parasols, my darlings,
On the hottest day.
Gents like pale princesses, darlings,
White as curds and whey
So keep away the freckles, darling,
That's the only way!

It might never catch on, she knew, because it wasn't really saucy like some of the popular songs but it gave Rose the chance to peep coquettishly from beneath the pink fringe which she had discovered flattered her enormously. She had also invented a mime to accompany the song. She began with the rolled up parasol hooked over her arm, then glanced up at the non-existent sky. Opening up the parasol, she fanned herself with her left hand to indicate the heat of the day. For the second half of the song she tripped daintily across the tiny 'stage' and pointed to her pale complexion, then ended by twirling the parasol coquettishly while she spun round so that her skirt flared out to reveal her legs.

There was no written music for the song but she had hummed the tune to young Harry, the pianist, and he liked it and soon picked it up.

Now she kept her eye on Harry and when he nodded she stepped forward and he played a short but boisterous introduction which alerted the customers that she was on stage and about to perform. One or two people turned from the bar to watch her, others continued their conversations.

Rosie's voice was not strong but it was sweet and she sang at the top of her voice. Harry had urged her to 'Belt it out!' and she was grateful for his advice.

Gratified, she saw that a few people were actually listening and nodding in time to the music. An elderly woman was tapping her foot and a small mongrel dog leaped to its feet and began to bark excitedly. When she sang it through for the second time Harry sang with her and by the time she came to the end and peeped out from under the pink fringe she earned a short round of applause for her efforts.

Harry stood up and said loudly, 'Words and music by Miss Rosie Lamore!' and there was a half-hearted cheer and a red-nosed regular cried, 'Well done, lassie!'

Inspired by the reception, Rosie sang another melody and then, catching the manager's eye, reluctantly took the hint and ended the performance. She could have gone on for longer, loving every moment, for she revelled in the knowledge that for a few brief moments she was the centre of attention. Rose thrived on the adrenalin rush that came with performing.

Stepping down regretfully, she made a circuit of the room, flirting with the men and winking at the women – making the tour last as long as she dared. She collected two shillings and threepence. As always she offered to share it with Harry but he refused, insisting that he was paid for his piano playing whichever day of the week it was.

Rose slipped on her coat and changed her shoes and was on her way out when she caught sight of a well-known face – Colonel Fossett. He was known as Colonel Brian Fossett, retired. People in the streets around Elm Tree Avenue felt that by living in a big house, he added a touch of class to the area, and they had invented a heroic service in the army for him, much of which might be true. A nice old boy, Rose thought. He was in the saloon bar but he had put his head round the door and now beckoned to her.

'You've got a nice little voice, my dear.' He slipped a sixpence into her hand. 'You need an agent. That's the way it's done. I'll keep my ear to the ground.'

She loved the look of him – every inch the military man with his large but neatly clipped moustache, sun-bleached hair from his years of service in Africa, and the still steely blue eyes. If she had been a soldier under him, she'd have followed him into battle without the slightest hesitation. Of course he was long since retired but he still had that indefinable air of authority that Rose admired. He was old enough to be her father but she could still imagine herself married to him and living in the nice house in Elm Tree Avenue with his elderly sister and the yappy little Scottie dog whose name she could never remember.

It was natural for Rose to consider any reasonable man as a possible future husband and age was no barrier. When eventually she wanted to settle down she would look for someone kind with just enough money to live a modest but happy family life. He need not be handsome or rich or even talented, she told herself, but he must love her and the children. And he must be straight as a die. No crooks would be considered for the role. But all that was in the distant future. Before that time arrived she wanted to be famous.

Another man appeared in the doorway and

greeted Rose. 'Have you heard? The colonel's been burgled again.'

'No!' cried Rose. 'Oh, that's awful!' She turned to him. 'That's so unlucky, Colonel. Have they any idea who it was?'

'None at all. I'm afraid after last time my faith in our local constabulary somewhat dwindled!' He shrugged. 'Not to worry! They didn't get the good stuff, thank the Lord. That's in the safe.' He patted her shoulder. 'Now don't give it another thought, Miss Lamore. That's for me to worry about. You concentrate on your career, my dear. You get along home before it gets dark.'

Rose took his advice but as she walked home she thought about the burglary and all her childhood terrors returned as dark memories, to heap guilt upon her slim shoulders once again. When she was five her father had gone away for a long time and nobody would tell her where he had gone. Her mother and grandmother wept over his disappearance while assuring Rose that there was nothing to worry about and she must forget all about it and she was thoroughly confused and frightened. When Alan Paton finally came home life had changed in a way she didn't understand but she somehow felt responsible. Much later, she was told by an interfering neighbour that he had gone to prison for robbery, that it was a terrible stain on the family's good name, and she warned Rose never to speak of it for fear of giving her mother a heart attack.

Halfway home, she realized that PC Stump had not put in an appearance and she finally caught up with another constable. He told her that PC Stump had been called to the hospital urgently because their baby was arriving early and there were complications. By the time she reached number twenty-three all her earlier excitement had faded and her father's news that he had won two pounds on a horse in the five thirty failed to cheer her up.

Marcus finished his breakfast and left the dining room. He had eaten very little, plagued by anxiety about the coming party. It was Marie's birthday and he was having doubts about the wisdom of introducing Rose Paton to his family. Marie would appreciate her but Letitia might be jealous of her looks and talent and Steven might flirt with her. His younger brother had a very flattering opinion of himself and rarely found it difficult to attract women. Janetta had so far proved a solitary disappointment to him but that may have been because Letitia had warned her friend that twenty-year-old Steven, like plenty of men of his age, was rather shallow, inclined to treat the fairer sex as brainless females.

Marcus made his way into the kitchen

where the birthday cake stood in a place of honour on the dresser, carefully covered by a muslin cloth. It was being admired by Letitia who lifted one corner of the cloth to show it to her brother in all its glory.

'Mrs Bray has made a cherry Madeira,' she explained, 'because we thought the fruit mixture might be too heavy for Marie to digest, and it will be covered with thick cream at the last moment and decorated with fresh rose petals. Not to eat, naturally, but they will look astonishing.'

Marcus ducked his head, inspected the big square cake and gave Mrs Bray a nod of approval. 'Wonderful!' he assured her.

Mrs Bray said, 'I shall pick the roses as late as possible and choose them as small as possible, then arrange them in two rows along the top edge. They'll be slightly over-lapping and that way they'll look like frills.' Her mouth quivered. 'Poor Marie, God bless her! I can't believe ... oh dear!' She fumbled for her handkerchief.

Marcus looked helplessly at his sister who said briskly, 'No sad thoughts today, Mrs Bray. We must all appear cheerful no matter how bad we feel inside. If Marie sees anyone crying it will spoil her day.' She patted the housekeeper's arm.

'I don't know if I can manage it!' She dabbed at her eyes. 'That sweet young girl...'

Marcus said, 'Of course you'll manage. You'll be fine, you'll see. We all will. And

45

Miss Lamore is coming. That will be great fun.'

Letitia said, 'We'll fetch you from the kitchen, Mrs Bray. You must be part of the audience when Miss Lamore sings. It's going to be very exciting having our own private performance.'

Mrs Bray had brightened and the handkerchief was now returned to her apron pocket. 'I did wonder if the cake needed a pink ribbon around the sides. The cream will only be on the top, you see, and I do have a very nice ribbon on my best hat. It would wash, afterwards.'

Letitia began to shake her head but Marcus intervened. 'A pink ribbon would be the final touch, Mrs Bray. How clever of you.'

Letitia smiled. 'Marcus is right. He frequently is ... but we shall see tonight if his unusual birthday present was also an inspired idea. Did he tell you that she might have to stay the night?'

Mrs Bray smiled. 'Oh yes, that's all taken care of. Thank goodness it's summer and we won't have to worry about hot water bottles.'

Letitia left them to it and Mrs Bray said, 'I was telling my old man about the party and everything and talking about you all. He said he saw Master Steven in The White Hart a couple of nights ago. Very excitable, he was, and what Bert calls hot-headed.'

'I can imagine!' Marcus knew she was being tactful. His brother frequently drank

46

too much and became rowdy. Once he had been thrown out. 'Don't tell me he was—'

'Oh no! Nothing bad, sir,' she hurried to reassure him. 'My old man was impressed with him. Said he would make a good soldier. The army needs men like him. That's what he said – and he knows because look what it did for our lad. A real hot-head, he was. In all sorts of trouble – but not now.' She smiled. 'We're very proud of him if you must know. The army was the making of him.'

'The *army*! Good grief.' Marcus had only been half listening, but now he stared at her. 'What has the army done to deserve my brother?'

'It's his spirit, sir. Your brother. He's high-spirited. That's what he reckons. Bold, that was his word. Bold and ... and forceful. They were his very words. Good in a military man, that is. A bit of training and they'd knock him into shape. Leastways, that's what my old man reckons.'

That evening the taxi drew up outside the door of number twenty-three exactly on time. Rose glanced out of the window and gave a cry of surprise. 'Oh Lord, Pa! Here's Mr Bennley, come for me after all! Well, I'm blowed!'

'But you wrote him a letter!'

'Must have gone astray, Pa. I suppose I'll have to go. I'll just fetch my outfit.' And

47

without giving him a chance to say more, she rushed upstairs, snatched up the bag containing her stage clothes and ran from the house, her face flushed with excitement. She gave a squeal of excitement as the taxi door opened and Marcus stepped out, a stiff smile on his face.

'I didn't know if you would come, Mr Bennley!' Beaming, she climbed past him into the taxi.

The taxi driver turned to smile at her, making no effort to hide his delight. 'Nice evening, miss.'

'Yes it is.' She gave him a coy glance. 'A very nice evening. I'm Miss Lamore and I've been engaged to sing at a private party. Did he tell you?'

'No. He hasn't said a word.'

Marcus climbed in beside her and slammed the door. 'I've had things on my mind.'

Her father had come to the door and now Rose blew him a kiss and waved. By the time she returned, he would have forgotten all about the letter – at least she hoped so.

Rose looked at her companion as she settled in the seat. 'Things on your mind? Such as what? Arrangements for the party?' Before he could reply she pulled her dress from the bag. 'Look! I added some new lace to my petticoat in honour of the occasion. It's got gold ribbon threaded through. I wanted to look really exotic for your sister.

What do you think?'

'Er ... Yes. Certainly.'

The taxi driver started the engine and began to weave his way through the traffic. 'I can't see from here but I reckon it looks very exotic, miss. Mind you, I should think an old sack would look exotic on you!'

'Oh! You dear man! Thank you!' Rose hadn't expected the evening to get off to such a flying start and felt a rush of confidence. She decided that although the taxi driver was almost bald he had a nice warm voice and she was sure he was happily married. Turning back to Marcus she asked again, 'Things on your mind such as what?'

Marcus lowered his voice and said, 'Such as my younger brother went out last night and stayed out all night! Fortunately he finally came back just before lunch with a sore head but in a foul temper.'

Rose rolled her eyes knowingly. 'Got a young lady, has he?'

'He didn't say. He's sleeping it off – whatever it was!'

Her eyes darkened abruptly. 'Do you remember the constable that night outside The White Horse? PC Stump? His wife's died and so has the baby. Isn't that dreadful? Poor man. He must be so unhappy!'

'Very sad. Yes.' He rubbed his eyes tiredly, then changed the subject. 'Marie is very excited. She came downstairs for an hour this morning to see everything – the decorations, the cake, the presents. Mother sent her a gold bracelet...'

'Will your mother be at the party?'

'No.' He hesitated. 'She lives near Boulogne with her second husband. She visits us from time to time but her husband is a farmer so he can't just leave it. And he doesn't like England. He's not too keen on the English, either, especially the men.'

'But your mother could come, couldn't she?'

He hesitated. 'Mother and my sister ... don't see eye to eye. Family business. I can't explain. Mother wants Marie to visit them in France while she still can but I'm not sure about the sea crossing. She's very frail but ... We shall see.'

Privately Rose thought them a rather odd family but, changing the subject, she said, 'So what do you think of my stage costume, Mr Bennley?'

'Very nice.'

She persevered, hoping for a better compliment. 'The parasol is part of my act and my pink satin shoes are in this bag. I shall be singing one song unaccompanied because there's no written music because I wrote the song and made up the tune.' She put her head on one side and gave him an upward glance. Surely he was impressed.

'Yes. Very nice.'

The taxi driver negotiated a horse bus that had collided with an army wagon and said,

'Sounds very pretty, miss. I'm sure you'll look a real treat!'

'Oh thank you! What a lovely compliment!' Rose hoped Mr Bennley would take the hint. To make sure he did, she whispered, 'What a nice man!'

Instead of the desired result, Marcus Bennley looked put out and muttered 'Nosy old devil!'

They sat in silence for a while until Rose said, 'So what presents did your sister have – apart from me, of course?'

It seemed that Marie had been generously supplied with gifts. 'She'll want to show them to you herself, I expect,' he told her. 'But – look here, Miss Lamore – could we use our Christian names? It would be less formal and it is a party after all. What do you think?'

Rose leaped at the idea. 'Of course we can. I'll be Rose and you can be Marcus – or is it Michael? My pa has got me all muddled.'

'It's Marcus.'

'Right. Marcus.' She gave him a beaming smile. 'Oh, this is grand, isn't it? I feel I know you all already.'

When they drew up outside Victoria House Rose hid her surprise at the size of it and instead offered to give the driver her autograph but they had nothing to write on so the idea had to be abandoned.

He said, 'Never mind, Miss Lamore. I shall never forget you. Maybe when you're

51

famous you can give it to me then.'

Minutes later Marcus had led Rose into the family home and a suitably bedazzled Marie was showing her the birthday presents which were arranged on a nearby table.

'Look at these beautiful slippers, Miss Lamore!'

'Please call me Rose.'

'Rose? Thank you, I will.'

'The slippers are delightful, Marie.'

'Letitia, my sister, chose them for me because she knows I like fur and these have rabbit fur linings. They'll be wonderfully warm in the winter ... and Steven, my lunatic brother, has given me a bottle of very, *very* expensive perfume and he said I am so sweet he wanted me to smell sweet! Wasn't that romantic of him, Miss Lamore – I mean Rose? He's not usually romantic – I mean, he's just my brother – but I think it suits him.'

Rose felt a tug at her heart strings. Would this lovely young woman live long enough to need warm slippers, she wondered, and how much perfume would she use before she died?

'The gold bracelet is from Mother and I hope to go over and see her soon ... Mrs Bray, our housekeeper, knitted me a bed jacket in pale blue because she knows that I love blue. Here it is!' She seized it from the table and held it up against herself. 'What do you think, Rose?'

'It's perfect for you. I wish we had a clever housekeeper.' Now a terrible thought struck Rose. She had not thought to bring a present. How could she have been so thoughtless! Stricken, she wondered frantically if she had anything about her that would make a suitable gift ... There was only one possibility and she hesitated. The parasol. Parting with it would be a wrench but she could buy herself another one with the money Marcus was going to pay her. Before she could change her mind she said, 'My present to you is a secret at the moment but I shall give it to you later on.'

'A secret?' Marie's eyes lit up. 'Oh how exciting! I've always loved mysteries.'

Just then a woman came into the large drawing room holding on to the arm of a handsome man and Rose guessed that this was probably Letitia and her fiancé.

She was right. Letitia wore a slim dress of dark lace with a string of pearls at her neck and she bestowed a gracious look in all directions before greeting Rose. 'I'm Marie's older sister, Letitia,' she told Rose, 'and this is Bernard da Silva, my husband-to-be.' Turning to him she said, 'This is Miss Rosie Lamore, who will sing for us later. Her performance is Marcus's birthday present to Marie. Wasn't it clever of him, darling?'

'Very clever, what!' He took Rose's hand and, smiling, kissed it gingerly.

53

As though she might be infectious, thought Rose, with a sudden inexplicable resentment. He seemed too cool and calculated – but then he was obviously a very superior person and she, Rose, was just a singer. Letitia, her hands clasped, was looking at him adoringly and Rose had to admit he was almost perfect – expensive clothes, gleaming shoes with laces tied in perfect bows, a handkerchief sticking out from the breast pocket of his jacket, a fancy embroidered waistcoat. The perfect fiancé.

And he had said 'what!' and in Rose's experience only rich people said that.

She smiled at him politely and said, 'Nice to meet you, Mr da Silva.'

Letitia said, 'I'm sure he won't mind if you call him Bernard just for tonight. You won't will you, darling?'

'Not at all.'

At once Letitia slipped her arm through his. Rose tried to imagine their wedding which would be very grand.

Mrs Bray came in and whispered something to Letitia and everyone made their way into a large dining room which had been tastefully decorated with flowers and ribbons for the occasion. There were other people who all seemed to know each other and when they sat down Rose counted thirteen. *Unlucky thirteen!* Had anyone else noticed, she wondered anxiously.

Marcus looked at Steven. 'Isn't your girlfriend coming?'

Steven frowned as though it was an effort to think. 'I may have said Friday,' he confessed.

Letitia said, 'Oh God, Steven! What an idiot you are!'

Accusing faces turned his way and he said, 'Or maybe I didn't. Maybe she's ill or something. How do I know?'

There was a fraught silence while everyone tried not to recognize the significance of the missing guest. Marie's eyes had widened fearfully and she covered her mouth with two fingers as she turned to Marcus for help. For some reason he glanced in Rose's direction and she sensed a growing panic. She jumped to her feet and pretended to do a recount. Then she smiled. 'No! It's only twelve. I'm not a guest, remember. I'm a present! I'm Marie's birthday present from Marcus!'

Within seconds everyone was laughing and the atmosphere relaxed and the threatened disaster was averted. Rose sat down feeling pleased with herself and Marcus sat down beside her. He leaned across and kissed her lightly on the cheek. 'That was very clever, Rose,' he whispered. 'What would we do without you?'

'More to the point, Marcus – what will you do if Steven's friend turns up?'

'We'll worry about that *if* she turns up.'

Mrs Bray, flushed with excitement, came

in and out with various trays and platters – cold ham, prawns in aspic and smoked salmon. Various bowls of salad and butter were already on the table and warm bread rolls were brought round. The wine flowed and so did the conversation. Rose could hardly believe that she was sitting there in such exalted company and at such a table. The cloth was white damask, the glasses glittered in the light from the candelabras and flowers floated in low glass bowls along the centre of the table. She reminded herself that she, too, was to marry a rich man as soon as she was famous.

Marcus rose to his feet and made a toast to his sister and everyone drank to her health and happiness. At the head of the table Marie positively glowed with pleasure.

Looking round at the rest of the smiling faces, Rose found it easy to pretend that their joy was not tinged with sadness.

Next morning Rose woke early and for a few seconds wondered where she was before the events of the previous night returned to put a broad smile on her face. An evening to be remembered, she thought happily. Her performance had been received with rapturous applause and later Rose had felt a great rush of pride when she saw tears of joy in Marie's eyes as she presented her with the parasol. Altogether, the birthday party had been a wild success. Letitia was delighted and even

Bernard had unbent sufficiently to join in with one of Rose's songs although he looked rather uncomfortable, Rose thought. Probably not used to being engaged in anything like that – she imagined him at the opera or the ballet. Maybe an orchestral concert where he could sit po-faced and look superior.

She stared at the ceiling, discovering a few slight cracks in the plasterwork. 'I didn't like him,' she said aloud. 'Sorry, Letitia. You obviously love him but I think he's stuffy.' Her gaze came down a little and she took in the large, ornate picture above the mantelpiece. It showed a bull-like creature with fancy horns and she thought it might be a stag. 'Bernard drank a bit too much,' she told the absent Letitia, 'and then he tried to wheedle me on to his lap!' Unsuccessfully, however. Rose smiled faintly. She was certain that a girl could lose her women friends by allowing their husbands to take liberties.

Climbing from the bed she padded across the bare polished floorboards and pulled the curtains open and found herself peering down into a small courtyard which was beautifully decorated with pots of flowering shrubs on to which the sun shone. The romantic picture thus revealed was rather spoiled by the sight of Mrs Bray pegging out serviettes and tea towels on a clothes line. Either the housekeeper was up very early or Rose had overslept. There was no clock in the room and Rose was undecided about what to do. Was it bad manners to go wandering about in other people's houses? Maybe the housekeeper would bring her a tray of tea and toast! Now that would be real luxury.

Opening the large wardrobe she found nothing but a smell of mothballs. The drawer below contained a selection of toys, mostly showing signs of loving attention over many years. Crumpled books, a box of ludo, a top but no whip, a wooden sailing boat with a damaged mast and a few skittles minus the box. She picked out an ancient pixie, handmade in green felt, and gave it a hug to prove it had not been forgotten. There was a blue knitted rabbit, a doll with yellow wool for hair and a small velvet mouse with button eyes. Rose loved them all on sight and wondered which toy had belonged to which member of the family. Naturally, the doll belonged either to Marie or Letitia, the rabbit might have been Steven's but the teddy bear definitely belonged to Marcus. Arms and legs ramrod straight, it appeared to be standing at attention. It gave no sign that it had ever been cuddled, its fur was fresh and unfaded and its brown glass eyes seemed to stare at her with cool disinterest.

'You're a dear, sweet thing,' she told it, rearranging the legs so that it could sit up on top of the chest of drawers. 'There! That's more comfortable, isn't it?'

Turning away, she examined the large, almost empty room. Velvet curtains, polished wooden floorboards with a patterned carpet – a far cry from her own room at home with its cracked linoleum and a rag rug made years ago by her mother. There was a washstand in one corner of the room with a jug of cold water and a basin, a folded towel and a soap and flannel. Rose made use of them and then dressed in her everyday clothes.

While she did this, she tried to recall the last few hours of the party when she had definitely drunk too much wine and hoped she hadn't made a fool of herself and let Marcus down. She remembered Steven proposing to her, going down on one knee and everyone laughing.

'I'm sorry,' she had told him, smiling down into those beautiful but cold blue eyes, 'but I've decided not to marry until I've made a name for myself in the music halls – but thanks ever so for the proposal. It's my first ever!' Which was a small white lie because a boy at school had asked her to marry him and she'd said 'yes' because at that time they were both six years old and she hadn't decided on her career path. Last night everyone had cheered Steven's proposal and her rejection and he had pretended to be heartbroken. Only Marcus had seemed unimpressed and she felt that, in his eyes, she had let herself down although she was unable to work out how or why. But she had seen the look on his face and it troubled her.

Ten minutes later, at five to seven a.m., someone rang the front door bell and roused the entire household. Letitia opened her eyes, looked at the bedside clock, kissed the photograph of her beloved Bernard, turned over and went back to sleep.

Marie awoke, wondered who it was but knew that it was not for her. She decided to stay awake and revel in the happy memories of the previous evening. Marcus had carried her in his arms to dance and had made her feel very important and said she looked glamorous. Bernard had also carried her round but had looked very self-conscious so that when he asked her a second time she had claimed to be too tired and had pretended not to see the relief in his eyes. Steven hadn't danced with her but she didn't care because she had never forgiven him for treading all over the sandcastle she had made when she was five years old.

The bell also awoke Marcus and he went downstairs but Steven was already at the front door.

'It's for me,' said Steven.

'How can you tell? You haven't opened the door yet.'

'I'm expecting someone. Go back to bed, you look awful.'

'You don't look too good yourself!' Marcus replied but he turned back and was halfway up the stairs before Steven opened the door.

As Steven had suspected, Andrew Markham stood outside. Part-owner of Andy's Supper Room, he was a man in his early forties, thickset with cold, grey eyes and a permanently aggressive expression.

Steven's heart quailed but he tried not to show his anxiety. 'What are you doing here? I told you never to come to my home.'

'And I told you I do what I like and if you don't want a home visit from me or my brother, you should pay your debts on time – and you haven't. You owe twenty-three pounds and eleven shillings and I'm here to collect!' He paused, took a deep breath and went on. 'And don't give me any sob story about your dying sister because I don't give a damn about her. She's your problem and you're mine!' His grey eyes were cold as stone.

Steven said, 'Give me twenty-four hours and I'll—'

'I want it now!'

'I can't give you what I haven't got!' He had lowered his voice and now glanced anxiously behind him in case his brother was lingering out of sight. 'I've had unexpected expenses. My sister has only weeks to—'

'My heart bleeds for you!'

'Christ! You're a hard-hearted brute!'

'You should have thought of that. You rang

61

up a bill and now you have to pay it.' He thrust out a meaty hand and instinctively Steven stepped back.

'I've told you – I'll give it to you tomorrow. Twenty—'

The blow from Markham's fist caught him under the chin and sent him flying.

'Jesus Christ!' he muttered groggily as he tried to pick himself up.

To his horror, Markham had advanced over the step and was in the hall. He loomed over him. 'Plenty more where that came from!' His voice was low but full of menace. 'How would you like me to break your arm? Or flatten your nose. You wouldn't be such a pretty boy then! Or I could set a couple of my lads on to you.'

Steven was terrified. He regretted ever setting foot in Markham's damned supper room and he certainly regretted running up a tab for food and drinks ... but from no-where an idea suddenly came to him. 'Wait a moment!' he begged as he scrambled to his feet. 'I've had an idea. You like pretty girls, don't you, Andrew?' He glanced over his shoulder to make sure he wasn't being over-heard.

'What if I do?' He hesitated, his fist at the ready.

'And you take on singers at your place.' Steven was already feeling nervous about his idea but it was too late to back out now. Time was not on his side. At any moment one of the family or the housekeeper would stumble upon them and awkward questions would be asked. Crossing his fingers he said, 'Look, get back outside. We can't talk in here. Someone might overhear us.'

Reluctantly Markham backed out of the door and on to the step and Steven followed him. Pulling the front door behind him he said, 'Suppose I could get you a girl – a very pretty girl. Very young. She wants to go on the stage and you could ... you could help her. Take her under your wing, so to speak. I'm not promising anything but...'

Markham looked interested. 'Single, is she, this girl?'

'Yes. I could bring her along one evening.'

He was obviously interested, thought Steven, and let out a sigh of relief. Markham had lowered his fist. Perhaps the danger was past.

'So what's her name, this singer?'

'Rosie Lamore. She's ... she's very new. Sings at The White Horse and writes some of her own songs. She could be big with the right manager.'

'Hmm ... And she's, you know, willing? She knows what it takes and who she has to please?'

Steven managed a short laugh and resisted the urge to feel his jaw which was very painful. Perhaps the blighter had broken it. If so he would have to fake a fall downstairs and blame it on the accident. 'That's for you to

63

find out!' he said. 'All I'm saying is ... if you forget the money I owe, just this once, I'll introduce her to you. The rest is up to you.'

'Forget the money? Pull the other leg!'

'She's got real talent. If you signed her up...'

There was already a gleam in Markham's eye, thought Steven. He set great store by his good looks. He thought of Rose and felt a twinge of conscience but tried to convince himself that he was doing Rose a favour. 'Plenty of talent.' Yes, he must concentrate on the fact that he was trying to promote Rose's career. Marcus must never suspect the truth.

'And pretty and young?' Markham narrowed his eyes. 'If you send me a scraggy old tart...'

'Would I do that to you?' Steven was sweating. He hoped none of his teeth had come loose.

Markham grunted. 'Bring her round Monday afternoon. If I don't reckon her, or she doesn't understand what's expected, you still owe me! If I take her on, we'll call it quits.'

He turned and walked away and Steven closed the door with a hand that trembled. As he made his way into the drawing room to pour himself a stiff drink, he told himself it would all turn out for the best. He had tried to do his brother's friend a favour. That was all. It was up to Rose now. No one could blame him if things went topsy turvy.

★ ★ ★

In number twenty-three Albert Street, the
day had also started badly for Alan Paton.
He was also awoken from a heavy sleep by
someone at the front door. He sat up and
looked at the alarm clock.

'What the hell? Five past eight?' He threw
off the bedclothes. 'I hope it's not Baby!' he
muttered as his mind raced. If it was Baby it
meant trouble.

He pulled on his trousers as the banging
continued and, abandoning the idea of a
shirt, rushed downstairs to open the door.

Two police constables stood on the step
and his fears multiplied.

'What?' he demanded, trying to brazen it
out. 'I suppose you do know the time!'

'Morning, sir.' The older man glanced past
him into the hall. 'Wondered if we could
come in and have a nose round. See if
you've—'

'Well, the answer's "No" so beat it.' He
hoped he sounded both confident and innocent, and regretted the absence of his
shirt and shoes.

Ignoring his comment, the two constables
pushed past him and made their way along
the passage to the living room, leaving him
to trail behind them. His heart thumped uncomfortably. Was this a random call or did
they know something, he wondered. If they
had got Baby and he had blabbed ... His
mouth felt dry but he knew he had to bluff

65

it out. If they knew nothing about the stolen goods, his best bet was to act innocent and outraged.

'You lot got a warrant?' he blustered. 'Cos if not then...'

'A warrant?' The young constable stared at him. 'Now why would you think that, sir? Got a guilty conscience, have you?' He grinned at his partner.

The older man said, 'Want to get anything off your chest? Come clean, as we say. Confession is good for the soul, sir. Did you know?'

They began to poke around, opening and closing the drawers, looking under the table and behind the chairs. One of them glanced up at the water tank and Alan's heart rate speeded up. He said, 'Want to rip up the floorboards, do you? Think I've got a dead body stashed away under there? Or enough explosives to blow up Buck House? Be my guest!'

Distracted, the older man glanced out of the window into the garden, his eyes narrowed. To his partner he said, 'Take a look round the shed.' When he had gone, he said, 'Your friend Baby is in a bit of bother and is down at the police station trying to explain away some stuff stolen from Colonel Fossett. Know anything about that, Mr Paton?'

'Stolen stuff?' He tried to look innocent. 'No I don't, and if you ask me you've got the wrong man. Me and Baby – we've both been straight for years and you lot know it.'

'Well, for your information we *haven't* got the wrong man, Mr Paton, because the pawnbroker identified him as the man who pawned a valuable clock the day after it was nicked! He claims he bought it from a man in a pub. Now isn't that original!'

He stepped into the scullery, opened a few cupboard doors and looked inside the oven. 'Dear oh dear! This oven needs a good clean. You want to speak to your house-keeper!'

'Oh that's very funny, that is. You should go on the stage.'

The second man returned from his visit to the shed, shaking his head, and was sent upstairs to 'take a gander aloft'. Alan was beginning to recover from his fright. They knew nothing. Baby had kept his mouth shut, thank the Lord! But using the pawn-broker! That was sheer stupidity and he would have something to say about that when he saw Baby.

They waited in silence until the constable confirmed that there was nothing to be discovered upstairs.

'I hope you haven't made a mess of my bedroom.'

'It's a lot tidier, sir, but you should try opening the window to let the fresh air in. Smells of old socks!'

'Open the windows? I couldn't do that.' He was growing bolder now. 'A burglar

67

might climb in!'

'You'd know about that, wouldn't you sir!'

They both laughed, drifting along the passage in the direction of the front door.

When they'd gone Alan gave a sigh of relief. He was grateful that Rosie was away at the party but she was bound to hear about it from the nosy neighbours. He'd have to tell her but he was going to get away with it. He mopped his face with a grubby handkerchief. That had been too close for comfort.

When Rose arrived in the dining room she found Letitia eating toast and marmalade.

'Come and join me, Rose,' she said with a smile. 'Marcus has already eaten and is in the garden. Steven is his usual uncommunicative self at this time in the morning. Marie is sleeping late but that's to be expected. Did you sleep well?'

'Yes thank you. I looked in the wardrobe – I hope you didn't mind – and saw all the old toys.'

'Not at all. Help yourself to eggs and bacon from the sideboard. Or there's stewed prunes.'

Rose hesitated. 'I don't know how much time I have. Marcus is calling a taxi.'

'Let it wait. You must eat.'

As Rose tucked into her breakfast with enthusiasm, Letitia said, 'Perhaps you would like to come to our wedding. Poor Marcus has no real friends so he could invite you.'

Rose looked startled. 'Oh no! I mean, I'd love to but...' What on earth would she wear? she thought desperately.

Letitia went on as though she had not spoken. 'It will be a grand affair, Rose. The da Silvas are a very wealthy family. Very highly admired. Marrying Bernard will transform my life. Not long now so I'm praying that Marie will still be with us, of course, and fit enough to attend.'

She reached for the toast rack and helped herself to another triangle. 'The trouble is, Rose, that she wants to spend time with Mother in France. Marcus is prepared to travel with her but she really needs a woman to help her with ... the womanly things of life – if you understand me. Personal things that a man doesn't need to know about.' As Rose opened her mouth, Letitia rushed on. 'And I refuse to accompany her. I know how it will be – she will arrange to go for a week and will then beg to stay on with Mother for another week and then another, and I will be stuck there with her when I should be here seeing to the wedding arrangements.'

Rose took a chance. 'Why doesn't your mother come here instead?'

There was a long pause and then Letitia said, 'Because I refuse to have that man in this house and Mother won't come without him!' She was breathing rapidly and avoided Rose's gaze.

Rose, concentrating on her breakfast, said nothing but she recognized the sudden anger and wondered what was behind it.

As though reading Rose's mind, Letitia forced a smile. 'Nothing for you to worry about, Rose. All families have secrets and the Bennleys are no exception. Please forget I said what I did. There was no need to involve you in our problems.'

Rose searched for a way to change the subject and reverted to the wedding itself. 'Are you marrying in a church near here?'

'No. Bernard's Uncle Henry and Aunt Sarah are hosting the occasion in their ballroom – they are quite hopelessly rich – as their wedding present to us. Isn't that wonderful?' She laughed. 'They live at Longley Manor – the family home for generations. The churchyard is full of tombstones bearing the da Silva name! They have acres and acres of land. They have no children so one day Bernard will own it all – you might say we shall be the master and mistress of the manor!'

There had to be a reason, thought Rose, why she was prepared to marry a rather stuffy man. Obligingly she said, 'How wonderful!' and wondered what Bernard's parents were like and whether he had sisters and brothers. The door opened and Steven joined them. He looked pale and ill at ease and Rose assumed he was suffering from the excesses of the party the night before. She smiled and wished him a 'Good morning!' but his sister was less forgiving.

'You look like death!' she told him crossly. 'It serves you right for drinking so much. You never know when to stop.' She looked at Rose and shook her head. 'Do you have a younger brother?'

'No. There's just me. And my father, of course.'

Letitia was watching her brother through narrowed eyes. 'You look terribly pale. Perhaps you should go back to bed.'

He put a hand to the left side of his jaw and said 'Toothache!'

Rose said, 'It does look a bit swollen. Poor you.'

Steven hovered by the table but made no effort to eat. Instead he said to Rose, 'I may have some good news for you. A friend of mine ... that is, a chap I know, name of Markham, runs a supper room. Nothing flashy but you could do worse ... I mean, you have to start somewhere in your line of business...' He stopped to clutch his jaw, then pulled out a chair and sat at the table opposite Rose.

Letitia stared at him, shocked. 'Not Andy's Supper Room? Heavens, Steven! That's seriously seedy! What on earth are you suggesting?'

He looked at her angrily. 'How would you know what it's like? You've never set foot inside it! Have you? Tell the truth!'

'I've never wanted to set foot inside it but I have heard of it. It's on Marlborough Street, a couple of miles from here. A run-down hall with a few tables—'

Rose interrupted their exchange, her heart fluttering with excitement. 'What about this place, Steven? You said I have to start somewhere. What did you mean?' She crossed the fingers of both hands.

Letitia dabbed her mouth with her serviette and stood up. 'I've heard enough. Take whatever he says with a pinch of salt, Rose.' She made her way towards the door and then turned back. 'Anyway, thanks again for last night's entertainment. Everyone was very impressed and Marcus is like a dog with two tails. I'll send you an invitation in due course.'

When she had gone Steven frowned. 'Invitation?'

'To the wedding.'

'Oh that!'

'I may not be able to come but—'

'Look here, Rose. About this chap I know – he called here earlier and I mentioned you. He's going to do me a favour and give you an audition – if you're interested. Take no notice of my sister. She's a stuck-up piece – and worse since she got engaged to Bernard. What a crashing bore that man is! I can't see what she sees in him unless it's the money, the aristocratic family, hobnobbing with the famous at society events!' His mouth twisted sourly.

Rose said, 'An audition? You mean I get to sing some of my songs? And then what?'

'Well, if he likes you I suppose he'll give you a spot in his stage show. But –' he held up a warning finger – 'I can't promise anything. You have to understand that. All I'm doing is mentioning you and you have to take it from there. Make your own decisions. What I mean is, if he *likes* you ... as a person...' He glanced away as his voice trailed off.

'It sounds wonderful! Really, Steven, it sounds too good to be true!' Her eyes shone as her mind filled with fantastic visions. She had hoped the private booking would lead to further such engagements but this leap seemed incredible. A personal introduction to a man who owned a supper room! 'Will he ... I mean, do you mean paid employment?'

He shrugged. 'I've no idea, Rose. As I said, all I did was pass on your name and say you were promising. The rest is up to you. Depends how good you are.' He winked. Crossing to the window, he thrust his hands into his pockets and stared out of the window. 'Don't blame me for anything that ... that goes wrong. If it does, I mean. It's a tough business, show business. You take the rough with the smooth or you get out.'

Rose was determined not to be dissuaded. 'If he's a friend of yours that's good enough for me!' she told him. 'I'm tremendously grateful, Steven.'

He closed his eyes. 'Just don't say I didn't warn you. I don't want everyone blaming me if you get ... led astray.' He fingered his jaw gingerly, cursing Markham – both for hurting his jaw and for putting him in an awkward position with regard to Rose ... If his brother ever found out there would be hell to pay. Steven knew that for a certainty. Not that he imagined Marcus felt anything for the girl, that was hardly likely on past experience, but he might feel responsible because he had introduced her to the family.

'I think you should go to a dentist,' Rose told him. 'Your jaw looks a bit swollen to me. Have the tooth out if he can't do anything with it.'

Steven gave her a long look which she found unfathomable, then got up and walked to the door. 'You'd better go and find Marcus.'

As he went out she jumped to her feet and rushed after him. 'When shall I go to Andy's Supper Room?'

'This coming Monday. I'll send a taxi for you but I won't be able to come with you. I've got plans for Monday. Don't worry. I'll settle with the taxi in advance so you can ride home but after that you'll have to make your own arrangements. Find out about the buses.'

'Aren't you going to wish me "Good

74

luck"?'

'Good luck, Rose!' He headed for the stairs and as he went up he muttered, 'You're going to need it!'

Three

When the taxi arrived to take Rose home, Marcus and Rose climbed in and settled themselves on the leather seat. Rose began at once to tell him about the wonderful opportunity that his brother had set up for her. He listened in a way that she found irritating, showing no enthusiasm whatsoever and occasionally shaking his head.

At last she stopped. 'You're as bad as your sister! You should be happy for me,' she told him. 'I thought you'd congratulate me but instead you're po-faced. Don't you want me to be famous?'

'It's not a very nice place, Rose. I do want you to be famous but not there. It has a bad reputation.'

The driver swerved to avoid a brewer's dray and Rose was thrown against Marcus who said, 'For heaven's sake! Not you, Rose, the driver.'

When she had regained her position she said, 'But Steven doesn't think so! He recommends it so how can it be a bad place? I don't understand.' Perhaps he was annoyed, she thought, because Steven was being so helpful. Maybe he was jealous that his brother was interested in her.

There was a silence and then he said, 'They ... that is some of them, are not nice people, Rose. Not to be trusted. I'm astonished that he recommends the man. What did Letitia say about it?'

'That it was seriously seedy but that doesn't mean—'

'You should listen to her. Steven has no right to interfere and you should take whatever he tells you with a pinch of salt. A large one!'

They sat in an unhappy silence until Rose said, 'Well, I'm going anyway, whatever you say. It's my first big chance and I'm not wasting it. I trust your brother even if you don't.'

'I know him better than you do, Rose, and he can be devious. I'm not trying to spoil the moment for you – why should I? Something tells me there's more to this than meets the eye and I don't want you to be exploited in any way.'

Minutes passed. Rose said, 'Letitia's invited me to her wedding. I suppose you won't approve of that either!'

'How will you get there?'

She glared at him. 'By bus, of course, if I have to but she said I can be your guest because you won't know anyone else!'

'That sounds just like Letitia.'

'Don't you have any friends?'

'I don't know. I've never thought about it.'

The taxi swerved again and the driver now shouted something rude to the driver of another taxi who retaliated by shaking his fist.

Marcus groaned. 'Of all the taxi drivers in London, I seem to have chosen the craziest...'

He smiled briefly. 'Letitia will be a happier person once she's married. It's important to her. Ever since she was a child she's had ambitions to be rich. Bernard is the answer to all her prayers.'

Rose was thawing a little. 'I suppose we all have hopes for the future – like me with the stage. What's your ambition, Marcus?'

He hesitated, opened his mouth to speak but then changed his mind. 'It doesn't matter.'

At that moment their taxi forced itself in front of the other taxi which came to a juddering halt. Two elderly women stared helplessly into their taxi from the window of the other one and Marcus swore under his breath. 'This is ridiculous!'

Rose, who was actually beginning to enjoy the excitement, said, 'It certainly is!'

'Oh no!' Marcus tutted as their driver nipped down from his cab and met the other driver who had also left his vehicle. They immediately began to use their fists and passing traffic hooted as the fight interrupted the traffic flow.

'We're getting out of this!' cried Marcus and, opening the door, he took Rose's hand and hauled her unceremoniously from the taxi. From the safety of the pavement they joined the crowd that was collecting and watched the two elderly women make their escape.

Someone somewhere blew a whistle and a policeman could be seen hurrying towards them.

Marcus said, 'Come on. I've seen enough.'

'But we haven't paid for the taxi!'

'And we're not going to. He's lucky we're not reporting him for dangerous driving.' He looked around him. 'Good job we're nearly there. I'll get you home in ten minutes.'

Clutching her bag, Rose resigned herself to the early end to her cherished taxi ride and trotted obediently beside Marcus. After a while she said, 'You were telling me about your ambition for the future.'

'I told you it doesn't matter.'

'It does to me.'

'Believe me, Rose.' He shook his head. 'It doesn't matter to anyone.'

Having been escorted to her home, Rose watched Marcus walk away and was immediately aware of a deep sense of anticlimax.

'Cinderella after the ball!' she muttered. Somehow the thrills of the previous evening had been thrown into shadow by the un-satisfactory ride with Marcus who, she now decided, was a mournful sort of person who had few friends, if any, and had a low opinion of the members of his own family. According to him, Letitia was a snob and Steven was not to be trusted. Marie alone remained a nice person in everyone's opin-ion. She felt she had been robbed of all the happy memories of the previous evening but she put on a cheerful expression and breez-ed in, determined to impress her father with the details of her overnight events.

He was slumped as usual in his favourite chair, reading *The Sporting News*. He had no shoes on and there was the inevitable hole in each sock where his big toes poked through. She knew at once, by the disgruntled look on his face, that she was about to hear bad news. As she deposited her costume on the table, he said, 'Ruddy coppers! Can't leave me in peace for a moment. Bang, bang on the door first thing this morning. I wasn't even up! Damned sauce I call it, waking decent folk at that time!'

'The police? What did they want?' She eyed him nervously. 'You haven't done any-thing.' She was immediately filled with doubts.

'Asking stupid questions. Routine enquir-ies, they call it. I know what I call it – harass-ment! That's what!'

Alarm bells were sounding at the back of

her mind but she dumped her bag on the table and joked, 'Someone been murdered, have they?'

'Murdered? Course not! They were coppers, not detectives. Making routine enquiries about some robbery or other. I gave them short shrift. Don't expect me to do your job for you, I told them. You get paid, you put in the leg work!' He scowled. 'Well, don't just stand there. Put the kettle on and make a pot of tea.'

Rose said, 'Was it Colonel Fossett's place?'

'Him and a few others. Fuss about nothing!'

'He lost a valuable snuff box which had sentimental value. He was at The White Horse and they were all talking about it the other night.' She regarded him anxiously. 'So they don't think you did it?'

'Me?' He gave her an indignant look. 'I should ruddy well think not! They were just trying to put the frighteners on me but I'm too fly for that sort of nonsense. They said they could come back with a search warrant. Come back with anything you like, I told them. Bring Scotland Yard with you! See if I care.' He sighed heavily.

Rose gave him a sympathetic smile. 'Forget all about them, Pa. Miserable lot! I'll make that tea and then I'll tell you about my private evening. I've got plenty of good news – oh! I nearly forgot. The housekeeper gave me some leftovers for you. They're in the bag wrapped in greaseproof paper.'

He perked up at once. 'Leftovers?'

'You know – sliced ham and a smoky sort of fish and—'

'Smoky fish? What, like bloaters? I'm very partial to a nice—'

'Not bloaters! I don't know what exactly but it's pink and smells fishy, and there's a slice of the birthday cake! Help yourself, Pa. They're ever so kind and I've got so much to tell you...' She fled into the scullery to make a pot of tea but while she waited for the kettle to boil she hurried back to him. 'There's a sister named Letitia and she's marrying this terribly posh man and she said she would invite me to the wedding!'

'Invite you to the wedding? Never!'

'She said she would! Because her brother Marcus – the one who collected me – does not have anyone he can take so...'

His expression softened. 'Look Rosie, you mustn't set your heart on it. See, people like that, they say things in the heat of the moment. They mean well but then they forget all about it. I don't want you to be disappointed, that's all. I don't want you getting all upset when the invite doesn't come. If it doesn't, I mean.'

'It will come, Pa. I know it will. Letitia is not the sort to—'

'Just don't get your hopes up, Rosie. That's all I'm saying.'

Rose swallowed an angry retort, knowing

82

that her father's concern was genuine.

He said, 'So did he pay you what he promised? Half a guinea, wasn't it?'

'Yes, he did! Ten shillings and sixpence! I feel rich for the first time in my life.' She grinned with delight but then looked serious. 'And I'm not going to spend it all in a rush but ... here you are!' She drew some coins from her pocket and handed him three shillings. 'Buy some cigarettes, Pa, or a few drinks – or even a few pairs of socks or a shirt.'

He took the money with obvious disappointment. 'Three shillings?' When she failed to rise to the bait he sighed loudly. 'And what would I want with a new shirt? I'm not going anywhere.'

'No, but I am. I'm going to a posh wedding and I'm going in style. Lord knows who I'll meet there and I don't want to look like the poor relation! I need a new hat and shoes—'

'You mean you're going to fritter it all on clothes!'

Rose sat down and regarded him earnestly. 'Pa, you have to understand something. Suddenly I've got chances to better myself and I mean to take them. For a start there's the wedding but there's something else. Marcus's brother is going to introduce me to a friend of his *who owns a supper room*! He might give me a singing spot. On stage! And my name might be on the programme.

83

"Starring Miss Lamore!"' She struck a pose, arms outstretched, and smiled at an invisible audience.

He seemed unimpressed so she rushed on. 'A real job, Pa, and I'll be paid regularly. I'll be on the way up! You can come and have some supper and watch me sing. You'll love it.'

Her father's eyes had narrowed, she noticed, and her heart sank. He was going to pooh-pooh it!

'Oh yes? A decent chap, is he, this man?'

'Well of course he is. Steven would never introduce me to somebody shady. I told you, the Bennleys are a very nice family—'

'No, Rosie. The Bennley's *seem* like a very nice family. You don't know what goes on behind the scenes, so to speak. All families put on a face for outsiders. They're probably no better and no worse than most.'

Mortified, Rose snapped, 'Like us, you mean. Like the Patons.'

'If you like, yes.'

'Dark secrets!' She regretted the jibe as soon as it was uttered but too late.

Her father looked uncomfortable. 'Just don't trust them a hundred per cent.'

'At least the police weren't knocking at their door before anyone was up!'

Rose wanted to hit him. Now her father was spoiling everything, pouring cold water on her wonderful news. She said spitefully, 'And please, Dad, don't lose all that money

84

on the horses.'

'The horses?' For a moment he looked puzzled; then he grinned. 'Oh! The horses! Now when do I ever lose on a race?'

'I wouldn't know, would I, because you only ever tell me when you win!'

Before the argument could become more heated she changed the subject. In a lighter tone she asked, 'Now, do you fancy some ham and stuff? I'll put it on a plate.'

'Ooh, we are la-di-da!' he mocked. 'Just give it to me in the paper, Rosie. It tastes just as good eaten with fingers.'

Fuming inwardly, Rose handed him the leftovers and brought in two cups of tea. Her father ate the food with exaggerated murmurs of delight, shoving it into his mouth with a total lack of finesse, and washing it down with slurped gulps of tea. She knew he was doing it to annoy her so she pretended not to notice and sipped her tea as serenely as she could and in silence. Aware of the unlovely spectacle her father presented, she was heartily thankful that he would not be accompanying her to Letitia's wedding.

That night, in Victoria House, Marie lay awake trying not to think about the fact that she was dying and that she would almost certainly be dead before Christmas. She had become accustomed to the idea but it still saddened her and the nearer her death came, the more she longed to be with her mother. Over the past months, the thought of dying in Victoria House appalled her. Letitia would become hysterical, Steven would make himself scarce, afraid of the embarrassment, and poor Marcus would struggle to deal with it, longing to help but unable to do so.

Her mother and Gerard would welcome her and her mother would be a wonderful support but how was she to get over to France? Letitia refused point-blank to go with her because it meant seeing and speaking with her mother and stepfather and that she would never do. Steven was out of the question. He would make a hopeless travelling companion, partly because he was utterly self-centred and partly because he would be seasick – which left Marcus. Marcus would do his best but she needed a woman with her and she had now seen a way in which this might possibly be achieved.

On the spur of the moment she rang her bell twice which was their code for Marcus. When he arrived, in his pyjamas and dressing gown, with his hair rumpled, she was reminded of Marcus aged fifteen, home from boarding school for the holidays. He never looked relaxed, his expression was always wary and even then she sensed a slight lack of connection to those around him. Now, not for the first time, she wondered what would become of him and wished she could live longer to be of some support.

He said, 'Not a moment too soon! I was just settling down,' and sat sideways on the end of the bed. 'How can I help?'

'Marcus, please don't be upset at what I'm going to say but –' she took a deep breath – 'I want to be with Mother when I die and not here in London.'

'Oh but Marie...!' he began but then stifled the rest of his instinctive reaction.

She rushed on. 'I know you'd all look after me and I know that if we begged Mother to come to us here she would come but then Letitia would leave and everything would be unhappy and I don't want to even think about how it would be. Please say you're not offended, Marcus.'

'I'm not offended. And stop worrying about everyone else. It's your life and—'

'And my death!' She gave him a smile that made him reach out and take hold of her hand. 'Mother would love me to be there with her. I know she would although how could she say so without stirring up old quarrels? The thing is, Marcus, I was wondering if we could ask Rose to come with me. I mean the three of us. We could pay her fare and something extra, couldn't we? We could all stay for maybe a week – Mother would love it – and then you and Rose could travel back. And we needn't tell the others I'm never coming back until it's all over. They could think it's just for a few weeks but then we could say I'm not well enough to travel or something.'

Marcus stared at her in consternation. 'But Letitia's wedding. You would miss it.'

She hesitated. 'The truth is I don't care, Marcus. I could write and say that I'm not well enough to travel home. Or Mother could do it for me. And we could send a present and a card. It needn't upset her.' She smiled wanly. 'She might not even miss me. It will be such a big day for her.'

He regarded her unhappily, considering the idea from every angle.

Determined, Marie went on. 'Imagine if I came and then collapsed or something, in the middle of everything! It would ruin the best day of her life!'

Marcus nodded. 'I take your point but ... I don't know about Rose. She might be willing to come with us but when? She is so set on her career and she has an interview coming up with the owner of Andy's Supper Room. I've advised her against it but she's determined to audition. It would be asking a lot from her, to give up that opportunity.'

For a few moments they sat in silence, thinking over the ramifications of the scheme, and Marie watched her brother hopefully.

At last he shrugged. 'I suppose we should take one step at a time. We must first ask Rose if she would do it. If not, that's an end to it. If she says "Yes" ... we'll take another step.' He patted her hand. 'How's that? Is that enough for tonight? Will that make you sleep better?'

Marie threw her arms around his neck and hugged him. 'That's wonderful, Marcus. And will you ask her tomorrow?'

'I promise. Mind you, I may not be able to stay there with you for the week. I may have to come back for my work but I could pop over to bring Rose back, of course. We can't expect her to sacrifice her plans for long.'

Marie was nodding enthusiastically. 'But at least I'll be with Mother. I shall feel ... safer with her and not so anxious. And I like Gerard. I can see why Mother fell in love with him.'

For a moment her optimism wavered. She had thought many times that she would never have time to fall in love and she felt that God had cheated her a little but she had never spoken of the matter to anyone and never would.

She watched Marcus leave and then she settled down in bed and smiled into the darkness. She couldn't believe that Rose would refuse but prayed earnestly to God, asking for His help. Then, to make doubly sure, she crossed her fingers anyway. Suddenly she had something to look forward to.

Rose felt that it was taking forever for Monday to arrive but it came at last and so did the taxi. She was disappointed to discover that, contrary to her expectations, Steven had not come with it, but at least the great moment had arrived. Her father came to the front door to wave her off and the next-door neighbour, Mrs Trilby, shouted 'Best of luck, Rosie!'

Throughout the journey, Rose talked non-stop to the driver, explaining the circumstances of her ride, and she felt that he was properly impressed. She was longing to arrive but dreading the interview in case she was turned down. It would be such a humiliation.

'Here we are, miss, and I'm to wait outside and take you home.'

Rose stared out of the taxi window and was suddenly lost for words. It was not quite as she had pictured it. The sign over the double doors said 'Andy's Supper Room' but it definitely lacked that show business magic she had expected. The painted sign looked a little faded but there were lamps at the edges of the sign and she tried to convince herself that it would look exciting after dark.

The driver said, 'This is it, miss. I'll be waiting. OK?'

'Yes.' Feeling breathless, Rose stepped down on to the damp pavement, which was littered with used tickets and crumpled sweet wrappers. Rose climbed out of the taxi, carefully avoiding a small pile of dog mess, thanked the driver and assumed a shaky smile.

She was wearing her best clothes and carried her costume, a new parasol and shoes.

The driver watched her. 'Well, go on then!'

Rose took a deep breath, pushed one of the doors open and went in. She found herself in the dark and had to wait for her eyes to become accustomed to the gloom. She could smell cigarette smoke, stale beer, fatty food and lingering perfume. From somewhere nearby an elderly woman appeared. She was scrawny, a little stooped, her grey hair was scraped back in a bun and she carried a tin of polish and a cloth.

'You Miss Lamore?' She peered shortsightedly at Rose.

'Yes.' Her eyes were now better focused and she could see that there were dim lights ahead at the end of a foyer.

'He's waiting in his office. I'll show you.'

'Thank you.'

The woman hesitated. 'Watch yourself, dearie. Just a word of advice, like. He can come on a bit strong, can Mr Markham. Know what I mean?'

'Yes. I will. I mean I do.'

'I'm Connie. I do bits and pieces for His Majesty!' She laughed wheezily as they made their way past the bar and cut diagonally across the supper room which held about a dozen large round tables, each one piled with upturned chairs. 'Ever heard of Madame Moyna? That was me in the old

91

days. I used to tell fortunes. Before that I was a dancer in the chorus, here, for Mr Markham's father. He was a nice old boy. 'Course it was a bit grander in those days. Better artistes. Better clientele. Better everything. Sign of the times, isn't it, dearie?'

Rose bumped into something in the gloom and there was a loud clatter.

Connie said, 'It's the umbrella stand. No matter ... Now where was I? Oh yes. I had an accident – fell down some steps – and my dancing days were over.'

'How awful for you. I'm sorry.'

'I survive.' She gave a short laugh. 'I hope you do. The last girl lasted three weeks, then got the sack. Uncooperative. Markham's got a one-track mind. He thinks women were invented for his amusement! He can't help it and he's no worse than lots of men I've known. Know what I mean?'

Rose hoped that she didn't. Surely not, she thought anxiously. Steven had vouched for the man, hadn't he? Andrew Markham was Steven's friend so surely Connie was exaggerating.

Ahead of her she saw the stage with its draped curtains and immediately she pushed aside her doubts. This was 'theatre land'! It was 'show business'! It might be a little drab but this was the first step on the ladder.

Connie turned left, knocked on an ornate wooden door, opened it and said loudly, 'Miss Lamore's here, Mr Markham.'

'Send her in.' The voice was gruff.

Just like that. No please or thank you. Rose felt a slight frisson of disappointment. In her mind she had rather glorified Andrew Markham and marked him down as the man who would set her on the road to stardom. She had hoped for a 'benevolent uncle' type who would nurture her talent. Now, it seemed, Mr Markham had less than perfect manners and a low opinion of women.

She went into the room and as she passed Connie, the woman winked at her and wagged a finger to remind her of the warning she had given. Rose found herself in a large room lit solely by table lamps, each in red silk with gold fringing. The carpet was thick, the walls were covered in gold and red paper and there appeared to be no windows, but there was a door at the far end which was partly covered by a heavy curtain. The room was heavy with cigar smoke and she choked back a cough.

Andrew Markham was sitting at a huge mahogany desk and made no attempt to get up and greet her. He was a large, bluff man with a ruddy complexion and massive shoulders. He was, Rose realized, what her father would call a 'bruiser'. As she crossed the room towards him she saw that his clothes were obviously expensive, and a diamond flashed in his tie pin, but there was no way he was a gentleman. Not that it mattered, she told herself quickly. He was the owner of a supper room and that made him a sort of theatrical agent and that was what she had been looking for. Now she had found him and there was no point in being critical.

'Good afternoon, Mr Markham,' she began. 'It's very kind of you to—'

'I'm told you can sing.'

'Yes. I write a lot of my—'

'Let's hear something then.' He leaned back in his chair and put his feet up on the desk. 'Can you dance?'

'Er ... I haven't had lessons but I—'

'Get on with it then.' He was smoking a cigar. Regarding her through narrowed eyes and so far he hadn't smiled once.

But he doesn't have to be Prince Charming, Rose told herself, glancing round for a pianist. 'Isn't anyone going to play for me?'

'Nope. Do your best.' He leaned back and blew smoke towards the ceiling.

'I like to wear my costume—'

'There's no time. Just get on with it.'

Dismayed, Rose forced a smile and struck a pose. She sang the first few lines of her parasol song and her voice quivered with nerves. She struggled on but already Markham was holding up his hand.

Rose waited, her heart fluttering with anxiety. She knew she had performed badly but he had made her nervous and she was annoyed with him for being so unhelpful.

'Not bad. We'll see how you go. Now, let's see what we've got. Pull up your skirt, Miss

Lamore.'

She hesitated but assumed this was normal and obeyed.

'Hmm. I bit on the skinny side but never mind. Forget the dancing lessons. You'll never make the chorus line. Now let's see what you have up top. Get your jacket off and unbutton your blouse.'

'Unbutton my blouse? But why?' She removed her jacket, watching him cautiously. 'No one is going to see—'

'Just do it and hurry up. I haven't got all day.'

She stared at him in disbelief. Was he within his rights to ask such a thing?

Removing his feet from the desk he got up from the chair and came towards her. He said, 'You obviously don't understand the way this works, Miss Lamore. You want the job, you do as I tell you. Play your cards right and I can make it all happen for you. This is show business – like it or lump it. I pay the wages, you see, and I call the tune! You give a bit, I give a bit. You play along and you'll become a star. You argue and you're out the door as fast as your skinny legs will carry you.' He ran his hands up and down her bare arms and laughed when she shivered at his touch. 'Well, well! I do believe we have a virgin here!' He smiled broadly. 'Am I right?'

Stammering, bright-cheeked with embarrassment, Rose protested that it was none of his business but that simply broadened his smile.

Without warning he pushed her back against the desk, grabbed her blouse and, fighting off her hands, tore open the buttons. He took a long look and she was deeply thankful for the chemise she wore.

'Pretty enough, I daresay!' he said, daunted by the row of small buttons. 'We'll save something for another day. I think we can do business. Mondays, Wednesdays and Saturdays.' Rose had backed away, clutching her blouse, her face scarlet. 'We'll call you "Miss Rosie Lamore – an innocent abroad"! We'll play up the virgin angle and they'll have their tongues hanging out for you!'

The virgin angle? Rose was mortified. 'Um … I don't know. Steven didn't say I'd have to … that is, I'll have to … to think it over.' She sidestepped him and reached for her jacket which she pulled on with shaking fingers. 'My father … He might object. I'll have to ask him…'

Ignoring her distress, Andrew Markham retreated to his desk, picked up a pen and scribbled on a notepad. 'Rehearsal Monday, two till three … We'll supply some extra clothes. Don't bother to write the songs. Let's say half a crown a night for the first six weeks, a little more if you do well. If not you're out.' He grinned at her and Rose was reminded of a wolf. 'You've got a lot to learn, Miss Lamore, but I'm a good teacher.

Ask Connie Wainwright. She's seen it all. She'll tell you. There's not much I don't know about this business. Do what I say, and you just might make it.' He stepped back, examining her critically with his head on one side. 'But you'll have to lose the "hare in the headlights" look! Innocent, yes, but you have to look sexy with it. That's what you have to aim for.'

He laughed suddenly and Rose had to resist the urge to turn and run. She tried to smile but her face seemed stiff and unresponsive.

He reached forward and tilted her head with one finger. 'But you don't know yet what sexy means, do you? Don't worry. I'll soon enlighten you. Steven Bennley was right. I can make something of you – if you let me. And you will if you know what's good for you!'

Rose, still poised for flight, hesitated. Seven and sixpence for three spots and an hour's rehearsal Mondays. Could she bear to accept his conditions? Could she afford not to accept them? Already her insides were trembling but if this was show business she told herself she must learn to live with it. Presumably this was the lowest rung on the ladder and the higher you went, the better you'd be treated, but it was a disappointing start. She had expected some respect for her small talent – a little appreciation – but Andrew Markham had showed her nothing but contempt although he had said she was pretty and he could make something of her. Her instincts were to turn and run but her head told her to at least give it a try. Six weeks, he had said, so if she could suffer the indignities for that long she might well find things improving.

'Yes or no?' he asked.

'Yes.' She intended to say 'Thank you' but the words wouldn't come. At least he wasn't asking her to sign anything that might prove to be legally binding. She took comfort from that thought.

He shouted 'Connie!' and the door opened at once which made Rose suspect that the old woman had been listening at the door.

The interview seemed to be over. Markham was fumbling in a drawer of the desk, paying her no attention. She stammered a 'Goodbye', hurried from the room and breathed a sigh of relief.

Connie smiled sympathetically. 'You'll get used to him, dearie. We all do.' She whispered. 'Don't let him worry you.'

Rose was moving firmly towards the door to the street through which she had entered. She was shocked and her confidence had taken a knock. Did she really know what she was doing, she asked herself. Was show business really as grim as this or was Andrew Markham an exception to the rule? And why on earth hadn't Steven warned her what to expect? Or had he? Maybe in her enthusiasm she had overlooked any warnings he might have given her. Or perhaps he had no idea how he treated women.

Connie had followed her to the door. 'I was wondering, dearie, where you live, because bus fares can run away with the money.'

'Albert Street, in Stoke Newington.' She spoke distractedly, shocked by the interview and full of doubts.

Connie's eyes widened. 'That's a fair old trot!' She had reached the umbrella stand and began to pick up the half dozen brollies that Rose had knocked over on the way in.

Rose said slowly, 'I may not be coming. I may not take the job.'

Connie straightened up. 'Not taking it? Why ever not?'

'He's ... He's not the sort of man I ever expected to work for. He was rather rude, Connie, if you know what I mean.'

Connie shrugged bony shoulders. 'You mustn't take it too hard, you know. I've met much worse in my time and you just learn to take the good with the bad. And he does know a lot of people in the business. Useful people.' She patted Rose's arm. 'I tell you what – I've got a spare room just round the corner. You could stay with me and I'd keep an eye on you. He goes too far and you tell me. How would that be?'

Rosie wavered. 'I suppose it would make things easier.'

Connie pounced. 'A shilling a week for the room and sixpence extra if you want me to do you meals.'

Rose got the impression that the old woman had made this deal before and probably more than once. 'That's very kind but I shall only be coming over three days a week and I don't want to leave my father on his own.' She didn't say that this was because she didn't entirely trust him not to get himself into trouble.

Connie persisted. 'But think of the money you'd save on fares and you'd be here, on the doorstep so to speak for extra rehearsal, costume fittings, dance routines. Oh yes!' she went on, noting Rose's surprise, 'there's always an ensemble number at the end which includes all the performers. You'd have to attend that. You see, it's not quite as easy as you might think. The final ensemble number only lasts for three weeks and then Jarvis works out a new routine.'

'Jarvis?'

'You'll like Jarvis. A bit precious, you might say, but he knows his stuff. He does a bit of everything – choreography, plays the piano, he even gives singing lessons on the QT so Mr Markham doesn't find out. Kids mostly. Sixpence a half hour lesson. Bit of extra cash always comes in handy.'

In spite of her doubts, Rosie now allowed herself to be drawn into the picture Connie painted and her initial fears about Mr Markham were fading. It appeared that other people worked for him and survived so perhaps he was not quite the monster she'd imagined.

Sensing her dilemma Connie said, 'Why not give it a week or two? If you don't enjoy it you can throw in the towel. Some girls do and no harm done. No questions asked.'

'You didn't throw in the towel.'

She laughed. 'I'm a tough old bird. But he's been good to me. My little attic flat belongs to him. The whole house does, in fact, but I get mine rent-free in exchange for the work I do here and I can rent out the spare bedroom. He reckons he owes me!' She gave a short cackling laugh and tapped her nose. 'I made myself useful over the years. Say no more!'

So maybe there was better side to Andrew Markham, Rose thought cautiously. It all sounded wonderfully exciting, like stepping through a door into another world. And without being callous, the idea of her own room so near to the Supper Room sounded more attractive than staying at home with her father. But she had to be realistic.

'I'll give it two weeks,' she told Connie, 'but I'll have to stay home with my father. He's not really fit and he needs me. I'll see how the money side of it works out.' She held out her hand and the old lady shook it.

'Thanks for everything, Connie. I'll see you next week.'

★ ★ ★

As Rose drew nearer to number twenty-three she was aware of a growing anxiety. Mrs Trilby from next door was standing outside with a man she didn't recognize and when they saw Rose the woman waved urgently, which seemed ominous. Her first thought was that her father was ill. She thanked the driver and jumped from the taxi full of dread. The expressions on their faces told her that there was bad news to come.

'What's happened?' she cried. 'Where's my father? Is he all right?'

The man, she now realized, was the landlord, Herbert Granger, whom she had met occasionally when the rent collector had been absent and the owner had called instead.

He said, 'It's not good, Miss Paton, I'm afraid.'

'Oh! He's not dead? Oh my Lord! Don't say he's...'

They exchanged uncomfortable looks and Mrs Trilby said, 'No, no, dear. Nothing like that.'

'Then what? In the hospital?'

The landlord said, 'Mrs Trilby will give you the details. Please call by when you can to discuss things.' He raised his hat, turned and hurried away.

Rose stared at her neighbour who said, 'Suppose I make us a pot of tea?'

'No!' Rose was struggling to find her key.

Failing, she banged on the door and shouted, 'Pa! It's me, Rose!'

Mrs Trilby took hold of her arm. 'He's not there, dear. They've took him away. We can't talk here – everyone's earwigging! Look around you.' She was tugging her gently towards number twenty-five.

Rose glanced up and saw several faces at windows, half hidden by the curtains. Something dreadful had happened. Her anxiety gave way suddenly to an over-powering weakness and she allowed herself without further protest to be led inside Mrs Trilby's house and seated in her living room. Mrs Trilby sat down opposite her.

'It was the police, Rose. They come back with one of them warrants and searched the house from top to bottom and found...'

Rose's hand crept to cover her mouth. 'Oh no!'

'They found some jewellery and stuff what they say your pa was hiding for someone else. Some chap called Babe, or Baby or some-such. Like a nickname, I suppose. They've arrested him for receiving stolen goods.'

'I don't believe it!' she cried, but in her heart she did. She simply did not want to believe it.

Mrs Trilby leaned forward and patted her knee. 'I'm sorry, dear, but they had the stuff they found, in a sack. It's the truth.' She shrugged. 'These things happen. No one's

103

pointing the finger at you. Seems like this other chap split on him. No such thing as honour among thieves. Now you sit tight and I'll make us some tea. It's been a shock and a cuppa will revive you.'

She bustled into the scullery while Rose, exhausted by the shock, tried to make sense of what she had heard. So what had the landlord been doing, she wondered, and followed Mrs Trilby into the scullery where a large tub of washing waited to be put through the mangle which she saw in the backyard.

'What was Mr Granger doing here?' she asked.

Mrs Trilby looked at her unhappily. 'Well, that's another bit of bad news, dear. Seems the police notified him that he was being taken into custody and charged and there was some rent owing so the landlord came round to—'

Rose gave a small cry. 'Oh, not the bailiffs! I can't bear it. I don't believe it. Pa would have paid the rent. He was never short of cash. He was so lucky on the ... horses.' She sank down on a stool and covered her face with her hands. 'Don't say he didn't win that money! Don't say he ... Oh Pa! What have you done?'

She wondered what the bailiffs would take if they were sent in to try and recoup the rent that was owed. They had so little that was of any value. And how would she pay the rent? The answer was that she could not do it. Her life, so exciting a few hours back, was now collapsing around her. She stood up unsteadily. 'I think I'm going to be sick!' she murmured.

'Not in here, you aren't!' snapped Mrs Trilby and, rolling her eyes, she pushed Rose none too gently out of the back door into the yard. Clinging to the mangle, Rose threw up on to a pile of ashes, recently raked from Mrs Trilby's stove.

The following day was Tuesday and by ten thirty in the morning Letitia Bennley was happily immersed in plans for the wedding. She sat at the table on the terrace in the sunshine surrounded by lists of people she wanted to invite, those she might invite and those she definitely would not invite. She wore a lightweight dress and jacket in pale green with matching shoes and a large straw hat and, framed by the white trellis behind her, she imagined that she presented the kind of elegant woman that the da Silva family would appreciate. She regretted the fact that only her two brothers were around to see her. Marie would not be down until later.

'Let me see...' she mused. 'Alison Wen-tropp? I'm having second thoughts about her because I'd have to include her mother and she's so awfully fat! She will certainly lower the tone and ruin the photographs!

Unless we make sure she is in the back row … Alison did invite me to her Easter Bonnet party and that was fun.' She put a question mark against the Wentropps. 'Although I do want her to see me on the day, not just in the photograph!' She circled the question mark and moved on.

The problem was that the da Silvas had so many friends and hopelessly outnumbered Letitia's. Bernard had hinted that the venue – his uncle's house – would easily accommodate fifty people. Letitia wanted to make sure that she had as many guests as he had but the Bennleys were a small family. Obviously her mother and Gerard would not be invited – she had decided to pretend, if questions were asked, that Mother was devoted to Gerard who was an invalid and refused to leave him in the care of others.

'Aunt Daisy…?' The maiden aunt who was crippled with rheumatism and never left her large cottage in Dorset. 'No.'

There were two uncles – one of whom was too fond of his drink to be invited although he had once been something unimportant at the British Consulate in Denmark and would otherwise have qualified for inclusion. She sighed. The second uncle, on her father's side, was a remote figure with whom they exchanged Christmas cards but had not seen for at least twenty-five years. Maybe they could risk an invitation. She added another question mark and glanced up as

Marcus approached and patted the seat next to her. He sat down, looking his usual awkward self.

'You'll be glad to know you are on my wedding list,' she told him cheerfully. 'So do please send me a decent present. I'm wondering whether or not to invite Uncle Henry...'

'Uncle Henry? We haven't set eyes on him for years.'

'I know but I'm sure he wouldn't accept. The point is to present a decent invitation list to Bernard's mother when I go to lunch on Thursday so she doesn't think we are completely beyond the pale! She'll be able to send out dozens of invitations. If the people on my list don't come no one can blame me – and they might send presents.' She added his name to the list and smiled at him. 'Don't look so gloomy, Marcus. You'll enjoy it on the day – and then you'll be rid of me!' She laughed, waiting for him to deny it.

Instead he said, 'Marie wants to be with Mother for a few weeks, or more. She needs her. It's understandable.'

Letitia's eyes narrowed and she set down the pencil, placing it carefully alongside the notebook. The excitement faded from her face. 'If you are going to ask me to take her over there, the answer's "No". You know my feelings. The man's a swine and Mother was a fool ever to allow him to...' She swallowed hard.

'Father wasn't anything to boast about, either. Just because you were his favourite you think he was a wonderful man but he made Mother unhappy.'

'She betrayed him!'

'If Father had treated her better she might have remained faithful.'

'You never liked him.'

'He never liked me! He made me feel like a freak. When you came along he was delighted – his little princess! He ignored me and made such a fuss of you that he and Mother argued about it. I heard them. Mama said he—' He was beginning to sound agitated and stopped abruptly.

He was annoyed with himself, Letitia realized with a small spark of triumph, for revealing the hurt he had felt all those years ago. She had revelled in her father's admiration.

Marcus went on. 'But we're getting off the point. Marie has asked me if I would take her over if Rose comes with us.'

Taken aback, Letitia frowned. 'Rose Paige?'

'Yes. I don't know if she'll agree but—'

'*I* don't agree. She's not at all suitable.'

'How can you say that? You've invited her to your wedding, haven't you?'

Flustered, Letitia cast her mind back. 'I may have said something but if she doesn't get an invitation she won't be coming.'

'But you promised her an invitation. You can't disappoint her! Anyway you said I can bring a friend. You actually said that she could come as my friend so I shall bring her with me.'

Letitia raised her eyebrows. 'Oh dear! Please don't tell me that you like the funny little thing.'

'She's not funny but yes I do like her but not in the way you mean. We all liked her, if you remember. Even Bernard.'

Letitia's elegant poise deserted her momentarily. 'Bernard? I'm sure he didn't.'

Marcus shrugged. 'To get back to what we were talking about – Marie's request that she should spend time with Mother. Of course we must make that possible and if Rose would come with us that would solve the problem. If Rose agrees, that is.'

Letitia thought rapidly. 'It would have to be a holiday for her. We don't want to pay her anything.'

'On the contrary, we would have to pay her as a travelling companion because she has work of her own as a singer and would be forced to miss it. She can't exist on fresh air.'

Letitia regarded her brother with something akin to loathing. Why did he have to spoil her morning? She had been feeling very cheerful with life and had been looking forward to making her invitation list and then Marcus had to blunder in and ruin everything. The way he always did when they were children, she thought.

'By work you mean ironing and singing in seedy halls. Well, she won't need much compensation for losing that!'

Marcus flushed angrily. 'I think what you mean is – "I hope she will agree to go with Marie and I shall be grateful that *I* don't have to make the journey"! That would be a generous reply in the circumstances but then generosity was never your strong point, was it!'

They glared angrily at each other and Letitia flirted with the idea of crossing her brother off the list but that would look odd and she didn't want the da Silvas to think she was at odds with members of her family. She swallowed hard and her anger turned to anxiety. What had Bernard said about liking Rose, she wondered uneasily. She desperately wanted to know but would die rather than ask Marcus.

He broke the long silence. 'Then I'll go in search of her and ask her if she'll do it for us. I also want to know what happened at her interview with that Markham chap. Steven seemed to think he was a reasonable man but I'm not so sure.'

'She's not exactly a shrinking violet, Marcus. I'm sure she can look after herself without you trailing after her. She's chosen a tough profession so she'll have to take the rough with the smooth. Let me know what she says.' She turned back to her lists, trying to hide the fact that the conversation had upset her.

He hesitated for a moment as if he was about to add something but she glanced up from beneath the brim of her straw hat and said, 'You still here?'

Four

PC Arnold Wicker smiled at the young woman on the other side of the front desk. 'And what can we do for you, miss?' he asked, smiling. 'Cat stuck up a tree, is it? Little brother got his head stuck in some railings?' He fancied himself as a bit of a wag. His mother always laughed at his jokes and so did Doris, his young lady.

This particular young lady did not even smile. She said 'Hilarious! I need to speak to someone a little more senior. Is PC Stump around by any chance?'

''Fraid not.' She was looking a bit stern but she was still pretty. Blonde curls were a weakness of his. 'Will I do, miss? Tell me what's wrong and I'll see if I can help.'

'I'd rather speak to PC Stump.'

'He's still on leave. His wife died. Did you know? Poor blighter. Knock you sideways, something like that. Funeral's Friday.'

'I'll talk to someone else then. It's about my father, Alan Paton. My neighbour says he's been arrested. I'm Rose Paton and I want to ... to make a complaint of wrongful arrest. It's got to be a mistake. I need to talk to him.'

His eyes widened. Of course. They had found stolen goods stashed away in his house earlier in the day and they'd caught him red-handed, so to speak. Some mistake! 'They found the stolen property, miss. Tipped off by his partner in crime. We've got them both under lock and key.'

That took her back a bit. He saw the doubt written clear as day on her face. Nice eyes. Shame about the father.

She pulled herself together. 'Then I want to be a character witness. I know him. He must have been led astray. Can't he be released on bail or something? He's not dangerous.'

He laughed. 'Sorry, miss, but can't be done. Rules is rules, as they say. They'll both be up before the magistrate – most likely next week. But I have to say they don't have a leg to stand on. They'll both go down.' He could almost see the thoughts whirring round in her brain. Plucky little thing.

'Then I'll make a statement. He's ... he's always been weak. I'll admit that. He might be stupid but he's not bad ... and the money he had came from his gambling. He liked a flutter on the horses and he was very shrewd. He ... he understood racing. Studied it all his life.'

He shrugged. 'Not up to me, miss.'

'But if I could prove that he didn't get any money from it? That would count in his favour, wouldn't it? I mean, if he didn't profit from the burglaries that would make a difference. If I can find the bookie's runner, I know where he waits for the bets, and—'

He interrupted her, leaning forward, glancing over his shoulder as though afraid of being heard. 'He said something, your father, about the rent. About he wanted to leave you a message but we don't encourage that sort of thing.'

'The rent?' She tried to look innocent of any prior knowledge. 'What about it?'

'Owing, I reckon, don't you? I mean, what else?'

Rose wanted to scream. It would be all round the neighbourhood at this rate. As if she didn't have enough to worry about.

The constable now glanced past her as the door swung open behind her. A man came in and said 'Rose?' and she turned, dismayed.

'Marcus! Oh no!' Why did he have to turn up and witness her downfall, she thought hysterically.

Without any warning, Alan Paton's daughter burst into tears and the two men exchanged discomfited glances.

'Women!' mouthed Arnold.

'It's all a mistake,' Rose insisted as she and Marcus hurried along the High Street in search of the man who took the illegal bets and rushed them to the bookie. 'The man's name is Wilf Todmore. Pa has often mentioned him. Look! There he is!' She pointed. 'On that corner by the pawnbroker's.'

Marcus said, 'Do you expect him to admit it?'

'If I explain the circumstances.' She speeded up and arrived at the corner almost out of breath.

The man saw them coming and glanced round nervously.

Marcus took hold of her arm but she shook him off.

'Mr Todmore, would you be willing to sign something at the—'

'I never sign nothing!' he told her.

'Please. It's nothing bad. It's just that my father was one of your clients – his name is—'

'I don't have no clients, miss. And my name's Sydney Cooper.' He looked at Marcus and tapped his forehead. 'Bit, you know, is she?'

'No I'm not!' cried Rose, her voice rising. 'Leave him out of this.'

Todmore put a finger to his lips and muttered, 'Keep your voice down, you silly cow!'

'Sorry.' She lowered her voice. 'My father's name is Alan Paton and he's a regular with you. He often gets lucky with the horses and—'

'Horses? Dunno what you're talking about, miss.'

Marcus looked embarrassed. 'He's not the

man, Rose,' he hissed urgently. 'Do please come away. You're making a scene.'

She rounded on him angrily. 'Stop interfering, Marcus. I'll make a scene if I want to. My pa is in a lot of trouble and I'm doing my best to sort it out. People like you wouldn't understand so mind your own business and I'll mind mine!' Her voice shook and a few more tears trickled unheeded down her face. She turned back to the bookie's runner but at that moment a large, elderly woman arrived. She was dressed in black from head to foot except for a sacking apron and a battered straw hat with faded red ribbons. She held out a few coins to the man Rose thought of as Wilf Todmore.

'Here y'are, Sydney.' She had lowered her voice. 'Three thirty, each way on Bright Star.'

Glancing quickly around him, he took out a small notebook, scribbled something, tore out half the page and handed it to her. 'How's hubby?' he asked.

She shrugged. 'He won't get no better but he ain't no worse, thanks for askin'.' She looked at Rose. ''Aven't I seen you at The White Horse? Aren't you the singer with the brolly?'

For a moment Rose brightened but then, remembering the present circumstances, she said, 'No. It wasn't me.'

'Well, you're the spitting image!' She

116

lowered her voice. 'Listen, dearie. Hot tip. Bright Star. Three thirty. Sure thing.'

'Oh, er. Thank you.'

The woman tapped her nose. 'We got this system, see. I do the tea leaves and my Bert, he interprets 'em. That's what it's called, see – interpreting, though some people call it reading but it's not the same thing. I saw a sort of star this morning in the dregs of his tea cup and right off he looks down the runners and blow me down – he sees Bright Star!' She waggled fat fingers by way of goodbye and they all watched her go.

Marcus asked him, 'Does it work, her system?'

'Hardly ever.' He turned to Rose. 'Satisfied? Now hop it!'

Marcus took hold of Rose's arm. 'His name's Sydney. He's not the one, Rose.'

Rose was reluctant to give up. 'Does a Wilfred Todmore ever come here?'

'I've never heard of him and that's the honest truth.' He looked at Marcus. 'Take her away, for Gawd's sake! She'll get my ruddy collar felt!'

Marcus took out his handkerchief, wiped Rose's tears and led her away. 'We'll find a café,' he told her, 'and have a cup of tea.'

Subdued by her disappointment she asked, 'What are you doing here? I don't want you following me around just now.'

'I've something to ask you, Rose. Something exciting.'

'Exciting?' She shook her head. 'No thanks, Marcus! I've had enough excitement for one day.'

'Are you going to explain why the bookie's runner was so important?'

'No. It's ... it's a private matter.'

'What was all that about tea leaves?'

'Forget about it, Marcus. I've got too much on my mind right now.'

'Aren't you ever going to tell me what's going on?'

'Probably not.'

Wisely, he made no reply.

Fifteen minutes later they were sitting in 'Maida's Café' with tea and cakes and Rose was listening half-heartedly to Marcus's offer.

'So you want me to come with you and Marie to take her to France, to your mother? Is that right?'

'To help look after her on the journey, yes. I thought you'd jump at the chance.'

He was obviously disappointed with the way she had received his exciting news and Rose understood. At any other time she would have jumped at the chance but now she had her career to think about and she also had to deal with her father's arrest and the possible arrival of the bailiffs. The latter was a deep humiliation to her and she was determined that Marcus should remain in the dark about it for as long as possible.

'I have three performances a week at Andy's Supper Room,' she told him with more than a hint of pride. 'How can I let them down? It's my big chance.'

'I see that. Couldn't you ask him to alter the dates – let you start later?'

'But I need the work. I have to live!' Already she had worked out that she would have to leave the house where she was born. With half the furniture missing and no contribution from her father – legal or otherwise – she was going to have to move out and Connie's place beckoned. If she went to France she might come back and find that someone else was renting Connie's spare room.

'But we'd pay you for your time,' he told her. 'Didn't I say that?'

'No you didn't.' Just like rich people, she thought bitterly. Money was of no interest. Even now he wasn't telling her how much they would give her and she would have to ask.

He said, 'It would be wonderful if you could find a way to do it, Rose. Marie seems to have set her heart on you coming with us – and you could meet my mother and Gerard. Marie wrote about you to them and I'm sure they would love to meet you.'

Rose tried to imagine herself sailing away from all her troubles for a few days, meeting pleasant people and enjoying an adventure. And helping poor Marie, of course.

'How long would we be away?' she asked cautiously. 'I can't just disappear.'

'Maybe a week, maybe a little longer.'

'And will she come home with us?'

'That hasn't been decided yet. It depends on several things – her health mainly – but if she wanted to stay longer we could come back together.'

Rose regarded him keenly, aware that he was holding something back. Just as she had with him. 'And Letitia won't go?'

'No.'

With a grin, she echoed his earlier question to her. 'Aren't you ever going to tell me what's going on?'

He laughed. 'I suppose I asked for that!'

'With Letitia and her mother, I mean.'

His expression changed. 'Father was a very difficult man to live with. If he didn't like you, you were made aware of it. He married Mother for her family's money and then never forgave her. He made her very unhappy and one summer, in desperation, Mother took off for France where her French mother lived and took me with her. There she met Gerard Feigant.'

'Who was kind to her.'

He nodded. 'They fell in love and ... the inevitable happened. Mother and I had to come home so that Father would think that the child was his.' He fell silent, allowing her to work out the consequences of what he had told her.

Rose stared at him, her eyes widening. 'You mean that ... Letitia is Gerard's daughter.'

'Yes, but you mustn't let her know that I've told you. That is why she hates him. Because she is not entirely 'one of us'. That's why she hates them both. Not that she has ever met Gerard. She hasn't.'

'But what about Steven and Marie?'

'They are father's children, as I am. But eventually, during a major quarrel, the truth came out and Father walked out of the house and never came back. It was a terrible time. Mother thought he might have killed himself and alerted the police, but then divorce papers arrived. It was in all the newspapers! After the turmoil died down, Mother went to live with Gerard and her aunt came to run the household here. She died some time ago but by then we were old enough to look after ourselves.' He threw up his hands in a helpless gesture. 'Not a very nice story, is it?'

Rose's reaction was one of gratitude. She was grateful that his family, too, had their share of 'skeletons in the cupboard', so to speak. Weak with relief she leaned forward and planted a kiss on his cheek which made him blush.

'Right then,' she told him, pouring them both a second cup of tea, 'I shall now tell you about *our* shady dealings, past and present, but first please order some more cakes!'

Letitia and Alicia da Silva sat at the large table in the morning room, surrounded by lists, address books and diaries, and Letitia had rarely felt happier. Her wedding was almost upon them and nothing had happened to cast a blight on their plans. Mrs da Silva, although not exactly enamoured of Bernard's choice of a bride, had bowed graciously to the *fait accompli* when Bernard asked his parents for their approval. There had been a young woman by the name of Carlotta Todd with whom Bernard had been involved for many years, the daughter of close friends of the da Silvas, and it had almost been taken for granted that she would be Bernard's choice. Unhappily for her but happily for Letitia, the latter had swept Bernard off his feet when they met and Alicia had been forced to hide her disappointment at the sudden change of plans.

Carlotta, plain but warm-hearted, came from a well-connected family, but Letitia had dazzled Bernard with her glossy dark hair and challenging brown eyes. At least, thought Alicia, they would produce handsome children.

Letitia handed over her neatly written list and sipped her lemonade, arranging her features into a serene expression while she waited with churning insides for any adverse comments. They weren't long in coming.

'Oh my dear! I don't see your mother's

name here, Letitia. It will arouse some comment, don't you think? I know you are not on the best of terms but we must surely invite her and her husband.' She looked at Letitia with raised eyebrows.

'She will have to refuse the invitation,' Letitia told her. 'My sister Marie is going to stay with them and, as you know, she is seriously ill and it's very likely that none of them will be able to attend.' She had rehearsed the little speech and delivered it with what she hoped was genuine sounding regret.

'How very sad. You must be heartbroken but it is quite understandable. They must all be sent an invitation – it's simply etiquette ... and they must write back and explain. Now let me see who else you have invited. Jane Coldwell?'

'I was at school with her. We've remained friends.' In fact, Letitia had lost touch with her but Alicia need not know that. 'She is always travelling so I shall use her most recent address.' It would be useful if they *did* manage to reach her because then Jane could tell everyone how popular and how clever Letitia had been at the exclusive boarding school both girls had attended.

'I see ... and Mrs Bray and daughter?'

'Our very devoted housekeeper.' Even to Letitia's ears it hardly sounded impressive but she hoped it sounded compassionate.

'Oh how kind of you, Letitia ... And the

Wentropps and Henry Bennley (uncle) and Marion Tant. Let me guess! Marion Tant is your godmother?'

'No, my godmother is dead, sadly. She was a great friend, actually, and would have loved to be present. I wish...'

Alicia glanced past her and smiled. 'Oh good, here comes Bernard! He can help us out. I've made out a list but he has a better memory than I do.' She beckoned him with a wave of her hand. 'Do come and join us, dear. Important decisions are being made.'

Letitia greeted him with a bright smile as he leaned down and kissed the top of her head. 'We're going through the wedding lists,' she told him, somewhat unnecessarily, but her hopes plummeted. He was sure to notice that Rose Paton's name was missing whereas Alicia would probably have been none the wiser.

Alicia patted the seat beside her so that he sat down opposite his bride-to-be. Peering over her spectacles, she continued to study the list. At last she said to her son, 'What was that young woman's name, dear? The singer that performed at Marie's birthday party.' To Letitia she said, 'My son was very impressed. Said she brightened up the evening.'

'That was Rose, Mother. I forget her other name.'

They both looked at Letitia for enlightenment. 'I'm afraid she won't be able to attend, either,' she told them firmly. 'Marcus has persuaded her to accompany Marie to France. A paid companion. Really, the timing is unfortunate but poor Marie is so much worse.

'Send her an invitation anyway, Mother. Even if she doesn't come she will like to know she has been remembered. Such a lively soul. Full of that hard to find *joie de vivre*!' Turning to Letitia he said, 'You found her quite charming, didn't you, dearest?'

'I did indeed.' She forced the words out. 'Very ... theatrical.' She turned to her future mother-in-law. 'All fluttering eyelashes! In the best vaudeville tradition!'

Alicia's eyebrows went up. 'Really? Bernard thought she was very modest and quite charming considering her chosen ambition.'

'She was certainly talented.' Letitia's mouth was dry. She longed for a change of subject but when it came it shocked her.

Bernard said, 'We're inviting the Todds, naturally. Simon and Nora Todd. Old friends of ours. I mentioned their daughter, Carlotta.'

Letitia felt a sudden coldness and her smile faltered. Not Carlotta! Bernard had assured her that the friendship was almost platonic except in the minds of the parents, but she suspected that Carlotta must have felt more for Bernard than she ever admitted. Or that Bernard admitted to *her*. There were photographs in the da Silva albums of the two as children growing up together and

125

as young adults with their arms draped around each other. Childhood sweethearts.

Alicia gave her a sharp glance. 'You don't mind, I hope. The young romance died, Letitia, the moment Bernard met you! Of course Carlotta was devastated but she's young and will find someone else eventually. These things happen.' She sighed. 'We haven't seen her for ages but she appeared on Monday, quite out of the blue, which I take to be a good sign.'

And Bernard had not said a word about the visit! Letitia stared down at her hands which rested on the table but, seeing that they shook slightly, she put them in her lap instead while she tried to find something casual to say. She knew without looking at him that Bernard had deliberately not told her that he had spent time with his former sweetheart. For whatever reason. Had they been alone together? It was ironic, she thought, that while she, Letitia, had been uneasy about Bernard's admiration for Rose, he had been keeping from her a meeting he had had with his former soulmate.

While she struggled to hide her emotions every second felt like an hour and the thought of a protracted lunch with the da Silvas was more than she could bear. She became aware suddenly that both Alicia and Bernard were staring at her anxiously.

'Is something wrong, Letitia?' Alicia was looking at her with concern.

126

Unable to speak, she shook her head and then, changed her mind and nodded. She would pretend to be unwell and would ask to be taken home.

Bernard understood only too well what was wrong and said, 'I haven't had a chance to tell you. It was nothing, Letitia. She came to see Mother because she wanted to know what to buy us for a wedding present. You know what they say about "too many toast racks"!'

Letitia nodded, then put a hand to her head. He laid a hand on her shoulder but she flinched at his touch.

Alicia said, 'You're very pale, my dear. You must come upstairs and lie down. No, I insist. I shall bring up a damp towel for your forehead. Come along, Letitia.'

Too upset to argue, she allowed herself to be led upstairs and settled on the bed in one of the guest rooms. Alicia closed the curtains and placed a bottle of sal volatile on the bedside table.

As soon as she was alone, Letitia sat up and snatched up the restorative, removed the stopper and sniffed gently at the pungent fumes. Almost at once her head cleared and she thought quickly. She was not going to faint but she would remain there for ten minutes, claiming the approach of 'a sick headache', just to satisfy Alicia's curiosity and maybe...

There was a knock at the door and Bernard came in with the damp cloth his mother had promised.

'I have a sick headache coming on, Bernard.' Hastily swinging her feet to the floor, Letitia stood up. 'I'm afraid I shall have to go straight home—'

'No wait, dearest. This is all my fault! I was going to tell you, Letitia – not that there is anything to tell. We didn't know she was coming and I was on my way out at the time. She—'

'Bernard, stop. I don't want to hear anything about it. My head aches. It's nothing to do with Carlotta. If you want to see her, you are free to do so. I have a sick headache and talking like this is making it worse.'

He regarded her helplessly – or, she wondered, did he look guilty?

'Letitia, there is no reason at all for you to imagine—'

'I'm not imagining anything. You told me you never felt anything for her other than affection but your mother spoke of a "young romance" and says Carlotta was "devastated" when you met me! Is it any wonder if I'm a little confused? Is it any wonder that I now have a thumping headache ... and as for Rose!' With horror she realized that her voice trembled and she was on the verge of tears. She had said so much more than she intended. Whatever would he think of her? She risked a glance at his face, saw that her wild words had disconcerted him and hastily looked away.

'What on earth has Rose got to do with this?' he asked. 'We were talking about Carlotta. I'm trying to explain how it was between us. We grew up as children together and were very good friends. I had no idea that her feelings towards me had changed because she said nothing to me.' He shrugged. 'Maybe I was naive but I didn't realize that the parents were hoping we would one day marry.'

'And you had given her no reason to think you loved her?' It was intended as a plea for reassurance but it came out like an accusation. Letitia took another sniff at the sal volatile. She must stay calm, she told herself. Calm and reasonable.

'You're saying I led her on? Really Letitia, I never thought to hear you say such a thing.' His tone was indignant.

She looked at him desperately. This was turning into their first ever quarrel, she realized, and she could not bear it. If only he would understand how much she needed reassurance. First Rose seemed to be a threat waiting 'in the wings' and now it was Carlotta! She was panic-stricken. 'So what did you decide on?' she asked. 'When Carlotta came to ask for advice about what she should give us?'

He looked puzzled and then his face cleared. 'Oh nothing, really. We just talked about this and that.'

'And I suppose she asked if you were happy?'

He considered. 'She did, as a matter of fact. How did you guess?'

Letitia drew a long breath. 'Because if I loved you still I would want to know if there was the smallest chance that you were regretting your decision. I would make a last desperate attempt to change your mind – even at this late stage.'

She saw then, with a sickening clarity, that he recognized the truth of what she was saying.

'What does it matter what she wanted or ... or why she came? She had her answer.'

'Are you sure you convinced her – that you loved me?'

'I'm sure.'

She could not read his expression. 'What exactly did you say to her?'

'That we were very much in love and that we had never exchanged a cross word.' He looked at her reproachfully. 'I may have added that we trusted each other.'

Frozen with a mixture of relief and regret, Letitia stared at him wordlessly – relieved that he had convinced Carlotta that he had never loved her but full of regret that she had revealed her own fears of rejection. For a long time neither spoke. She thought that if Bernard turned from her and walked from the room she would know that she was not forgiven. It would be all over.

Instead he held out his arms and she stepped into their familiar warmth and clung to him. But in spite of his belated words of reassurance Letitia's heart raced and the panic refused to subside. It felt to her at that moment that something had changed between them and a shadow had been cast over their once bright future.

That evening, several hours after Letitia had gone home after a very subdued lunch, Bernard looked up from the evening paper to see his mother bearing down upon him. He had expected it and folded the newspaper and set it aside.

'We have to talk, Bernard,' his mother began, settling herself on the nearest sofa. 'Your father and I need your reassurance about your forthcoming marriage. I am not insensitive, Bernard, as you know, and I sense that all is not well. Talk to me.'

A large tabby cat had followed her in and now jumped up on to her lap. Alicia picked it up, said 'Not now, Tabsy!' and dumped it ceremoniously on to the floor. 'Shoo!'

Offended, the cat ran from the room and Bernard wished he could do the same.

'I don't know what to say,' he began. He had spent hours wondering how much he dare tell his mother and he had come to no conclusions.

'Then answer me this. Why *did* Carlotta call in the other day? Was it only about the wedding present? My intuition says it was not. I thought it odd at the time but let it pass.'

Bernard ran anxious fingers through his hair.

'Bernard! Talk to me!'

'No, it wasn't only that. She ... Carlotta wanted to know if I really was in love with Letitia.'

'And you told her ... what exactly?'

He avoided her gaze. 'I hesitated and she at once—'

'You *hesitated*?' Appalled, she sat up straighter, clutching her necklace. 'Good heavens, Bernard. Have you taken leave of your senses? A hesitation speaks volumes! How could you have been so foolish? The poor young woman must have thought that you had doubts! Don't you see that? What did she say?'

'That she still loved me and ... and that it wasn't too late. She would forgive me for everything and we could make a fresh start.'

'Oh Bernard!' She fell back in the chair, staring at him. 'I can't believe this is happening. Only weeks before the wedding and everything arranged. Your father will be furious when he knows.'

'Why does he have to know? Why can't it stay between the three of us?'

As his meaning became clear, hope shone in her eyes. 'You didn't tell Letitia all this?'

'No. I lied to her. Does that please you?'

Alicia thought about it, a hand to her head. At last she said, 'What did you say to Carlotta ... exactly?' He hesitated and she groaned. 'Oh Lord! You didn't give her hope, did you?'

'Of course not. I said that it was much too late to change things and that I do love Letitia but ... but that I hoped she would always remain my dearest friend. My closest friend.'

His mother now had one hand protectively across her throat. She was shaking her head slowly from side to side. 'Tell me you didn't say you hoped she and Letitia would become friends!'

'Why ever not, Mother?'

'You *did*!'

'You are being melodramatic!' he said irritably. 'You know how I hate it when you do that!'

'And you are being extremely optimistic, Bernard, not to say foolhardy. Answer me this question with total honesty – did you tell Carlotta that you still loved her?'

He jumped to his feet and stared down at her, his face reddening. 'I may have said something of the sort but ... I couldn't bear to hurt her feelings. I think I said I loved them both in different ways. Something tactful like that. I'm not a complete idiot although you obviously think I am!' He was glaring at her now. 'What the hell does it matter what I said to her? I'm marrying

133

Letitia and that's the end of it. Carlotta understands that. She was very reasonable about it. Now I really can't take any more of this ... this inquisition. Excuse me!'

He turned and almost ran from the room, through the house and out into the garden. He headed for the summer house where he threw himself down into one of the faded chairs. 'Well Bernard,' he told himself, 'that didn't go so well, did it! First Carlotta, then Letitia and now Mother! You've upset everyone except Father but Mother will now upset him!'

The cat appeared and looked up at him warily. Bernard stared down at him. 'Where did we go wrong, Tabsy?' he asked shakily.

The cat blinked and, with a deep sigh, Bernard leaned down and picked him up. At once the cat settled down in his lap and began to purr and as he stroked it, Bernard wondered enviously if he would ever feel that happy.

As soon as Rose had sent Marcus back to his family, she set off in the direction of Garret Street where the landlord lived at number seven. To her surprise she was invited in by an elderly lady who led the way to an ornately decorated sitting room, severely shaded by heavy curtains in faded brown and only one gas light which flickered and spluttered as if it was on the verge of going out. On the mantelpiece a large mahogany cased clock showed the time to be three minutes to one although Rose knew it was much later.

'My son will be with you in a moment,' the old lady announced. 'How are you getting on?'

'Er ... I'm very well, thank you.'

'You'll never regret the lessons, you know. Everyone says that. It's quite an asset in later life.' She clasped her mittened hands and nodded encouragement.

Rose began to think that she had come to the wrong house. 'I've come to see Mr Granger, the landlord of number twenty-three Albert Street.'

'Ah! A landlord, is he? Nothing surprises me. I always said he could turn his hand to anything. He was only eleven when I said to my husband, that boy has the potential to ... Oh, here he comes.'

Footsteps sounded in the passage and the door opened to admit a tall, thin man. He regarded Rose with surprise.

'I'm Rose Paton, the daughter of your tenant at twenty-three Albert Street. My father...'

'Oh yes, of course. Arrested for receiving. I remember you – you're his daughter.' He regarded her with ill-concealed curiosity. 'You take after your mother, I assume.'

His mother interrupted eagerly. 'She's come for her lesson, William. I was just telling her that playing the piano is an asset you will always appreciate. I started to play when

I was six years old...'

He shook his head. 'Mother, that was William. He taught the piano, not me. He died. Do try to remember.'

'William died?'

'Yes. I'm Herbert, your other son. Now please go and give Mrs Lake a hand in the kitchen while I sort out this little problem.'

Although he spoke kindly, the old woman looked at him fearfully. 'Herbert?'

'Yes, Mother.' He held the door open for her.

She said, 'How silly of me.' To Rose she said, 'I get a bit muddled these days.'

Rose smiled. 'Life can be a bit of a muddle for all of us.'

'Off you go, Mother.'

'Yes, dear. I'm going.' She smiled at Rose and whispered, 'Good luck with the lesson. You'll be fine.'

Rose, already feeling fraught, fought down an urge to cry for the second time that day. Was there anyone in the whole world who was not feeling lost and bewildered, she wondered, and began to consider her visit here a mistake.

Herbert Granger said, 'Sit down, Miss Paton. You've come about the rent arrears, I assume.' He waited for her to sit, then followed suit. He chose a high-backed chair and crossed his legs. 'The bailiffs are due at your house at eleven tomorrow morning. If you are in you will be able to discuss with

136

them which furniture they remove. If not they will have a key and will remove...'

He speaks nicely, thought Rose, and he dresses well. Reluctantly she was impressed, both by his appearance and his manners. His trousers were well cut from good quality cloth and his high-collared white shirt was spotless. His shoes shone and his fingernails were neatly manicured.

She heard herself ask the all-important question. 'How much do we owe?'

'In monetary terms it's sixty shillings, which is three pounds.'

'I can't pay it. You know that my father has been arrested? He may be ... away for some months.' He nodded, his face stern. 'I have an idea, Mr Granger. I shall have to find other accommodation – a rented room – and will not be needing any of our furniture. Neither will my father for the foreseeable future.'

He raised his eyebrows and Rose felt that he was impressed with her little speech and she at once felt a small surge of confidence. 'This is my suggestion, Mr Granger. If you work out the value of *all* the furniture, you could deduct what we owe, keep all the furniture – since I have nowhere to store it – and give me the difference.'

If he was surprised he hid it well. 'And why should I do this?'

'Because then you could rent out the house as furnished instead of unfurnished and I could use the money to start paying the rent for a furnished room somewhere.' She had Connie's spare room in mind. 'It would be to your advantage as well as mine.'

He was watching her closely without giving any clue as to his possible answer. At last he said, 'What do you do for a living, Miss Paton? When you are not negotiating financial deals, that is.'

'I'm an artiste, Mr Granger. My stage name is Miss Lamore and I sing. If you want to find out more come to Andy's Supper Room Monday, Wednesday or Fridays.' She added untruthfully, 'I'm something of a favourite, although I say it as shouldn't!' It wasn't exactly a lie, she assured herself, because she certainly *would* be a favourite before long. She rather hoped he would check up on her one evening. It would be fun to spot him in the audience. He might even call out to her during the applause. 'Well done, Miss Lamore!'

His eyes widened. 'An artiste? A *favourite* artiste! Well, well!'

While Rose was trying to decide whether or not he was mocking her, the door opened and his mother came in.

She said, 'Oh sorry, William. I was looking for...'

He said, 'Miss Paton is a singer, Mother, in a supper room. Isn't that exciting?'

'Oh yes, dear, very exciting. Mrs Lake says to ask you...?' She frowned.

138

Rose jumped to her feet, unwilling to watch any further confusion. She would be old herself one day, if she lived long enough, and this glimpse into old age was not encouraging. 'I have to go,' she told the landlord. 'May I have your answer, please?'

He said, 'I agree. Call in again tomorrow around this time. I'll have a look at the furniture in the meantime and will leave the balance with my mother if I cannot be here myself. Mother, will you please show Miss Paton out?'

'Indeed I will.' She was all smiles. 'Come along, dear.'

They parted cheerfully on the doorstep and Rose hurried home, glowing with a sense of cautious triumph. Her father might not be too pleased but he was not in a position to carp since, had it not been for his stupidity, she would not be in this situation. First thing in the morning she would get in touch with Connie and then she would return by eleven to pack a few of her belongings and anything she felt her father might want, such as clothes, when he came out of prison. It was surprising, she told herself, buoyed up by her small success, just how easily a problem could be turned around if you put your mind to it.

Rose arrived at the church with fifteen minutes to spare and huddled beneath her father's black umbrella, thinking about poor

PC Stump and his dead wife and child. The rain was little more than a drizzle but she had taken great care with her hair and didn't want her curls to frizz. Finding herself alone in the church she had returned to the churchyard where she huddled in the lee of the building, immediately beside the church porch out of reach of the brisk wind.

Alone with her thoughts, some of the previous day's pride had faded and she now suspected that accepting Connie's spare room had probably been a step too far. Small, barely furnished and without even a rug, it smelled of damp and there was an ominous stain on the wall which hinted at a leaky roof.

Connie, naturally, had been delighted by her decision to move in and had asked for four weeks' rent in advance but Rose had persuaded her to take three instead. Would she, she now wondered, be able to stay there for four whole weeks? Could she bear it? Too late she realized that she should have asked to see the room before committing to renting it. The first evening's 'supper' had consisted of a thin mutton stew with onions and carrots and a large chunk of bread. They had shared the meal in Connie's living room, accompanied by loud snores from her ancient dog – a small mongrel.

Her self-pity was now interrupted by the first mourners who trailed sadly past her without so much as a curious glance. She

140

waited until the clock above them struck three when the funeral procession arrived and the coffin was carried into the church by six unhappy people. Rose followed them in and sat in solitary splendour in the back row.

There were no choristers but the vicar did his best. For Rose it was an ordeal. It brought back sad memories of her mother's funeral. Rose was almost glad she was dead because she was spared the humiliation of her husband's arrest and the knowledge that he had broken his promise to stay on the straight and narrow.

PC Stump sat in the front row, separated from his sobbing mother by his small daughter. Or was the sobbing woman his mother-in-law? Or a sister of the deceased, maybe? He wore a black suit and looked smaller than he did in his uniform.

Rose looked at the coffin and wondered where the dead child was – tucked into the same coffin as the mother, presumably, because there was no smaller coffin. Safe in her mother's arms, thought Rose, and felt a little comforted.

After the service they made their way to the new grave and the umbrellas went up again. Rose caught the young widower's gaze across the grave and gave a little nod because a smile seemed so inappropriate, but as soon as she got the chance, she dropped her single rose on top of the coffin and slipped away, leaving the family to their private grief.

She paused at the church gate and glanced back and the realization hit her that before long she would probably be attending Marie's funeral, and she stumbled from the churchyard with two large tears rolling down her face.

Five

Monday afternoon found Andrew Markham lolling in a chair in his office, smoking a cigar. Through the smoke he regarded Connie whom he had just summoned. She stood in front of him, not having been invited to sit, and clasped her hands anxiously.

'So, Connie,' he said. He had sat through the afternoon's rehearsal. 'What do you think of her? Our Miss Lamore, the people's favourite!'

'Oh, she was good, wasn't she!'

'Was she? Is that your considered opinion?'

'Yes. Yes, it is.'

He wondered what had happened to her since the two of them had been more than friends. Then she had been a bright spark – a beautiful, somewhat fiery individual, full of confidence. A challenge, in fact. He had set his heart on having her but she had tried to resist his approaches. Poor Connie. She had thought it a game. She had wanted a romance. A chase. He had soon put her right. It had taken a few hard slaps – more than a few, in fact – before she understood who held the whip hand.

He said, 'So you don't think her legs too thin?'

'Oh no! ... At least, maybe just a bit.'

He sucked on the cigar and blew out a smoke ring, watching it float upwards, smiling a little. Poor old Connie. She still needed to humour him.

'So you thought her voice reasonable? Or nothing special ... or disappointing. Weak, perhaps.' Pointedly, he waited for her opinion.

'Er no ... that is ... it's early days. It'll grow stronger. Her voice, I mean. She's never had a singing lesson.'

'And what about the rest of it? You reckon she'll be agreeable to my suggestions? The after-show performance, as you might say?'

Connie knew immediately what he meant, even without the leering tone and the wink. She swallowed. 'I couldn't really say. She's very young and—'

'All the better! I like them young and tender. A revelation for both of us.' He laughed. 'A bit more than a revelation if she says "No", eh?' He snatched the cigar from his mouth and leaned forward. 'Bit of a revelation for you, wasn't it, all those years ago! But you fought back. Proper little scratch cat!'

She said nothing, startled by the outburst.

'Oh, don't look so scared, woman. She won't be the first or the last to be taken by

144

surprise – and I've got a bottle of champagne to soften her up. She won't be in a fit state to argue. She won't want to argue.'

He leaned back in the chair. Poor old Connie She was a shadow of her former self – scrawny now, haggard, her spirit crushed many years ago. Closing his eyes he visualized Miss Lamore. She owes me a lot, he reminded himself. No real talent, a waiflike, child's body and no voice to speak of. But she was pretty and she had blonde curls. He would let her think she was on the way to a glamorous future.

Connie looked at him uncertainly. 'I'll be off then, shall I?'

He waved her away, pulled out his gold watch and studied it. Only a few more hours and Rose would learn that there was more to show business than she had ever imagined.

That same afternoon, Steven was running a nervous finger round the inside of his collar as he waited for the solicitor's answer to his question. Mr Gideon was a neat little man, young, with a thin frame and plain features, and had been with the firm since he was twenty, which made him around twenty-three. Steven heartily disliked him. Unfortunately, the man had a strong grasp of the workings of the trust and Steven always felt he was going to enjoy refusing his requests. He was never pleasantly surprised, but this time Steven felt it to be a matter of life and death.

'I'm sorry, Mr Bennley, but as I have told you before, the wording of the trust fund is perfectly clear.'

Steven, having eased his collar, now found himself almost breathless with fear. This refusal was going to cost him dearly. He had to make the man understand that this time it was different. This time he was in fear of a possible beating – all depending on Rose – but obviously he could not put that into words. If Rose rejected Markham, Steven could expect the worst. And when Marcus found out, there would be hell to pay. The only way to prevent damage of one sort or another was to repay the debt.

He said, 'Mr Gideon, I don't think you quite understand the seriousness of the problem. It is absolutely imperative that you advance me the money I have requested. It's a business matter of the utmost importance. A ... a pledge is involved and I like to think I am a man of my word. You surely understand that.'

'Mr Bennley, you are being very guarded about this business matter but even if you were to give me each and every detail, my answer would have to be a refusal. I am not allowed to tamper with the trust in any way. You are asking me to behave unethically.'

Steven looked at him with something approaching hate. How satisfying it would be to lean across the desk and punch the smug

146

little man in the face! Without the money, he, Steven, would receive much more in the way of physical force. He imagined himself lying in the gutter being kicked and stamped upon by two thugs who were paid to cause their victims maximum pain and distress. Worse still, poor innocent Rose might find herself at the mercy of Andrew Markham and he desperately wanted to prevent that from happening. In a rash moment he had used Rose to save himself but he was ashamed of that fact now and was desperately trying to rescue the situation. If he could persuade this wretch to advance him the money he would go straight over to Andy's Supper Room and hand it over. He would then find Rose, take her on one side and give her a serious warning about the sort of man Markham really was so that it would then be up to her. She could walk away from it all or take her chances. He would be glad to wash his hands of the affair.

An idea came to him suddenly. What would happen to Marie's money when she died? Presumably it would then be shared between himself, Marcus and Letitia ... but then maybe once the latter married the trust would no longer apply to her. For a moment he brightened but then shook his head in despair as a fresh wave of guilt washed over him.

'Mr Bennley, I have a suggestion to make, if you'll pardon the intrusion. Have you considered finding some occasional paid work that would supplement your money from the trust fund?'

Steven stared at him, his temper rising. The nerve of the little wretch! He jumped to his feet. 'I don't at all pardon the intrusion. I find your suggestion rude and offensive!'

'I am simply trying to help...' The solicitor appeared quite unmoved by his client's response and Steven fought down a desire to lean across the desk and throttle him with his own bare hands. Instead he pushed back his chair so forcefully that it fell over. Then he snatched up his hat and strode out of the office before he could lose control and make an utter fool of himself.

... 'Dear Rose, A cautionary word in your ear – Markham can be pretty powerful. He's that sort of chap. Don't let him talk you into anything you don't fancy ... Steven'

Rose frowned, then glanced up at Connie, who had delivered the note to the dressing room when Rose came off stage.

Connie said, 'He seemed a nice enough fellow. A bit flustered but I expect he was in a hurry. Your young man, is he?'

'I haven't got a young man but I do know him. He's the brother of a friend. "Pretty powerful"? I wonder what that means exactly.'

'Can't you guess?' Connie raised her eyebrows. 'Some men have ... urgent desires.

They can get ... carried away .That sort of thing.'

'But it was Steven who arranged the audition for me. He didn't say anything about ... about this.' She looked bewildered. 'Mr Markham has promised me a glass of champagne when the show ends tonight. To celebrate what he calls my debut on the professional stage.' She smiled. 'My debut! Isn't that wonderful! He's going to ask a friend of his to come and hear me sing. A theatrical agent! Steven said he had influential friends – Mr Markham, I mean. I daresay the agent is one of them.'

'Well dear, one glass of champagne won't hurt you but if I was you I wouldn't go any further. Keep your wits about you.' She glanced over her shoulder and lowered her voice. 'It can be hard to say "No" to a powerful man.'

Rose stuffed the note into her pocket. 'One glass, then. Mind you, I have drunk champagne before at Steven's sister's birthday party. It's lovely.'

'I've drunk pints of the stuff!' Connie boasted. 'In the old days, that is. I liked it but I do prefer a nice drop of gin. It seems to—'

'Did you see me on stage, Connie?' Rose began to struggle out of her costume. 'I thought it went well. Not a lot of applause but then it is Monday and there weren't many people eating. I expect Friday will be

149

a better day – and maybe when I've got a bit more experience, I'll have a spot on Saturday. What d'you think?'

'Very likely – if you play your cards right. Be nice to him but not too nice. Let him think that maybe next time...' She shrugged. 'I'll wait up for you, Rose, seeing as it's your first time.'

'Oh, Connie, that is sweet of you. I expect I'll have lots to tell you.' She had changed into her best clothes and now did a little twirl. 'What will he think?'

'You look lovely.'

Rose laughed. 'Do I look like a star?'

'Almost there. Give it time.' She fumbled in her bag and produced a small package wrapped in paper. 'Here, eat these. Jam sandwiches. You can't go drinking champagne on an empty stomach.' She thrust them into Rose's hand, turned and hurried away.

Rose looked at the sandwiches and then decided that there would be a bit of a wait until the show ended and Mr Markham was ready for her. She had taken the first bite when the door opened and one of the waitresses put her head in.

'I'm to tell you he's waiting in the office. Best get a move on, ducks!' She winked and withdrew.

Abandoning the idea of a jam sandwich, Rose made her way round the edge of the supper room and headed for the office. She had just reached it and was about to knock when it opened and a man came out.

She stared. 'Marcus!'

He smiled. 'I thought I'd collect you and take you round to your room. I've explained to Mr Markham.'

Andrew Markham appeared in the doorway behind him, looking none too pleased. He said, 'Another time, then, Miss Paton. I was telling your friend, Mr Bennley, that you did well tonight. A good start.' He closed the door with a little more force than was necessary.

Rose and Marcus looked at each other.

Marcus said. 'You did do well, Rose. I thought I'd come along and have supper and watch your first real performance.' He peered at her face, surprised by her expression. 'What's the matter?'

'Nothing's the matter,' she told him through gritted teeth, 'except that you're here and you've ruined everything!'

As Rose marched furiously back towards Connie's house, Marcus strode to keep up with her.

'What's the matter?' he demanded, utterly confused. 'Didn't you want me to watch the show?'

'Of course I did, but I didn't want you to come to meet me. You made me look like a ... like a child who needed looking after.' She threw him a sideways look which would have troubled a lesser man. 'If you must know, Marcus, I was going to have a glass of champagne with Mr Markham.' She turned to face him, her expression stony. 'I don't suppose he'll ask me again now. I wanted him to think of me as a ... a sophisticated woman!'

'But you aren't a sophisticated woman, Rose! You're a young, very sweet, very innocent—'

'Oh for Lord's sake! Even a young woman is entitled to a glass of champagne to celebrate the evening. My first professional performance.' Her voice trembled. 'What on earth will he think of me now?' She was close to tears but her anger outweighed her frustration. She knew she was being unfair but she had buoyed herself up for the big romantic moment and Marcus had snatched it away.

He hesitated. 'Rose, I don't think you understand what might have happened. He might have given you too much to drink and tried to...'

She marched on and he ran to catch up with her. She said, 'So what if he wanted to kiss me. It's nothing! So what if he wants to look at my legs? I might want him to. Really Marcus, you don't know anything about me – and it isn't up to you to tell me how to behave.' She regarded him with irritation. 'Mr Markham's got friends who are agents. Don't you understand? Connie says he might get a bit amorous. Some men are like that. They need women around them. They—'

'You know nothing about men like him, Rose. I'm trying to ... to protect you from his sort.'

'And if I don't want you to?'

He was silent.

'I have to grow up sometime, Marcus.' Abruptly she came to a halt. 'This is where I live with Connie. She'll have a bit of supper for me. I must go in.'

'No, wait. I've got the dates for the trip to France with Marie. We need to talk about—'

'Not tonight! Come round tomorrow.'

Marcus sighed deeply. 'I'll bring a bottle of champagne. We'll celebrate your—'

'Don't bother. It won't be the same.' As soon as she said the words she regretted hurting him but she was in no mood to worry about it. Eager to be rid of him, she banged on the front door and called up to Connie's window. When it opened she relented slightly and turned to say 'Goodnight' but he was already disappearing into the gloom of the street lamps.

Steven went down to breakfast next morning in a very anxious frame of mind. He was wondering what exactly had happened between Rose and Markham and if whatever it was had satisfied Markham. Sitting in moody isolation, he helped himself to porridge and added honey and cream. Five minutes later Marcus appeared looking lost in thought. He chose stewed fruit and sat down without a word.

Steven said, 'Rose's first performance. I wonder how it went.'

His brother shrugged. 'Nothing to cheer about. She's very sweet but her voice was not strong enough for such a large room. I think she should restrict her work to private groups.'

'Did they applaud?'

'Yes but it was hardly rapturous.' He frowned.

Steven wondered how he could best approach the subject uppermost in his mind. 'What was Markham's verdict? Was he pleased? It was I who recommended her, remember. I said she was very promising.' He tried to sound casual.

'Markham? I didn't bother to ask him. I don't trust the fellow. I went in to collect her and he had a bottle of champagne on the desk and two glasses. They were going to celebrate, apparently, and I interrupted the proceedings. Rose wasn't very pleased.'

So what exactly did that mean, Steven wondered, his hopes faltering. 'You interrupted them? How exactly? What were they doing?' He almost held his breath.

'Nothing. I got there first and he lost interest and I walked Rose home. She was very upset with me for interfering.'

Steven lost his appetite and pushed the plate away. So Markham had lost his promised sweetener! Hell! A shiver ran through him. Markham was an impatient man. He would hate being thwarted and he would take his revenge. He would now want his money and, without it, he, Steven, could now expect the beating. If he could fight Markham fair and square, one to one, he might well win because he was younger and quicker. At the moment he would willingly have had it out with him, but that wasn't Markham's way. He never laid himself open to physical harm but would send two of his thug friends and it would be an unequal fight which Steven would lose. It was now or never, he decided.

'Look Marcus, could you lend me some money? I'll pay it back.'

Marcus rolled his eyes 'You never have done before. Why should this time be any different?'

'Because ... I've got the chance of a job ... Marcus! You're not listening.'

'I'm not listening because I've got things to think about that are more important than your debts! And don't pretend you've got job prospects because I've heard that before, too.' He leaned forward, his expression grim. 'We've all lent you money over the years and you've never repaid a penny so the answer's "No"! Now for heaven's sake, leave

155

me in peace. I've got worries of my own.'

There were times when Steven hated his brother. Times when he hated the whole family – except Marie and Mother. Letitia was a smug little madam with her wonderful Bernard, and Marcus was too wrapped up in his own little world to care about anyone else. They all had money from Grandmother's trust fund but Marcus earned money from his stage designs and must surely have money to lend. Marcus was just selfish. Perhaps when Markham's bully boys had broken every bone in his brother's body, he would be sorry.

Marcus glanced up suddenly. 'What's the matter with Letitia, do you know? She's in a funny mood lately. Yesterday I thought she'd been crying but she—'

Steven banged his fist on the table so hard that the crockery rattled. 'Why should I care what's the matter with her? She doesn't give a damn about me or anybody else. She won't acknowledge her own father! She won't take Marie to France. She's a cold and selfish bi—' He stopped just in time. 'God help poor old Bernard! That's what I say.'

He went out of the dining room, slamming the door behind him, and almost cannoned into a small, mousy woman. This was Miss Evans who stood in for Mrs Bray on her days off.

'Oh Master Steven, I was wondering if Miss Letitia was feeling unwell. She hasn't

156

come down to breakfast. It's not wise to miss a meal. Should I take her something up?'

He hesitated then shook his head. 'No. Let her sleep. If she needs any help she'll ring her bell. We all have one for emergencies.' And I have my own emergency to deal with, he told himself, though God only knows how I shall do it. Ringing a bell won't save me.

Upstairs in her room, Letitia sat up in bed, her knees drawn up, her hands clasped around them as though for protection. Her face was drawn in misery and her complexion was pale. She had gone up to bed the previous evening without waiting for the evening meal, pleading a headache, but she was actually suffering from extreme fear. She had parted from Bernard on Thursday and had spent the days since then wondering how much she could trust his repeated assurances that he did really love her more than Carlotta. She desperately wanted to believe him and had decided to send him a letter asking for forgiveness for her lack of trust; she had written three but, on reflection, each one had been torn up. It might be better never to refer to the incident again. That way he would not be able to change his mind and confess that he *did* prefer Carlotta.

'Don't leave me, Bernard!' she whispered

again and again like a mantra. 'I can't live without you. You said you *adored* me. You swore it on your honour.'

She sat up a little straighter. Suppose she asked him to swear on the Holy Bible ... but he might refuse. He might repeat that she did not trust him and use that to wriggle out of the marriage. And if he did agree to swear on the Holy Bible? Would it suffice or would doubts linger?

She put a hand to her head which ached abominably; her stomach rumbled with hunger. If only Mother had stayed with them instead of going off with that dreadful Gerard. She would have understood Letitia's plight and would almost certainly have sympathized. She might have brought up a dish of warm bread and milk sprinkled with sugar, the way she did when they were children, in need of sympathy or otherwise out of sorts.

Letitia smiled faintly, then slid slowly beneath the blankets. She was so tired from the awful confusion she was feeling, and sleepless nights had left her a prey to depression. Was it possible to die of grief, she wondered, twisting on to her right side, and pulling the pillow further under her neck in an effort to find a comfortable position. Was it possible, in extreme circumstances, to lose your mind from an excess of anxiety? Suppose Bernard were suddenly to arrive to speak with her – that could only mean one thing. That he wanted to cancel the wedding. Unless it was to reassure her of his love. Either way she would have to refuse to see him. She felt and looked so terribly exhausted. Miserable and worthless.

And it was all Mother's fault for falling in love with a stupid French farmer and bearing him a child. An oddity. A dark-haired child in a family of fair heads. She had grown to dread the jokes about the milkman which unaware friends innocently made. She had seen herself as a cuckoo in the Bennley nest! She had never expected any man to want to marry such a person and Bernard had never been told the truth. Bernard, she felt, was her only chance of respectability. Bernard and the da Silvas. Whatever happened she must never lose them.

Marcus sat in the study behind the desk which had once been his father's, leaning back in his chair and surveying his half finished sketch through narrowed eyes. He was designing a backdrop for a stage production of *Swan Lake* which was destined for the local theatre later in the year. It was the second commission he had received since he finished his art training and, determined to make a career for himself in theatre design, he told himself it was a promising start. That way he need not immerse himself in the hustle of business but would hopefully be able to work from home where he felt at ease.

Nearby, propped on a small easel, was the finished painting he had produced for his first commission – the scene from *Macbeth* where the three witches meet on the heath – a dark design full of lowering clouds and wild and rugged heathland. He was looking forward to producing a very different mood and had initially sketched in three graceful trees set against a clear blue sky with sunshine filtering through the branches.

'A little bland, maybe,' he wondered anxiously. 'A little predictable?' But a scene with a lake and trees was required for the backdrop to the dancers who represented swans, and for the moment he could not see how to give it a fresh and original slant.

Success was very important to Marcus. As a child his father had mocked his early artistic talent, declaring that he lacked the necessary imagination, and only his mother had supported him. Although his father was long gone from his life, the need for Marcus to prove him wrong remained.

'Suppose I include the far edge of the lake and edge it with clumps of rushes...' he muttered, 'or better still bulrushes. And maybe a heron?' Or would the heron be at odds with the swans?

There was a tap at the door and before he could say 'Come in!' it was opened to admit Letitia. He stared at her in dismay. She was still in her nightwear, her hair dishevelled and her feet bare.

'Marcus, I must talk to you. I have to ask a favour of you.'

He thought her voice trembled. 'Are you ill?' he asked, adding, with his usual lack of tact, 'You look dreadful.'

It told him something about her state of mind that she did not protest at the last comment. She sat down in the seat nearest to him and wrapped her dressing gown more tightly around her. 'I'm not ill yet but I soon will be.'

Smothering a sigh at the interruption to his work, Marcus waited for her to explain.

In faltering tones she told him what had happened between her, Bernard and his mother, and he listened intently. He was surprised and flattered that she needed his help and he pushed thoughts of his design work to the back of his mind and concentrated on her plight.

'The thing is, Marcus, that although he promised me there was nothing for me to worry about, I sensed that he was hiding something; that perhaps they both were. This Carlotta is besotted with him. I know it in my bones.'

Her anguish was very real and Marcus hesitated. It was pointless for him to try and convince her that all was well while he had no way of judging the situation. Looking into her troubled eyes, he searched for something reassuring to say but she rushed on.

'I'm sorry to burden you with my problems but Mother is miles away and I can't upset Marie when her health is so precarious. Steven has his own problems and—'

'Has he asked you for money?'

She nodded. 'And not for the first time. But forget about Steven. He must sort out his own problems. I have to know, Marcus, before I walk up the aisle, whether or not Bernard has put this other woman out of his life. If I knew that I could rest easy but until then ... I shall be a bundle of nerves!' She wiped away the first tears with the back of her hand and blinked furiously.

Marcus looked at her with growing compassion. 'Suppose you write to him? Tell him how you—'

'No, Marcus. If I put my fears into writing and then it turns out I'm right and he marries her ... she might read my letter. I know you'll think that pathetic but I'd hate her to know my desperation. She'll gloat, Marcus. Don't you see? I would be utterly humiliated. No.' She took a deep breath. 'I want you to go to the da Silvas and talk to him, man to man.'

A shiver of alarm ran through Marcus's body at her words. Confrontation. He had never learned it and certainly never sought it. His whole being shrank from the idea but even as his mind formed a tactful refusal he knew he would have to agree. He had never seen his sister in such a pitiable state and he was shocked. Letitia was always so cold, calm and collected; always so ready to scoff at others for their weaknesses; so desperate to forget the unfortunate circumstances of her position in the family. He had never felt close to her but now that she was begging for help, he felt an unexpected spark of sympathy. She was human, after all, he thought with surprise.

She had covered her face with her hands but now glanced up at him, white-faced. 'You're going to say "No" I can tell. I knew you would but—'

'I haven't said "No",' he corrected her. 'I'm ... I'm simply trying to imagine how I would go about it. I can't think ... I would hardly know what to say. Certainly I'll try but I'm not good with people. You know that. Suppose I make things worse!'

'How could they be any worse?' she cried passionately. 'All you need to do, Marcus, is speak to him, pretending that I don't know anything about it. Don't tell him the real reason why you are there – or that I asked you to approach him. Pretend you are worried about me and wonder if he has noticed a change in me. Ask if maybe there is something wrong between us – and notice how he replies.' She swallowed hard. 'Whatever you do, don't mention Carlotta because if you do he'll know that I've told you about her.

163

Forget Carlotta. Just see if you think he is ... prevaricating.'

'How will I know?' Marcus regarded her unhappily, baffled by the complexities of the prospect ahead.

'You just will!' she told him. 'You're not stupid, Marcus. You may not be good with people but you are very intelligent. You can do it. Please.'

Marcus could see hope in her eyes and was torn between a feeling of pride that she believed he could help her, and a dread that he might wrongly interpret the 'signs' and make matters worse.

Cautiously he nodded. 'But you have to promise that whatever comes from our encounter, you won't blame me. I'm not going to accept responsibility for—'

'Oh thank you, Marcus!' Her expression changed. 'Oh I knew I could rely on you! I won't forget it, Marcus. If you ever need my help...'

Inwardly he prayed that he never would need it, but he returned the smile which now lit up her previously forlorn face. He thought that maybe he never would understand women. He had tried to help Rose and she had been furious. Now his sister was flinging her arms round him in a brief hug before rushing out of the room. That was certainly out of character, he thought. She made him feel like a hero and he rather liked it.

Left to himself he tried to return to his work but she was soon back.

'I forgot to ask when you would go over there, Marcus. What about this evening? The waiting is more than I can bear!'

He sighed. Getting to his feet he drew the cloth over his sketches. The work would keep, he told himself. To Letitia he said simply, 'I'll walk round now.'

A maid opened the door and he asked to speak to Bernard.

'I don't know,' she replied. 'They have visitors.'

'It's rather important,' he told her. 'I'm Marcus Bennley. They know me. My sister is going to marry Bernard in a few weeks' time.'

Her eyes opened as her interest quickened. 'Oh! I'll go and see, then. You'd better wait in the morning room.'

She left him there without inviting him to sit down and he looked around the room with interest but then he moved to the window and stared out over the gardens.

Minutes passed and Marcus tried to remember exactly what he had planned to say to Bernard. Most of it had flown from his mind and he tried to recall his sister's instructions. Don't say that she had been in tears. Don't say that she was worried about Carlotta. Don't even mention Carlotta. Just say that Letitia was unusually quiet, that she wasn't eating properly and that she could not sleep. He was also going to say that he wondered whether Bernard knew of anything that might be troubling her.

When at last the door opened it was Mrs da Silva who entered. There was a smile on her face but it lacked warmth and Marcus felt the first prickle of unease. They shook hands and she said, 'Do sit down. I hope this won't take long as we have visitors and are almost ready to go into dinner.'

'I appreciate that, Mrs da Silva, but I'm sure that you understand how ... sensitive a young woman can be prior to her marriage. I simply want a few words with your son about er ... certain matters. I'm sure Bernard would want to help if he can. One brother-in-law to another!' He tried to make light of his visit.

She looked a little startled and he wondered if he was making too much of a mystery of it.

'I do appreciate, Marcus, that your sister has no mother to confide in – at least she has, but she is not in the immediate family circle. I am very willing to talk to her if those certain matters...' She left the sentence unfinished.

Marcus had the distinct impression that his mother had been slighted but hesitated to rush to her defence. Letitia would not want him to cause any further difficulties. Instead he said, 'If I could speak to Bernard for ten minutes you can then resume your evening's entertainment.' It sounded rather stilted but it was the best he could do.

'I'll speak to him.'

Marcus took out a handkerchief and dabbed at his face. He wondered if he had handled the conversation well and decided he probably could have done better. The mission had caused him a certain amount of stress and he suspected that his talk with Bernard would be equally difficult.

Bernard, however, hurried in with what seemed to be a genuine smile of welcome. 'You need to speak with me,' he began. 'I hope nothing is wrong.'

They sat in adjoining chairs and Marcus envied Bernard the casual way he relaxed into the chair. He looked slightly flushed – possibly a few drinks had brought that about – and the smell of cigarette smoke lingered around him.

'Not wrong, no,' he said, 'but I am a little concerned about my sister, though she doesn't know I'm coming to see you. She mustn't know.' He leaned forward. 'I wondered if you had noticed any change in her lately. To us she appears rather quiet, almost subdued, and she isn't eating properly.' He watched the other man's expression closely and thought he saw a flicker of alarm. 'I've tried to talk to her but she maintains there's nothing wrong.'

'Then I'm sure there isn't. Letitia has a

very sensible head on her shoulders—'

'She hasn't slept properly for several nights and I've been urging her to see our family doctor—'

'See the doctor?' He sat up a little straighter. 'Surely there's no need for that. I believe it's quite usual for brides-to-be to be a little anxious.'

'I'd like you to be frank with me, Bernard. If there is anything wrong between you I feel now is the time to—'

'Nothing at all.' Abruptly he got up and closed the door, then resumed his seat. 'Look, Marcus, there was a young woman in my life before I met your sister but she now means nothing to me except ... except that she cannot quite accept that. You know how women can be.'

Marcus shook his head. 'I've never been in that situation.'

'Well, lucky you!' He gave a short laugh. 'Carlotta came to see me and Letitia found out about it and ... well, she may have read too much into the incident.'

'So this other young woman—'

'For heaven's sake, man!' His cool manner was suddenly evaporating. 'The wedding is only weeks away! It's much too late to change anything ... even if I wanted to. Which I don't. You can tell your sister that there will be no change to our plans.' He gave Marcus a look of irritation. 'Will that soothe her fears, do you think?'

168

A strained silence fell between them. Marcus felt a sudden chill. All was not right.

Bernard realized he had spoken too sharply. 'I'm sorry. I didn't mean to sound callous but my mother has been nagging me and now...'

Marcus's thoughts swirled unhappily. He had been told not to make things worse. Was he doing that? He said, 'Do you love her? Letitia, I mean?'

'Of course I do.' He ran his fingers through his smooth hair and rolled his eyes. 'Women! They can be the very devil!'

'This Carlotta...?'

'Forget her! She's history!' He sat up and leaned forward confidingly. 'Look, Marcus, tomorrow I'll send Letitia a bouquet of flowers...'

'Don't send them. Bring them. She needs to be reassured.'

Bernard sighed. 'Very well, I'll bring them and I'll reassure her. How's that?'

Marcus was feeling distinctly uneasy. Bernard didn't sound like a man who was deeply in love and soon to be married. Feeling rather disloyal, he wondered if Letitia was more keen on the match than Bernard. He had denied that Carlotta was important to him, yet he didn't appear to be that concerned for Letitia either.

Abruptly Bernard stood up. He forced a smile. 'There. Nothing but a storm in a teacup. I'm so sorry you've been worried about your sister but we'll soon put that right. Trust me, Marcus.' He looked pointedly at Marcus who was still sitting down. 'I'll have to get back to our guests but I'm glad we've had this little talk.' As Marcus rose to his feet Bernard reached out and they shook hands. 'If we don't meet again, I'll see you on the big day! Give Letitia my love.'

'I can't do that. She doesn't know I've come to see you.'

'Oh! How stupid of me.' He was leading the way out of the morning room and along to the front door. 'Steady as you go!' he joked as he opened it.

Marcus paused on the step, looking up into Bernard's handsome face. He felt there was more he should say but words failed him. The truth was he was glad to be out of there and, nodding briefly, he turned and began to retrace his steps.

His doubts crystallized as he made his way home and he knew that he was no longer confident of Bernard's feeling for Letitia. However, he could never tell her that ... and maybe he was wrong. Had he read the signs correctly or jumped to the wrong conclusions? Somehow tonight he would reassure her and when Bernard came the next day they might well recover the feelings they had originally had for each other. He told himself he had done his best. The trouble was that he now doubted the wisdom of his visit. Instead of returning with confidence he was full of doubts which he felt unable to share.

'Damn and double damn!' As he let himself back into the house he promised himself that, sister or no sister, he would never again put himself into such an invidious position.

Six

Dressed in her best clothes, Rose sat in the seats at the side of the court and waited for her father's name to be called out. A magistrate's court was a new experience for her and she glanced round in awe at the panelled walls, large, high windows and stark wooden pews. It reminded her of church and that was appropriate, she thought, for important matters of good and evil were dealt with within the walls. She wondered if she offered up a prayer whether God might listen but probably he was busy in the various churches.

The magistrate looked very small behind his high desk but the gavel he used to good effect helped his air of authority as did his dark robes and stern expression. He had a white moustache and beard but very little white hair on his head yet still maintained a certain dignity due to his position. Rose was glad she was not going to face him.

On her left was a very fat woman who snorted with every wheezy breath and filled the surrounding air with the smell of onions. To Rose's right a thin woman dressed in black sat with a rigid back, staring at the magistrate while he discussed the case of the young man who was her son.

The magistrate, peering through his spectacles, read from his notes. 'You are accused of carelessly pushing a barrow loaded with logs which overturned in—'

'Your honour, it wasn't me being careless. It was—'

The court official interrupted him. 'Do not address the bench while the charge is being read out.'

'I only meant—'

'That will do!'

The young man turned to stare helplessly at his mother who shook her head by way of a warning.

The magistrate continued. 'The barrow overturned in the middle of the street and startled a baker's horse which then reared up and came down on an elderly man who is now in hospital receiving treatment for his injuries...'

Rose's mind wandered. She tried to imagine her father waiting somewhere below the court in some kind of dungeon, sitting with other ill-doers. Perhaps they sat in gloomy silence ... or maybe they chatted to each other, discussing their alleged crimes and denying that they were guilty. How could her father deny anything? The stolen goods had been found in his premises and his partner in crime had also been arrested and had given her father's name to the police.

The best solicitor in the world could not save him from whatever sentence the magistrate handed down. He was going to prison. She sighed. For herself, she was deeply ashamed of his behaviour and selfishly pleased that no one else knew what he had done. Except Marcus and he didn't count because she had sworn him to secrecy and she trusted him. On reflection, she was now sorry that she had been cross with him at Andy's Supper Room because she knew he meant well.

The magistrate's voice interrupted her thoughts. 'I see here that you do not hold the required trader's licence. Is that correct?'

'Yes, your honour but it's not my fault because—'

'It seems that nothing is your fault.' He gave the defendant a withering look.

The sound of her father's name jerked her back to what was happening around her. The young man was being led away and his mother was forcing her way out, her expression grim. Rose crossed her fingers, hoping that she might never be in that position.

Her father suddenly appeared at the top of the steps and he immediately searched the row of seats for her. When she gave him a discreet wave and smiled she expected him to show relief that she had turned up to support him but instead he looked embarrassed and made no effort to acknowledge her. Hurt by the rejection, she told herself that he was obviously ashamed and didn't want her to watch his downfall.

'You know him, do you?' whispered the fat lady.

Too late to pretend otherwise, Rose thought, and nodded.

'Your pa?'

The court official glared across at them. 'Silence in court!'

The charge of receiving stolen goods was read out while her father stood, twisting his cap in his hand. Rose saw him suddenly, not as her father but as a stranger – a small, abject figure. She was all he had in the world, she realized. No money, no job, no home. Stricken by his plight she jumped to her feet. 'Please may I speak in his defence? He's my—'

Every face in the room turned in her direction. The court official roared, 'Silence in court!'

But she plunged on while she had everyone's attention. 'He's my father and he's had a hard life and he's not a bad man at heart. He's weak but—'

The magistrate was banging his gavel and Rose found herself seized by the arm and dragged, with considerable difficulty, past the fat woman who grumbled 'Oi! Watch it!'

'He was led astray!' she shouted, struggling to prevent herself being swept off her feet.

Despite her protests, she found herself in the corridor, panting with anger, facing a man in a uniform she didn't recognize.

The man gave her a final shaking and then released her. He said, 'Think yourself lucky, woman! You might have been done for contempt! I've done you a favour!' He was a beefy looking man with a florid complexion.

Rose glared at him angrily. 'Well, I don't think myself lucky. You nearly pulled my arm out of its socket! And I wanted to help my father. He's—'

'I should reckon that little outburst has made it worse for him, poor wretch. You was in contempt of the court and the judge could have had you taken down into the cells. That would have been hard for him.'

Shaken by this assertion, she said, 'Made it worse for him? Oh but that wouldn't be fair. I was only—'

'You were making a disturbance in court and it's not allowed. Learn something from it. Now I have to get back.'

He left her standing irresolutely in the corridor. She felt foolish and lonely, largely ignored by the various people who hurried past. Slowly she made her way down the stairs and out into the sunlight.

At first she stood there feeling sorry for herself. She had made a mistake in the court and it had all been pointless because her father was going to be given a prison sentence.

But as the minutes passed, her own natural optimism gradually returned and she reminded herself that all was not bad. There were good things in her life, too. She was going to France at some time, with Marcus and Marie, and she had Letitia's wedding to look forward to. Finally, as she set her face towards Connie's house, she was smiling again.

'Excuse me, Miss Paton. May I have a word with you?'

Surprised, Rose swung round to find Mr Granger waiting to speak to her. Her first reaction was to expect bad news in some form but then she realized he was smiling.

'It's about my mother, Miss Paton. You remember the two of you met when you called at our house last week.'

'Ye–es,' Rose replied. Keeping her tone neutral and not knowing what to expect.

'You recall that she is often confused.'

'She mistook you for your brother.'

He nodded. 'And she thought you had come for a piano lesson!'

They exchanged sympathetic smiles.

'My mother has now decided that you are a family friend and wants to see you again. I wondered if you might find time to visit twice or three times a week say, for an hour. To chat and read to her. She loves the Bible.

I would pay you.'

Rose's first inclination was to jump at the chance of a little paid work but she gave it careful thought. 'I do have my career, Mr Granger, and there are rehearsals and three evening performances each week. And I am also about to travel abroad – to France – on a mission of mercy!' She rolled her eyes to show that this was an exaggeration and then explained about the trip to Boulogne with Marie.

He said, 'A travelling companion. Lucky Marie ... So what do you think? I gave your proposition consideration. Maybe you will return the compliment. My business takes me away from home quite frequently and Mother is on her own too much. Mrs Lake is too busy to cope with her lapses of memory and I suspect that Mother's vagueness makes her nervous. It can be rather disconcerting. I think my mother gets lonely.'

'I now live some way from Garret Street, Mr Granger. Would you pay my fares on top of the rest of the money?'

'I would. I was thinking a shilling an hour.'

'I was thinking one and sixpence.' Her eyes met his. She thought his mouth twitched.

'Shall we say one and threepence?'

'Why not!' She held out her hand and they shook on the transaction. She shrugged. 'Mind you, the Bible is not my favourite book but I shall try to wean your mother off it and on to something lighter.'

'That will be interesting!' After a moment he said, 'Your father? What happened? Was he convicted?'

'I don't know. I was dragged out of court for trying to plead for him. They said it was contempt of court.' She shrugged. 'I'll make enquiries later on. So I am the daughter of a criminal. Should you be inviting me into your home?'

'I'm prepared to risk it, Miss Paton.'

'Then I'll call tomorrow about half past ten. Will that suit?'

'Perfectly. I'll make a point of being there but in future I'll leave the money in an envelope with Mrs Lake.'

He seemed pleased, Rose thought, as they separated and she went on her way with a lighter heart.

One o'clock came and two o'clock and Letitia was becoming nervous. Her brother had told her that Bernard was proposing to call in during the morning but there had been no sign of him. Marcus had hidden himself away once more in the study, working, and her pride would not allow her to approach him again. She had taken great care with her hair, had dabbed on some 'Bonjour Paris' – a perfume Bernard had given her – and was wearing her most attractive dress.

The lunchtime meal was now over and she had been unable to eat more than a few mouthfuls of the cold chicken and salad which she had had to force down her unwilling throat to avoid comments from her brothers. Now she sat alone in the drawing room with a magazine, trying not to look too often at the clock on the mantelpiece.

When at last the bell did ring she abandoned her nonchalant pose and hurried to listen at the door of the room as Mrs Bray passed on the way to the front door. Her relief faltered when she failed to recognize the male voice. It wasn't Bernard!

'Dear God!' she whispered, frozen with disappointment. She was still there when the door opened abruptly and almost knocked her over.

'Oh! Sorry Miss Letitia. I didn't expect anyone to be—'

'Flowers! Oh how beautiful!' Letitia stepped back to admire the enormous bouquet which the housekeeper was holding out for her.

'Aren't they lovely!'

The flowers were wrapped in a gold patterned paper and tied with gold ribbon. She stared at them as she stammered her thanks.

Mrs Bray smiled. 'I wish someone would send me flowers like that!' She withdrew, closing the door quietly behind her. Letitia, feeling ultra-sensitive, wondered if she had guessed or known that Bernard himself was expected.

'He's not coming!' In a moment of anguish

she hurled the flowers on to the nearest armchair and pressed trembling fingers on to her eyes in an attempt to stall the tears that threatened to betray her.

The door opened again and the housekeeper handed her an envelope. 'I almost forgot it,' she told Letitia. 'I slipped it into my apron pocket.'

The door closed again and Letitia stared at the envelope which bore her name in Bernard's familiar handwriting. But what on earth was the housekeeper going to make of the bouquet upside down in an armchair! With a groan, Letitia sat down and opened the envelope.

My dearest Letitia, I wanted to visit you today but something has come up and Mother is in a state and insists she cannot do without me! You know how she can be and the wedding preparations are proving a little more daunting than she expected. Poor Mother...

'Poor Mother indeed!' Letitia tossed her head indignantly but she accepted the fact that it was normally the bride's parents who organized the wedding. Since her mother now lived in France the responsibility had shifted to Bernard's family. She knew she ought to be grateful and she was.

Everything has to be absolutely perfect or she isn't satisfied! Instead I will come tomorrow if that is convenient to you. It seems an age since I held you close and I am desperate to see you again. Please accept these flowers as a symbol of all you mean to me, my adored Letitia. Before long we will be together for ever and I for one cannot wait. All my love, dearest. Yours, Bernard...

'Oh my love!' Letitia held the letter to her heart and smiled through the tears of relief. He did love her and he would come tomorrow. She trusted him. The letter had changed everything.

She reread the letter and then glanced guiltily at the abandoned flowers. Hurrying over to retrieve them she took the time to study the selection of blooms in more detail – white rosebuds, pink carnations, frothy white gypsophila and deep red chrysanthemums. They must have cost a great deal of money, she thought with satisfaction. Bernard loved and valued her. Her doubts faded as her smile broadened.

'Mrs Bernard da Silva!' she whispered, the dream restored to a forthcoming reality.

Content that her future happiness was once more assured, she let out a long breath. She would find a suitably large vase and arrange her beautiful flowers.

When Rose arrived at Andy's Supper Room that evening she was told to go straight to Andrew Markham's office.

It occurred to her immediately that perhaps he was going to offer her the promised glass of champagne, but the pianist's next remark put paid to that hope.

'And he didn't look too happy,' he told her. 'I'd step carefully if I were you, Miss Lamore. He's got a temper on him.'

She tapped on the door of his office and heard nothing so tapped again.

'Come in!'

She found him in his usual place, at his desk, but this time there were other people with him. Two burly men stood behind him as though they were his bodyguards. Or soldiers on parade who had been told to 'Stand easy!' Their feet were apart and their hands were clasped behind their backs. Neither of the two men smiled as she entered.

'Oh, Mr Markham,' she began earnestly. 'I'm sorry about the other night. I was so looking forward to—'

'Who the hell is he?' Markham glared at her.

'Just a friend. He—'

'You're telling me that's all he is – a friend?'

'Yes, Mr Markham. We met recently ... I hardly know him actually but he's very kind and—'

'He seems to see the situation differently, Miss Lamore. He claims he is going to marry you.'

She stared at him. 'Marry him? Oh no!

You've misunderstood whatever he said to you ... Unless it was a joke.' But Marcus didn't make jokes, she remembered. So why on earth had he said it?

The two men glanced at each other and grinned but Markham wasn't grinning. He scowled at her. 'He's a damned nuisance, Miss Lamore. I don't like men hanging round my performers. Do you understand? I need you to concentrate on your act.'

'He only came that once. He just wanted to see me perform at a real venue. I mean, not in a public house like The White Horse in Stoke Newington.'

He took his feet off the desk and leaned forward. 'He says he's going to meet you every time you perform. Steven didn't warn me that he had a brother who was going to make a pest of himself! We had an understanding, Steven and me. He suggested that you were unattached. He misled me.'

'No he didn't!' she said with genuine indignation. 'At least he told you the truth. I am unattached.' She was trying to hold back her growing anger. How dare Marcus tell her boss that she was going to marry him! 'I'm sorry, Mr Markham. I really was looking forward to our little celebration on Monday night. I'll speak to him. I'll make it clear I don't want him hanging around. I can't break off the friendship altogether because I'm going to France with him one day soon to take his sister...' Seeing his expression change she faltered.

His eyes narrowed. 'Does Steven know about this trip to France?'

'Well, yes, he must do ... but he's not coming with us. Just me and Marcus and Marie. Because Marie is desperately—'

'Never mind Marie! You say Steven knew.'

She nodded, wondering where this uncomfortable conversation was leading. Hoping to steer it on to something less serious she gave him a nervous smile. 'I could come along after tonight's performance – if you still want me to.'

He ignored her offer. 'That little swine has double-crossed me! I didn't think he'd have the nerve.'

He was speaking to the two men, she realized.

One of them said, 'Maybe we should have a word with him, Mr Markham.'

The other said, 'Or two or three words!' and they both laughed.

Markham nodded. 'Ask for the money. If he has it, that's fine. We're square. If he doesn't ... Yes, I think a word or two will do the trick. But be careful. Don't go too far. And don't get caught. Got it?'

They both nodded.

'Then get out of here!'

When they'd gone Rose began to speak but he waved her away. 'You too. Get out!'

Shaken by his tone and manner she didn't argue. Outside she paused to recover her poise and the pianist called across to her.

'Crossed swords?'

'You could say that. I can't make him out.'

'Don't let it worry you, Miss Lamore. He can be an awkward devil when he likes. On about young Bennley, was it? Money's usually at the root of it.'

'Money?' She made no attempt to hide her surprise. She had thought the Bennley family reasonably wealthy.

'He's run up a biggish debt at the bar. Drinks and a game of chance. Plays regularly, does Bennley, and owes money. Mr Markham takes a dim view of that. Not that he's the only one.' He closed the lid of the piano with a bang and reached for his jacket. 'Yep! Funny thing though – it's usually the toffs. Know what I mean? The ones that ought to know better.' He adopted a genteel accent. 'The ones who get dear old Pater to bail them out!' He gathered his sheets of music and put them in the piano stool and reverted to his normal voice. 'We had a chap once, middle of last year, ran up a big tab at the bar and his father was Sir Somebody! Very posh. Not that it helped. He refused to cough up for his baby boy and...' He shrugged. 'I'm off for ten minutes. I fancy a mutton pie but I'll be back by three if you want to run through any of your pieces.'

He turned to go but Rose said, 'What happened to him? The toff, I mean.'

'Don't rightly know. He disappeared.

Never set eyes on him again. Police looking for him and everything. I reckon the chap did a runner.'

He grinned and wandered off, whistling under his breath, leaving Rose with something new to worry about.

That night Rose found Marcus outside the stage door. She tried to storm past him but he caught her hand and forced her to stop.

'Marcus! How many times do I have to tell you I—'

'I don't care, Rose. I need to look after you.'

'You don't! I can look after myself. I always have done.' She glared at a few spectators who were enjoying the argument. 'Heard enough, have you? If there's one thing I hate it's nosy parkers!'

One of them laughed but the others drifted away, discomfited. Rose glared at him until he, too, finally followed them. She turned back to Marcus who was looking embarrassed by the exchange. 'Oh! Have I embarrassed you?' she cried. 'Well, now you know how I feel when you keep appearing like my fairy godmother! If you have to look after somebody, look after Steven. He seems to be the one in trouble, not me! He owes Mr Markham money. Did you know?'

'Of course. It's nothing new. I'm tired of saving him. He has to learn the hard way.'

She remembered another grievance which

distracted her from Steven. 'And what's this about you marrying me? How dare you tell Mr Markham such a whopping lie!'

He had the grace to look disconcerted. 'Oh that! I just wanted him to know that you were important to somebody. That somebody was looking after your interests. I thought it might as well be me as anyone else.'

'Indeed, then you were mistaken! I do not want him to think that I am about to be married to you or anyone else. He has to know that I'm dedicated to my career. If I marry I might have a child and then bang goes my future!' She had started to walk home and he fell in beside her.

'You would still have a future,' he pointed out. 'You would have a family and a devoted—'

'I don't want that, Marcus. I don't want a family and I don't want a devoted anything! I want fame and fortune. Can't you understand? Don't you want to be famous for your stage designs?'

'Famous? Good Lord no!' He sounded genuinely horrified. 'I can't think of anything worse.' After a moment's thought he said, 'Suppose you don't become famous. What will you do?'

'Why shouldn't I?'

'You might not be good enough. No one can guarantee you success.'

She stopped abruptly in the middle of the

pavement and stared at him in disbelief. 'Not good enough? But I can sing and I'm pretty and I'm going to learn to dance. Why are you being so unkind, Marcus?'

'I'm not being unkind. I'm trying to save you from disappointment. You've set your heart on fame and fortune and it doesn't just happen.'

'You don't like my singing, then?'

'It's fair enough but...' He shrugged. 'You're very pretty but you don't know yet how well you will dance. Success depends on so many things like ... like luck. You might not be lucky.'

He had rattled her but she was determined not to show it. 'Well, Marcus Bennley, for your information, I will dance well and I will be lucky. I don't doubt it for a moment and I thank you not to be so gloomy. Now I won't talk about it any more. Not another word!'

Minutes later they reached Connie's house and Rose glanced up and waved to her. 'I wonder what we're having for supper,' she mused. 'Poor Connie is a terrible cook but I can't bring myself to say so. She's been so kind to me.' Her mind gave another sideways hop and she frowned. 'Tomorrow I have to go back to the police station to ask about my father's sentence and where he is.'

'It's fifty days' hard labour and he's been sent to Pentonville.'

Her mouth dropped open with shock. 'You

189

asked the police about my father?'

'I thought you'd want to know.'

'I was going tomorrow! You really are the most exasperating man I know! It was none of your business.'

'It is in a way, Rose, because I wanted all the ends tied up for you before we go to France with Marie and I've bought the tickets for this coming Saturday. She is fading fast and I'm terrified she will pass away before we reach Mother. I was trying to help. I'm sorry.'

He looked so forlorn that Rose's anger disappeared and she at once forgave him and concentrated on Marie's plight.

They arranged that the following day Rose would write to her father in prison and explain that she would be out of touch for an unspecified time. After she had posted the letter she would make her way to Victoria House and discuss the trip with Marcus and Marie. He wanted to make it as much fun for Marie as they could and Rose was eager to help. Naturally, in the circumstances, neither of them gave a second thought to Steven.

The moment she set foot inside the door Connie appeared. In her ancient dress and grubby apron it was hard to imagine that she had once been even remotely glamorous and, with Marcus's words ringing in her ear, Rose was struck by the contrast of an ageing failed artiste and the successful woman she herself expected to be. She would hate to end up like Connie, she thought uneasily. Her hair was tied in rag curlers and her feet were encased in broken-down slippers.

'I saved you a nice bit of bacon roll,' she told Rose, 'and a few spuds. Nice and filling, bacon and onion roll. My mother always made it on a Saturday. She reckoned it filled all the corners!' She led the way into the corner that passed as a kitchen. 'Mondays it was usually kippers and cabbage, Tuesdays was either bangers and mash or stuffed hearts. Pigs' hearts, that is. Lovely, they are...'

Rose took off her jacket as the plate was set before her. The suet crust looked cold and soggy but she thought the bacon might be edible. She was hungry and began to eat.

Connie sat beside her on a hard-backed chair that wobbled ominously, due to a missing strut beneath it. 'Nice young man you were with!' she remarked hopefully. 'It looked like that Mr Bennley.'

'It was.' She poked at the bacon but as she did so cold bacon fat escaped from inside the rolled crust.

'Stepping out, are you?'

Rose had a mouthful of bacon and could only shake her head.

'Looks like a gentleman,' Connie persisted with obvious envy. 'Romantic, is he?'

'Romantic? Certainly not.'

'Don't let our lord and master know about him. He—'

'Your lord and master?'

'Mr Markham. That's his nickname here. He can be very jealous – and spiteful with it. But this Mr Bennley – is he good to you? Flowers and chocolate and things?'

'Hardly!' She sighed. 'Mr Bennley interferes too much for my liking but he means well. He actually went to the police station to find out what happened to my pa. I am rather cross about that.'

'And what has happened to him? Your pa, I mean.'

'Fifty days' hard labour. He's in Pentonville.' Sighing heavily, Rose added salt and pepper to her food but it made little difference. There were some pieces of half-cooked onion and she managed to swallow them down.

Connie pursed her lips, sucked in air, then shook her head for good measure. 'Pentonville eh? I don't envy him. Nasty reputation, Pentonville. I know a man – he was our next-door neighbour years ago when I was a girl – who went there. Spent hours, he did, on one of those treadmills. Walking up and up this giant wheel and getting nowhere. Agony, he said it was, on his legs. Torture's what I call it. Mind you, you got a short break now and again and a cup of tea but it was soul-destroying. That's the very words he used.'

Rose was staring at her in horror. 'But Pa will never manage that. He has a gammy leg and limps quite badly.' She frowned. 'Perhaps that's only for the very bad cases. My pa isn't really *bad*. I mean, he's not wicked. Not like some people. He hasn't murdered anyone or burned down someone's house.' She shrugged. 'It wasn't much of a crime. I suppose you could call him a minor criminal.' She glanced hopefully at Connie. 'He might be treated with...' She searched for the word. 'With leniency.'

'He might be and he might not. I mean hard labour has to be hard, doesn't it? Although if he's lucky he might just do the oakum. Picking this horrible tarry rope for hours on end. Still, look on the bright side, eh. They have to be punished if they've done something wrong like your pa.'

'He was led astray, Connie!' Rose protested half-heartedly. Her mind was on other things by now.

'They all say that, Rose.' She gave a short snort. 'I was led astray, m'lud! You can hear them all saying it.'

Rose pushed aside her plate.

'Aren't you going to finish it?' Connie demanded. 'Give it here. Waste not, want not!' She took the plate and reached for a clean fork.

'By the way, Connie, remember I told you I was going to France for a few days – well it starts Saturday and I may be away for the whole week.'

'But you've paid me for your suppers.' She looked anxious.

'Doesn't matter, Connie. You keep the money. It's not your fault I shan't be eating them and Mr Bennley is going to pay me for the trip and everything.' She sat back. 'Imagine me in France! I can hardly believe it. I just wish it wasn't going to be so sad.' Briefly Rose explained the reason behind the trip. 'It will be interesting to meet Marcus's mother and her new husband but I can't stay away too long because I don't think Mr Markham's going to be very pleased. I've only just started at the Supper Room and I'm taking time off.'

Connie narrowed her eyes. 'Talking of him, how d'you get along with him, Rose? He can be rather demanding. Some men are like that. He certainly was with me. Couldn't take his eyes off me.'

Rose considered, her head on one side as she tried to analyse her feelings towards her employer. 'He's quite nice but ... he's rather intimidating when he wants to be. I thought he liked me but now I'm not sure.' She decided not to tell Connie about the way Marcus had interfered on her behalf because it made her feel foolish.

One way and another she was beginning to feel depressed and after a few more minutes she made her excuses and went to bed.

★ ★ ★

While Rose was drifting into an uneasy sleep, on the other side of the Channel Clarice Feigant lay wide awake, thinking about her daughter's approaching visit and trying to keep calm and not give way to grief. She had to be strong for Marie's sake because she wanted her last days or weeks to be happy. She told herself that she must never let her daughter see just how devastating her death would be to the whole family.

'Gerard, are you awake?' she asked in a low voice, not wishing to wake him if he had been fortunate enough to find sleep. There was no reply and she trusted him not to pretend. He understood how anxious she was about the forthcoming visit and how much she valued whatever time the three of them would have together, and he, too, wanted Marie's stay with them to be as pleasant as possible. They understood that the end was inevitable but Clarice had notified their local doctor that her daughter was coming in case, towards the end, Marie needed medical assistance of any kind to ensure a peaceful, pain-free death.

No one would ever know how much pain Letitia had inflicted on them by her attitude towards Gerard but they had lived with it now for many years and had come to accept that nothing would change. The knowledge that Gerard was Letitia's father had effectively broken the family and Clarice deeply regretted telling the truth about it. It had

195

been a mistake, she now realized, but at the time Gerard had longed to see his daughter and she had thought it only fair that he should, especially after her divorce.

Sitting up, she glanced down at her husband, his weathered face and black hair dark against the pillow. He was handsome in a French way, with dark eyes and defined cheekbones that gave him an almost saturnine appearance which belied his warm heart and passionate nature.

She slipped out of bed, slid her feet into her slippers and went downstairs. Sometimes it helped her to sleep if she drank warm milk and she went into the big farmhouse kitchen where the ancient stove still gave out a little heat. Pouring milk into a pan she left it to warm and wandered to the back door and out into the yard.

There was a brand new rocking chair which they had bought from the local 'cabinet maker' whose work was sturdy but unsophisticated. It creaked as it rocked but it was a soothing sound and the chair would last for many years. It was a present for Marie but now Clarice sat in it. It had been a warm day but the night air was cool with no wind. Tomorrow the temperature would rise and there would be high humidity. Fortunately the old farmhouse had been built to keep out the summer heat so that July and August would always be bearable.

Gerard had reminded her that July the

fourteenth was the *Fête de la Fédération*, when the revolutionaries had stormed the Bastille fortress in Paris. There would be celebrations throughout France and even the smallest villages would remember Bastille Day with a party and a few fireworks. Hopefully Marie would be able to sit in the rocking chair and watch the display from a distance. Would God spare her that long, she wondered, with the familiar frisson of fear.

Clarice stared out over their land which lay still and secretive beneath the clear night sky. The farm stretched ahead towards the village of Wissant on the Opal coast, near Boulogne. Beyond the little fishing village, the wide currents of La Manche separated them from England's southern coastline – and beyond that, London and her family.

'What will you think of our farm, Marie?' she murmured.

Currently they had two pigs, a small vineyard, a small orchard with apples and pears and three large meadows in which they grazed milk cows and a few sheep. She hoped against hope that Marie would live long enough to become close to Gerard. He had grown from a young man to middle age without the joys of family life. He had missed so much. At least she had enjoyed the children when they were younger and had many happy memories. Gerard had nothing but he had never once reproached her.

'But soon, Gerard, you will meet with

Marcus and Marie,' she murmured into the darkness, 'and also young Rose who has so impressed Marie. If Marie loves her then I will love her also.'

For a little while she rocked gently in the new chair, imagining her daughter sitting there surrounded with cushions and a rug for her lap. When Marie was finally taken from her, Clarice would sit in the rocking chair and imagine that she was Marie and that somehow they were close to each other. Closing her eyes she said softly, 'Please God don't take her too soon.'

Seven

Steven ached all over and was finding it hard to breathe. They had knocked him down and kicked him and left him unconscious in the gutter. Apparently he had been discovered and brought to the hospital where he now lay in extreme discomfort and trepidation. But anger simmered within him and there was a desperate longing for revenge.

For the time being, however, Steven was pretending to be unaware of his surroundings because a nurse was standing by his bed, describing his injuries to a young policeman who no doubt waited, with his trusty notebook at the ready, for the gory details of the attack.

'He was found early this morning, Constable, by a market porter on his way to work. Gave the poor chap quite a turn because he thought he was a dead body. No one knows how long he was lying there. He's got—'

'Hang on a minute. I can't keep up!'

'Oh, sorry.'

No doubt a slow writer, thought Steven. The nurse continued at a slightly slower pace. 'He has two broken ribs, as far as we can tell, and received a severe blow to the head which led to concussion. Sister said it was a nasty beating ... there are various contusions. He still appears to be in a stupor and we can't get a word out of him.'

Steven clutched gratefully at this snippet of information. A stupor. He would prolong it while it suited him. He needed time to plan his excuses.

'So you don't know who he is.'

'No, we have no idea, but he was wearing decent clothes, his hair's been well cut and his shoes weren't cheap.'

Damn. Steven almost groaned. He had been hoping to remain anonymous but it looked as though they might ferret out the truth. If he could leave the hospital without revealing his identity it might be possible to tell the family that he had had a serious fall somewhere. That way they need never find out about Markham's thugs and his own humiliation at their hands.

The policeman said, 'Then someone will be asking about him. That type always do. He'll be a 'missing person'. Shouldn't be difficult to find who he is and why they picked on him. Just a matter of time.'

'He must have been quite good-looking – under all the bruises.'

Good for you, thought Steven, holding back a wan smile which would have been painful considering the split lip and aching jaw. He wondered what he looked like and shuddered. What grieved him most was his inability to inflict similar injuries, which he could have done if there had been only one attacker. Two made it pretty impossible to retaliate with much effect.

The nurse said, 'When are you coming back? I'd reckon another hour or so before he comes round. If he knew his attackers you might find them. They must be animals, the men who did this to him.'

When he was alone again, Steven began to consider his options. If he named them, it would become known that they had put him in the hospital and that would offend his dignity and damage his self-respect. If he was unable to claim that a bad fall had been responsible, his family would find out and whatever they said by way of sympathy, they would be thinking it served him right for his profligate ways and might teach him a lesson. That would be hard to live with.

What he really wanted was to search out each of his attackers separately and beat the living daylights out of them but if he did, they could name him and then the whole story of the debt would come out and he, Steven, might even get arrested for assault. To confuse matters even more, he still owed Markham money.

With a groan that was a mixture of pain and frustration, he turned over cautiously in the bed and almost immediately fell asleep.

★　★　★

Mrs Granger came into the room with her hands outstretched in welcome. 'My dear Miss Paton, this is so good of you. William tells me you are going to visit me and read to me. That will be such a treat.'

'I will be coming fairly regularly,' Rose told her, 'But not immediately because I have to go to France for a—'

The old lady's expression changed. 'To France? Oh dear! Are you sure?' She sat down and Rose did the same. 'I don't entirely trust the French, you know. My mother didn't like them at all.'

'I have to go with a friend,' Rose explained, 'who is not well enough to make the trip on her own. Most likely it will take less than a week and I'll be back. But I thought I would read to you for an hour today before I go.'

'Well I'm most grateful, Miss Paton. Now what are you going to read? My mother loved the Greek legends – King Midas and those Argonauts and the man who had wings and the bull in the cave...' She frowned. 'Do you know those stories?'

Rose confessed that she had never heard of them. 'But I thought you—'

'I used to read to the boys when they were young.' Mrs Granger smiled at the memory. 'They loved adventure stories. Tales of "derring do"!'

'Do you have a Bible handy, Mrs Granger?'

'A Bible?' She frowned. 'Most certainly I do. It's on my bedside table ... Do you play the piano, my dear? William is a very patient teacher. Everyone says so.'

Rose thought how sad it was for Herbert Granger that his mother seemed unaware of his existence. Not that he seemed to mind. He accepted his mother's lapses of memory with good-natured resignation. 'I don't play the piano,' she admitted. 'But I can sing.'

Mrs Granger smiled. 'Well, dear, that's better than nothing.'

Rose felt slighted. 'I have a very sweet voice – so I've been told. I perform on stage. That's my career.' This produced not a flicker of interest from Mrs Granger so Rose hid her disappointment. 'So, do you want me to read to you from the bible? I'm only here for an hour and I don't want to waste your time.'

'Oh you won't do that, my dear. I'm always busy. William will tell you that.' Her smile faded abruptly. 'But do you have to go to France? They can be very perverse, the French. That's what my mother believed. That's her very word. And it's such a long way and such a big country. And the English Channel ... well really!' She tutted with disapproval. 'Do give it some thought, Miss Paton.'

'I will,' said Rose. 'Now what about that Bible?'

She was beginning to realize that the

money she earned from her time spent with Mrs Granger was going to be well deserved.

Later that same evening, in Victoria House, Rose, Marcus and Letitia were together in the drawing room although Letitia sat apart at the small table in the window bay while Marcus and Rose sat on the sofa. The latter were discussing their forthcoming trip to France but Marie had gone to bed early with a headache, insisting that they would manage very well without her and she needed her beauty sleep!

Letitia had spent the afternoon at the dressmakers, trying on her wedding dress and finding it unsatisfactory in several ways. She now sat with a pencil and a sketching pad, trying to work out some improvements.

She glanced up. 'What do you think, Rose? Can you spare a minute?'

Obediently, Rose crossed the room to peer over her shoulder. Letitia had kept the design of the dress a close secret but now she needed a little help.

'The waistline was nipped in too tightly, Rose – I felt it was rather old-fashioned so I suggest keeping a line right down the front but not separated into skirt and bodice. What do you think?'

The sketch had been skilfully drawn.

'It looks very nice – and certainly more modern,' Rose hazarded nervously.

'I'm glad you agree ... and there were three

frills down the front of the skirt which looked rather overdone. A little excessive. I don't want to seem flamboyant. The da Silvas would not approve of that.'

Rose said, 'Is it white – or shouldn't I ask?'

Letitia lowered her voice confidingly. 'The silk is grey and white stripes. Very narrow stripes. And there's no bustle as such but the jacket at the back is full and softly pleated over the hips.'

Rose was genuinely impressed. 'It sounds wonderful! You will bowl Bernard over!'

'Oh Rose, I do hope so!'

'What will you wear on your hair?'

'I shall wear it swept up, naturally, and I thought a cluster of white roses – silk, of course. Or do you think blush pink would be softer? I am wearing long gloves and carrying a prayer book and a single lily.'

Rose thought about it. 'If you wore blush pink roses you could maybe match the gloves.'

Letitia looked at her, hesitating. 'That's a very good idea, Rose! Thank you. I'll speak to the dressmaker tomorrow for her opinion.' She smiled. 'Now you may go back to Marcus. I'm sure there is a lot to talk about for your journey.'

Ten minutes later, Rose and Marcus had decided that they should reserve four inside seats in the ferry boat so that Marie could lie down if she was tired.

They were interrupted by the front door

bell and Mrs Bray appeared to say there was a police sergeant at the door.

'He says there's been some kind of a to-do,' she told them breathlessly, 'and Master Steven is in hospital.'

Marcus left the room hurriedly and the two women looked at each other in alarm.

Letitia said, 'I wondered where he was at breakfast this morning but I didn't give it another thought.'

'Maybe he was run down by a motor.'

'At least he's still alive or they would have told us.' With a sigh, Letitia closed her sketching pad. 'He was like this as a boy. Always in some scrape or other. After Mother left us he became worse. Mother always referred to his temper as 'a short fuse'. She said he didn't need to go looking for trouble because trouble came looking for him!' She glanced up as Marcus re-entered.

'He was set upon by three men,' Marcus told them. 'He can come home but he has to rest in bed for another day or two.'

'That I would like to see!' exclaimed Letitia. 'When did he ever do what someone wanted him to do?'

'I've sent for a taxi, then I'll fetch him home.'

Steven came in half an hour later with an attempt at bravado which fooled none of them. He was moving cautiously, lowering himself into an armchair with a few groans.

Letitia stared at his bandaged jaw and left cheek and winced. 'You look terrible!' she told him unhelpfully. 'Anyone would think you'd met a herd of stampeding elephants!'

Mrs Bray appeared and tutted at his battered appearance. 'Shall I make you some hot milk?'

He rolled his eyes. Moving his mouth carefully he said, 'I could do with a whisky! Make it a double!' It came out as a mumble but Marcus guessed what he'd said and moved to the sideboard to pour the drink.

Letitia said, 'Should you be drinking alcohol? Have they given you any medicines?'

Steven ignored her.

Rose said, 'I hope the police catch them, Steven – I mean, whoever did this to you.'

Mrs Bray, her hands on her hips, shook her head. 'I don't know what the world's coming to. Streets full of thugs! People robbing houses! Smashing church windows! And what's the government doing? Nothing, if you ask me.'

Steven said, 'There'll be an extra one for dinner tonight, Mrs Bray.'

She nodded. 'Did they starve you in that hospital?'

'I couldn't eat properly. My jaw...'

Rose frowned. 'Oh, you poor dear!'

Mrs Bray said, 'I'll make it an easy meal – invalid food! I'll make soup followed by ... let's see now ... fish pie with a mashed potato topping. You'll manage that all right.' She gave him a cheerful smile and hurried back to the kitchen.

Steven drank the whisky in three mouthfuls and held out the glass for a refill. Seeing that he was about to demand serious attention, Letitia rose to her feet. 'Rose and I have things to talk about,' she said by way of explanation and the two women made their exit.

Being left alone with his brother was not at all what Steven wanted. He knew there would be questions and he had not yet perfected his story. He drank the second whisky and handed back the glass. 'I'm going to lie down,' he said. 'I need some sleep.' He held up a hand. 'No, I can manage the stairs, thanks Marcus. Just leave me in peace for a couple of hours. Don't worry about me. I'll be down in time for dinner.' He gave Marcus a brave smile. 'Don't fuss, old chap. I'm a survivor!'

Saturday dawned and Rose was delighted to see blue skies and to note that the wind had dropped to a light breeze. The taxi took the three of them down to the quayside at Folkestone and Marcus carried Marie while Rose struggled with their luggage which they had reduced to a minimum but which still weighed a considerable amount.

Because the weather was good and the crossing promised to be a smooth one they sat on a bench on deck to enjoy the adventure. Marie was dressed warmly although it was midsummer, as they had been warned that there might be cooler winds out in mid-channel. Marcus also carried a travelling rug in case she needed it.

No one from the family had come with them – Steven because of his injuries, and Letitia because she had another meeting with the dressmaker who was having to make late alterations and was not happy about them. The wedding was only a week away – on the fifth of July – so Marcus and Rose were planning to return on the Wednesday in plenty of time to be of help and support to Letitia.

A few blasts on the horn announced that they were setting off and the crew dashed to and fro, casting off the ropes and coiling them on the deck in preparation for their arrival in Boulogne. Rose and Marie sat side by side while Marcus went below deck to find a warm drink for Marie. Fellow passengers crowded the rails and the general mood was festive. Rose could see that Marie was enthralled, her eyes shining, her hands clasped excitedly against her chest.

Rose said, 'Your mother must be very excited – and Gerard also.'

Marie nodded happily. 'I can't wait to see them or the farm. Mother says there are cows and hens and some friendly pigs ... and they make their own cider and apple brandy – and I may have some of both!' She laughed. 'Not too much though or I may get drunk, like Steven.' She leaned closer to Rose and lowered her voice. 'I know he gets drunk sometimes and I don't believe he was attacked by thugs. Why should anyone attack him? They didn't steal anything from him. I think he may have got drunk and stumbled around in the road and been knocked down by a horse and cart or even a motor car! But don't tell Marcus I said that. He's rather strict with Steven.'

'I won't tell a soul.'

'And especially not Mother. I don't want her to worry and Marcus says we needn't tell her about him being in the hospital. I think – oh, here comes Marcus now with the drinks.'

He had brought three mugs of hot chocolate and they quickly settled down to enjoy the crossing.

At five to seven Clarice Feigant went to the back door, watching impatiently for her loved ones to arrive. Gerard had taken the horse and cart to meet Jean-Philippe's small fishing boat when it returned to Wissant from Boulogne with the visitors. Her husband, full of enthusiasm, had first cleared out the cart and polished the woodwork. The cob had been brushed and his harness polished. Gerard had filled the cart with rugs and cushions for Marcus and Rose but Marie, wrapped in blankets, would fit safely and snugly beside him on the seat. Her husband had been as excited as she was about the visit, she thought gratefully, and neither had spoken of the fact that they would be sharing Marie's last weeks; nor could they bear to talk about what would come next.

She had waved Gerard off early in the morning in a fever of anticipation. Covering the distance from Boulogne to Wissant wouldn't be easy but they had solved the problem. Jean-Philippe, the son of Gerard's oldest friend, would sail his fishing boat to the port of Boulogne to meet the ferry around eleven o'clock in the morning. He would then bring the three visitors back in his boat to Wissant where Gerard would be waiting with the horse and cart to transport them the last stretch of the journey.

Clarice had then filled the waiting hours with preparations for their evening meal. She had prepared a large terracotta dish of her own version of cassoulet which contained duck, sausage, ham and beans as well as herbs and this had been simmering for hours in the large farmhouse range. Marie, she had told Gerard, needed nourishing food to give her stamina – the fresher the better! She had made bread to go with it, to be spread lavishly with butter from the milk from their own cows. In the large larder there was a game pie.

They would have omelettes from their own

eggs, stews from the rabbits in the surrounding fields and salad stuff from their vegetable garden. They would even drink the wine made from their own grapes the previous autumn and Jean-Philippe would take out his boat and bring back fish from the sea. Secretly, Clarice planned to keep her daughter alive 'by hook or by crook!'

Her sharp ears caught the sound of hooves and the rattle of wheels which grew closer. They were coming. Clarice pressed her hands together. 'Thank you, God!' she whispered.

She had searched the shops for books to read to her daughter and had told her in her letters about the Bastille Day celebrations they would attend on July 14th. She had made up her mind to give Marie countless good things to look forward to. She would give her precious daughter little time to contemplate dying but plenty of good reasons to stay alive!

A long excited discussion of their journey meant that they did not settle to their meal until just after nine o'clock when Jean-Philippe joined them. Rose had taken to him immediately when she saw him waiting for them on the jetty – a burly figure with wild hair and a broad smile on his face. Now she sat opposite him, watching him enjoying the cassoulet. She found herself wishing that she belonged to a family like the Bennleys and envying Marie. The girl had brothers and sisters, good friends, a mother and a French stepfather – an interesting past. Gerard spoke good English with a strong accent but Jean-Philippe's grasp of the language was not as good although that did not prevent him from joining in the conversation.

When Marcus told him that Rose was planning a career on the stage he was puzzled by the word.

'Stage,' Marcus echoed. 'That is the theatre. *Théâtre.*'

Jean-Philippe's cheerful laugh rang out and Rose had the impression that he was not taking her seriously.

Marie said quickly, 'Don't laugh, Jean-Philippe. Rose can sing and she will soon learn to dance. She's going to take dancing lessons.'

His bright blue eyes gleamed with fun as Jean-Philippe wagged a warning finger at Rose. 'Eez not ... you, *le théâtre!*'

'Not for me? But why?' she demanded, trying not to be impressed by his rugged good looks and confident manner.

'*Ce n'est pas convenable,*' he explained. 'No ... good.' He reached for another slice of bread.

Marie and Rose exchanged exasperated glances and looked at Clarice for a translation.

She hesitated. 'He says it is not ... not very respectable. Rather unconventional.'

Marcus, seeing the expression on Rose's face, said quickly, 'He doesn't mean to be rude, Rose. The music hall *is* unconventional, you have to admit. Even legitimate actors are thought by some to be slightly beyond the pale.'

Rose glared at him. 'Some might say we are more creative.'

Marie patted Rose's hand. 'What does he know about the theatre? He may never have been to one. And he's French, remember. Maybe they just think differently or...' She let the sentence die, substituting a shrug for the words.

Rose stared at her shoes.

Marcus smiled at her. 'Marie is right. How much do you know about fishing? You are both experts in your own line of work and know nothing about the other.' He reached out and gave her hand a comforting squeeze.

'True.'

Clarice said, 'Take no notice, Rose. Jean-Philippe is teasing you. Now, would anyone like any more cassoulet?'

They had all dined well and groaned, protesting that they were full, with the exception of Jean-Philippe who nodded eagerly.

His plate was refilled, their tumblers were refilled with wine and they all chatted while he enjoyed his second helping.

Gerard asked, 'How is our daughter, Marcus? Our little Letitia? Very excited, yes?' He smiled. 'The wedding is a very wonderful day for her.'

Marie answered his question. 'She is very thrilled – but very nervous. No one has seen her dress. It's a big secret but I know how it will look because we discussed it together.'

He nodded, pleased. 'And this man – this Bernard? Bernard da Silva. He is the good man for her?'

Marie nodded enthusiastically. 'He seems very nice and he's rich and his family are—'

'Rich? 'He shook his head. 'It is not about the money. It is about the happiness. The love. Does he love her?' Gerard leaned forward and now, Rose thought, he looked a different man. Very intense. Almost stern. 'Does he adore her? This man must make her happy for the rest of her life!'

Taken aback, Marie regarded him warily. 'Most certainly he loves her!'

Clarice threw a warning glance at her husband but Gerard appeared not to notice. She said, 'Letitia wrote very lovingly about him, Gerard. You've forgotten.'

He said passionately, 'It is so easy to make the mistake – to marry the wrong man. She is my only child. *Our* only child. I want ... your mother and I want only her happiness. That is for all of you the same. We want you to be happy and to be loved.'

Rose felt a frisson of envy. Did her own father care so passionately about *her*? Did *anyone* care that much about her? Certainly

215

her mother would have cared but Pa was different. How wonderful to have such a loving father. She felt a moment's fierce irritation with the absent Letitia who refused to appreciate Gerard, and wondered if Marcus was thinking along the same lines. She glanced at him but he was very quiet, apparently lost in thought.

Feeling that the cheerful dinner conversation was taking a less than jolly direction Rose said brightly, 'It will be a splendid day!' Smiling, she picked up her tumbler. 'Here's to Letitia's wedding!'

Marie looked at her gratefully and did the same and soon they were all sharing a toast to Letitia's long and happy marriage.

Marie turned her attention to Jean-Philippe. 'Do you have a wife?'

He looked at his friend who translated.

Jean-Philippe threw back his head and laughed. 'A wife? *Mais non!*'

Clarice said, 'He's a confirmed bachelor. Or maybe no one will have him!'

He listened to the translation then rolled his eyes. *'Peut-être.'*

Clarice translated. 'Perhaps.'

Gerard grinned. 'Pity the poor woman!'

Clarice looked enquiringly at Rose.

Rose shook her head. 'No one,' she said firmly. 'Marcus told my employer that he was going to marry me! I knew nothing about it, of course, but I had told my employer at the Supper Room that I was concentrating on my career.'

All heads turned to Marcus who had the decency to colour slightly. 'I was simply trying to protect her.'

Clarice narrowed her eyes. 'So has she turned you down?'

'He hasn't asked me.'

'But if he did?'

Now they all turned to look at Rose.

She shook her blonde curls. 'How can I answer that? I am not going to marry anyone until I'm famous. Not until I'm known as the famous Miss Lamore!'

Jean-Philippe said suddenly, *'Quand je trouverai la femme parfaite, je la reconnaîtrai.'*

Rose regarded him blankly but Clarice smiled. 'He'll recognize his perfect woman when he sees her!'

Clarice began to collect the empty plates and Rose helped her. Her thoughts lingered, however, on what Jean-Philippe had said. Was it really as easy as that? What happened if you didn't recognize the right person? Had Letitia recognized Bernard? She had heard about love at first sight but did it always happen like that? Clarice had made a mistake the first time she fell in love ... unless it was equally easy to fall out of love. Rose decided she must bear that in mind and keep her eyes open. How terrible if the perfect man slipped past her.

Soon the table was reset with a cheese board and crusty bread, and a large dish of fresh fruit. Marie, tired but happy to be with her mother, refused to go to bed and the evening continued with good food and equally good humour.

Monday, June 30th found Steven hurrying downstairs in his pyjamas and dressing gown, cursing roundly. He had been woken by the sound of the front door bell and Mrs Bray seemed to be missing. Possibly in the garden fetching some vegetables for the evening meal. Letitia never answered the front door. God help Bernard!

As he ran down the stairs he shouted 'I'm coming, damn you!'

He peered cautiously through the coloured glass in the door to make sure that Markham's thugs were not standing on the doorstep. The unfamiliar outline was too small, he decided, so he plucked up his courage and opened the door. An elderly woman stood there and for a moment he stared at her in dismay. Who was this old hag, he wondered. Were there gypsies in the area? They didn't usually appear until the apples needed picking.

'Yes?'

'I need to speak to Rose Paton.'

'Why come here? She doesn't live with us. She lives with some crackpot woman...'

She drew herself up a little. 'She lives with me and I'll ask you to mind your language! I'm Connie and I need to know when she's

218

coming back. Our lord and master's expecting—'

'Lord and master?'

'That's what we all call him. He's our landlord, see.' She started again. *'Mr Markham's* expecting her for tonight's performance and he's sent me to look for her. It's lucky I knew her address here.'

Recognizing the name Connie, Steven regretted his use of the word 'crackpot'. This woman, according to Rose, had once been Markham's lady friend. Must have been donkey's years ago, he thought, eyeing the lined, powdered face, dirty hair and shabby clothes, but he had no wish to cause Markham any further aggravation. The less contact he had with that sadist the better.

He assumed a friendly smile. 'Oh Connie! You're the lady that makes the bacon rolls!'

'Bacon and onion actually but yes, that's me.' She thawed a little, he thought. 'I'm a dab hand with suet crust. I do her a bit of supper and I think she appreciates it. She needs fattening up a bit. Poor little legs like sticks! So she's a friend of yours.'

'Not exactly. She's friendly with my brother Marcus.' He put a hand to his back which was beginning to ache.

'So, can I have a word with her?' Connie asked.

'I'm afraid they're not back yet. You knew they were going to France, I suppose, to take my sister over to Mother's place?'

'Yes, but I forgot the dates and he wants to know whether or not to include her in the show this evening.' She shook her head. 'He won't take it kindly if she doesn't turn up. He's got a bit of a temper and he'll be thinking she's let him down.'

'They didn't leave until very early Saturday and they wouldn't be back quite so soon. It's quite a journey.'

'I thought they were going to Boulogne.'

'So they were but Mother lives at Wissant some miles further along the coast.' He felt uneasy under her scrutiny.

'You'd be Steven. She's spoke about you.'

'None of it good, I suspect!' Smiling was an effort and he fingered his aching jaw. There was hardly an area of his body that wasn't sore. The Sister on the hospital ward had tried to persuade him to involve the police but he had fought shy of that, insisting that he had taken a tumble down some steps while under the influence. She hadn't believed him but finally gave up.

Connie frowned. 'So what should I say to him? Back tomorrow maybe? He's not going to like it.'

'Look here,' he said. 'Don't say you've seen me. Don't mention my name. There's a dear.' With one hand to his back, Steven disappeared into the sitting room, telling her to 'Wait a moment!' and reappeared with a florin which he pressed into her hand. 'Buy yourself a drink or something, Connie.' Or a dozen bars of soap, he thought. 'Just say you spoke to the housekeeper. I'd rather not get involved.'

She regarded the florin with obvious disappointment. 'So when am I to say then?'

'Say she's expected back soon because we've got a wedding on the fifth – that's Saturday. Now, if you'll excuse me ... I've been unwell. I had a fall down some steps.'

She nodded, unsurprised. 'You do look a bit battered – as if you've gone ten rounds in the boxing ring but didn't win!'

A damned sight worse than that, he reflected. Stupid old cow! He bit back a rude comment about her own sorry appearance. 'I'd better get back to bed.' He closed the door firmly, crossing his fingers that she would deliver the correct message.

No doubt she knew Markham well enough to choose her time. If she waited until he'd been drinking he'd be in a foul mood and she might get the back of his hand across her face. He closed his bedroom door. 'Rather you than me!' he told her as he fell back in the bed, pulled up the bedclothes and prepared to go back to sleep.

Connie made her way home, stopping only to call in at the Dog and Bone to spend some of her florin. As it happened, the pie man called in while she was drinking her third gin and she bought two mutton pies to eat when she got home. Food cheered her

221

up and she felt in need of solace. She missed Rose's company more than she would admit but now she blamed her for being in France and out of Andrew Markham's reach because that put Connie in the firing line. The three gins were intended to boost her courage when she next saw her employer.

As she let herself in by the front door of the house, Mr Coates, the downstairs tenant, came out to meet her, a nicotine-stained finger pressed to his lips in warning.

'What?' cried Connie in alarm.

'Shh! He's up there, Connie! Our lord and master! Pissed as a newt!'

'Up where?'

'Your flat. He let himself in. I thought he was after me for the rent I owe but he simply ignored me. He could hardly get up the blooming stairs! Fall down 'em, you miserable sod, I thought. Fall down and kill yourself!'

Connie hesitated. She had the two pies and she could give Markham one of them. They could have a bite to eat and a nice chat and *then* she could tell him about Rose letting him down. Sometimes she could sweet-talk him into a better mood – a more romantic mood, maybe. Deep down she still had a reluctant affection for the man. Andrew. She smiled at the memories. He'd been young and handsome once and she would have walked over hot coals for him!

Mr Coates was waiting for her answer, a

puzzled look on his face. 'Come back later, Connie,' he advised. 'Let him sober up a bit. He's a bad-tempered bugger when he's drunk. You know he is!'

Still she hesitated. Her head told her his advice was sound. She could just slip away and come back later. Her heart, however, said that maybe he needed her and somehow they might rediscover a little of the old magic. It was a long time since anyone had cared for her. She was old and had lost her youthful charms but Andrew had nothing to boast about except the money he had made, and his good looks were fading fast. He could only just claim to be good looking. Overweight and unfit, he had made many enemies. He was not a happy man.

'Connie! Hop it while you still can.'

She gathered her wits together and gave him a sad smile. 'I remember him when he was twenty-one. His birthday party! I was invited. The girls went mad for him then but he only had eyes for me.' She started to go up the stairs.

'More fool you, then!' he snapped.

Connie heard him slam the door of his kitchen in disgust but she pushed aside the last remaining doubts. When she reached the door of her flat she found it wide open. There was no sound from inside the flat. Probably fallen asleep, she told herself with a smile. Well, in that case she would tiptoe round, laying the table with a decent cloth if she could find one, and maybe a candle. A pity she didn't have any flowers. A single red rose. That always looked good on a table laid for two. A single rose *meant* something. She stepped inside the door but he was waiting behind it.

Even as her smile faltered, a hand clamped itself around her throat and she was jerked backwards off her feet.

'Where the hell have you been?' His voice was thick, his words slurred. 'And where's that girl?'

She couldn't answer because she was half choked and struggling for breath. Suddenly he gave her a push and she tumbled head first into the room.

Shocked, she stared up from the floor as he towered over her, his fists clenched, his eyes narrowed into mean slits. 'Where's Rose?' He tried to smile. 'Where's the wonderful Miss Lamore?'

She scrambled into a sitting position, searching for a lie that would pacify him. Mr Coates's warning flashed through her mind and she decided to lie. 'Rose is …Yes, I think she'll be in later … at the Supper Room.'

'You *think* so?' He swayed. 'You're supposed to *know*.' He put out a hand to the wall to steady himself. 'You always were a stupid cow!'

She prayed that he would collapse and then sleep it off. He would be in a better mood when he woke up again. If that didn't

224

happen she must somehow get past him and out of the flat. There was no way she was going to talk him into anything while he was in this state and her fear grew. Cursing her stupidity, she glanced round for something with which to defend herself if the need arose. She said, 'I've brought us a bit of dinner, Andrew – I mean Mr Markham.'

She thought of the poker and took a step back to be nearer to it but, as drunk as he was, he read her intentions in her face. He lunged forward, she snatched it up but he took it from her and threw it across the room. It struck a picture and shattered the glass before falling on to the ancient sofa.

Markham laughed at the expression on her face. 'What? Going to hit me, were you? Who're you kidding?'

They faced each other across the room, Connie white-faced, holding her breath, Markham red with anger and fuelled with drink.

She watched for a chance to dodge past him and escape through the door but he held his arms wide. 'Come on, Connie! Make a run for it!'

He took two steps towards her and she imagined his hands closing again around her neck. If she retreated she would soon have her back against the wall. If she ran forward...

'Andrew! I mean ... Please don't...'

★ ★ ★

Downstairs in the hallway, Mr Coates stared upward, wondering what was going on in the attic flat. Asking for trouble, she was, going up there when they all knew what he was like when he was drunk. Usually he sent his bully boys to do his dirty work but when drink got the better of him his temper took over from any common sense he might have.

Suddenly he heard a scream followed by silence. Then he heard a thud.

Above him a door opened and Mrs Jupp, from the first floor flat, came down. She had her apron on and clutched a duster in her free hand. She said, 'What's happening up there? Is Connie all right?'

He explained the situation and they regarded each other fearfully.

'D'you think we should go up and see?' she asked.

'That thud must have been him falling down. Dead drunk, most likely.'

Suddenly they heard heavy footsteps on the top stairs.

'That's him!' Mrs Jupp clutched at his arm. 'At least he's on his feet again.'

They froze momentarily.

When the footsteps reached the landing, however, Mr Coates grabbed Mrs Jupp's arm and pulled her into his front room and closed the door. The erratic footsteps thundered down, the front door opened and as one they rushed to the window. Peering out they saw Andrew Markham staggering along the pavement. For a moment he clung to the pillar box long enough to vomit, then continued his erratic journey.

'Ugh!' Mrs Jupp wrinkled her nose. 'The filthy pig!'

For a long time, listening, neither of them spoke again.

Mrs Jupp broke the silence. 'Well ... good riddance to him!'

'D'you reckon she's all right?'

'Course she is. She's a tough old bird. None of our business.' She rubbed her eyes. 'I'm not trailing up any more stairs than I have to. The doctor says I have to rest with my feet up on a pillow. My legs have ached like crazy these last few weeks. I can hardly walk.' He was not listening, she realized with a shrug.

'I told her not to go up.' He scratched his thinning hair. 'I couldn't stop her. It's very quiet up there. Maybe he knocked her out.'

Mrs Jupp nodded. 'My neighbour had a run-in like that once. Husband knocked her out with a coal scuttle! She had to have stitches. Good thing it was empty ... Poor old Connie. She'll come round.'

He frowned. 'Maybe we should see how she is.'

'She'll be embarrassed.' The thought of finding Connie on the floor in a dishevelled state was immediately distasteful and it overcame Mrs Jupp's natural curiosity.

Mr Coates wavered. 'She might need help

but he might come back while I'm up there. We could lock the front door.'

'But it's his property, Mr Coates. He's in a nasty mood already. He might have a go at us. Might kick us both out for interfering!'

They thought furiously until Mr Coates suggested they wait for an hour or so. 'When we hear her moving about again you could go up to her. Woman to woman. Like you said. You know.'

Finding she had talked herself into a corner, Mrs Jupp resigned herself to the inevitable. 'Right you are. Soon as I hear her on the move I'll pop up with a mug of tea.'

Eight

When the taxi pulled up outside Connie's flat the following day, Rose and Marcus saw a constable standing on the doorstep. It had been raining and he was an abject figure, huddling into his damp uniform for whatever warmth he could find. His feet were apart and his hands were clasped behind his back. He looked as though he had settled in for a long stay, thought Rose, surprised.

'What on earth is happening?' she asked.

'Something serious,' said Marcus. 'I'd better see you in before I go home.'

'There's no need. I'll be fine. You go on back to Victoria House. I know you're tired. I certainly am.'

The taxi driver turned in his seat. 'Looks like trouble. They don't stick the Old Bill on the doorstep for nothing!' He leaned sideways to get a better view.

Rose was already out of the taxi and hurrying towards the constable. 'What's going on? Why are you here? Has something happened?'

He put his hands on his hips, effectively barring her entrance. 'You could say that, miss. Why are you here?'

'I live here. In the top flat with Connie.'

By this time Marcus had joined them. 'Is something wrong?'

'You could say that.' He regarded Rose with narrowed eyes. 'So you're the one who lives with Miss Wainwright, are you? So where were you yesterday?'

Not liking his tone, Marcus said firmly, 'She was with me, on the journey back from Wissant, in France. Why are you asking? What has happened here?'

'So you are giving this young woman an alibi.'

Rose's heart seemed to stop. 'An alibi?'

Marcus said, 'An alibi? Certainly not – because she doesn't need one.'

Ignoring him, the constable stared at Rose but before he could say any more the side window of the bay was pushed up and Mr Coates poked his head out. His eyes were wide with shock. 'It's Connie! She's dead! He killed her! Our lord and master killed her!'

Now robbed of his chance to tell Rose the dramatic news himself, the constable turned on him irritably. 'You've been told not to gossip about the murder.'

'But she lives up there. She's going to find out for herself soon enough.' He turned back to Rose. 'It was him that done it! Markham. We heard this scream sort of cut short and then nothing ... except a thud and then he was down the stairs and away, drunk out of his mind and staggering. He done it. He strangled her! Her neck was all bruised. And he's scarpered. Well, he would.'

Rose had started to tremble with shock and she felt Marcus's arm go round her. Markham had *murdered* Connie? Was it possible? She said, 'I must go up to her.' Her voice shook. 'Oh, poor Connie!'

'Sorry, miss. No one's allowed up there. It's a crime scene and there are investigations going on. Anyway, she's not there. Wainwright's body was taken to the mortuary.'

Wainwright's body. It sounded so horribly impersonal, thought Rose, as though Connie had ceased to be a person.

The front door opened and a sergeant came out. The constable briefed him and Sergeant Cooper looked Rose up and down.

Marcus said, 'We've just come back from a trip to France. We know nothing about it.' Briefly he explained their situation and gave the name and address of his mother and stepfather in Wissant for purposes of corroboration.

Rose said, 'But why did he kill her?'

Sergeant Cooper said, 'That's for us to find out, miss. We'll be taking statements from all the tenants here, the staff of Andy's Supper Room and all his friends. All in good time. And if Markham makes contact with you, Miss Paton, you must notify us immediately.' He made to go back inside but then turned. 'I suppose you don't know where he is, Miss Paton? It's a crime to withhold information.'

'I have no idea, Sergeant. How could I? We've only just come back from—'

'He might have mentioned something last time you saw him, before you went away.'

She shook her head. 'He didn't.' She was about to mention Steven Bennley but stopped herself in time.

Sharp-eyed, the sergeant asked, 'What? You were going to say something.'

'I wasn't. It's nothing.' The two men were friends and Steven would be questioned like everyone else. Once they told him about the murder, he would no doubt offer the police any information he might have. It was not up to her.

Marcus said, 'You'd better come back with me, Rose, to Victoria House. You can stay until the wedding and then make whatever plans you wish.'

She nodded, saying nothing, as a fresh thought entered her head. Not only had Markham killed Connie, he had also, by his terrible crime, put an end to Andy's Supper Room and thus to her career. At once she was ashamed of the selfish thought. What kind of person was she, to put her own needs ahead of Connie's frightful death? But it was a sobering thought. She now had no home and no job – except for the few hours when she read to Mrs Granger.

Marcus shook her arm. 'Rose! You're not listening, are you? I said you must come back with me for the time being.' He gave his address to the sergeant and said they would be available for further questioning if it were necessary.

Rose was refused entry to Connie's flat so she and Marcus returned to the taxi and had barely travelled twenty yards down the road when they saw Mrs Jupp making her way slowly back to the house. She carried a basket of shopping and walked with a stick.

'Stop the car!' cried Rose and jumped out. 'Mrs Jupp! Isn't this terrible! Poor Connie. I can hardly believe it.'

Mrs Jupp set down her shopping basket. 'Our lord and master – a murderer! I still can't take it in. Mind you, I never did like him. A bit of a bully. That's what he was. Lord knows where he is now. Hiding himself in the south of France most likely. All he has to do is change his name and grow a moustache or a beard! He'll get away with it. His sort always do.' She shook her head. 'It could have been me ... or you! Or Mr Coates. When I think of it ... the danger we were in.' She sat down on a low brick wall, leaning well forward to escape the privet hedge behind her. She began to rub her legs, making the thick brown stockings wrinkle. 'If my husband was alive he'd go berserk. Fancy living in the house of a murderer! He never did like the man. He never liked the flat, come to that, or the street. Said it was a comedown but beggars can't be choosers.'

Marcus called from the taxi. 'Rose. We should be going.'

She said, 'They'll catch him, Mrs Jupp. I'm sure they will. Try not to worry.' She helped the old lady to her feet and handed her the basket. 'You take care.'

As soon as the taxi moved off, tears filled her eyes and she rested her head on Marcus's shoulder and sobbed.

Soon after Rose's discovery of Connie's death, Alicia da Silva went in search of her son and found him staring moodily out over the rain-sodden lawn. Hearing her come in, he did not turn but said, 'If it's like this on Saturday Letitia will be furious. A rainy wedding! Can you imagine!'

For a moment she stared at his uncompromising back with compassion but then she settled herself on the sofa. 'Come and join me, dear,' she said, her voice deceptively calm. 'We have to talk.'

He turned reluctantly. 'Do we?'

'I've just said so, Bernard.' She pointed to the adjoining armchair. 'And I think you know why.'

He sat down but with a bad grace. 'What is it now, Mother?'

He sounded sullen which reinforced her fears. Taking a deep breath she said, 'You had a letter this morning from Carlotta.'

He was shocked, she saw. No doubt he had thought himself the first person to see the morning's post, but she had been down before him. 'I think I should know what it was about, Bernard.'

His defensive attitude fell away at her words and she saw by the look in his eyes that his mind was in a turmoil. 'I ... I can't show it to you,' he stammered. 'She has told me not to. Her words are for my eyes only. I owe her that much, surely.'

'You owe her nothing, Bernard. She is a close friend who developed a schoolgirl crush on you. That is all. I thought better of her, to tell you the truth. She is obviously trying to make mischief between you and your bride-to-be.' She held out her hand. 'I want to see her letter, Bernard. The wedding has to go ahead on Saturday with no loose ends and if necessary I will write to Carlotta myself.'

'I'm not going to show it to you!'

Alicia rose to her feet. 'Then I shall go to see her, face to face, in front of her parents and—'

Bernard also jumped to his feet. 'No! Don't you dare do such a thing. If you do I ... I shall leave this house and never come back!'

She shrugged 'That's your choice to make. I will not be thwarted, Bernard. I want to see that letter. I need to reassure myself that—'

'It won't reassure you. Quite the opposite in fact.'

She gave him a long, hard stare. 'Go and get the letter.'

He gave in as she had known he would. Poor Bernard. Not much backbone. His father had seen the weakness in him when he was much younger. As soon as he had left the room she sank back on to the chair and tried to compose herself. Her heart was beating rapidly and she took several deep breaths. Somehow she had to stay strong. Bernard had to marry his fiancée on Saturday and no one must ever know of these last-minute setbacks. The affection in which she had previously held Carlotta had been finally dispelled by her meddling.

It was anathema to Alicia that a woman should be unable to accept that a man had stopped loving her – or vice versa. Admitting such a failure, if that is what it was, was naturally humiliating but continuing the fight to keep the beloved was even worse, involving such a deep loss of dignity.

Did her parents know what was happening, she wondered. If so they must be appalled. If not then perhaps she, Alicia, should tell them. If that meant a break with Carlotta's family then so be it. Bernard's happiness, his marriage to Letitia and the family prestige came first, she reminded herself. If necessary, friendships would have to be abandoned for the greater good.

Bernard returned, tossed her the letter and then resumed his study of the lawn. His hands were in his pockets, she noticed with disapproval, and his shoulders sagged. She reached for her spectacles and opened the letter. With a sinking heart she read,

My darling Bernard, I cannot let another day pass without reaching out to you. You know just how much I love you and I know that you still care for me. Letitia was a mistake but there is still time to put matters right. Tell Letitia the truth. Beg her forgiveness and then, whether or not she gives it, you and I can make plans for our future. We can run away, marry somewhere far away from the families and live happily ever after – as you know we will...

'Dear God!' She glared at her son's unresponsive back. 'This is so immature! Lovesick babbling!'

He said nothing and she read on.

... Come to the barn this evening and I will give you the courage you need to break with Letitia. I can be strong for both of us, my very dearest Bernard. I will be there at nine o'clock. I know you won't fail me. I know you will not break my heart. Your devoted Carlotta...

In spite of her anger and her previous comment, Alicia was reluctantly forced to admit that the wording of the letter had a genuine ring to it. She must accept that the poor woman loved her son. Poor besotted creature. If only she could accept that Bernard no longer loved *her*.

She resisted a dramatic urge to tear the letter into pieces and hurl them into the empty grate. That would incense Bernard. Instead she said, 'Do you intend to meet her, Bernard?'

'I don't know what to do.' He turned wearily. 'Whatever happens I shall make one of them deeply unhappy.'

'If you abandon Letitia you will make *everyone* unhappy – including me and your father. To desert her at this late stage would ruin her life ... and probably yours also. You would be branded an utter cad, Bernard, and Carlotta would be to blame.'

'I know all of that, Mother!' he said hoarsely. 'Do you think this wretched business hasn't been in my mind for every minute of every hour of every damned day? God!' He let out a long breath. 'I sometimes wish I had never met either of them. Maybe I am not cut out for married life. All this emotion ... I cannot deal with it. Last night I tossed and turned and ended up wishing I could put an end to everything!'

'What does that mean?' she asked, her voice rising in alarm. 'Of course you can deal with it. Be a man, Bernard. Stand up for what you want ... Put an end to everything? I hope you don't mean...'

He recrossed the room and threw himself into the armchair. 'No, Mother. I don't mean *that*.' He frowned. 'I mean disappear to the ends of the earth where nobody knows me and nobody even *wants* to know me – let alone marry me!' He looked at her, frowning thoughtfully. 'Kill myself? At least I have never thought of taking that way out before today, Mother. I daresay I'm too much of a coward to put an end to my life.'

'You're not a coward, Bernard, and I can prove it to you. Write to Carlotta ending it, give the letter to me and I will meet her at nine o'clock. Where is this barn?'

He shook his head. 'No, Mother, I'll go. I have to do it myself.' He sighed heavily and muttered something under his breath which Alicia pretended not to hear. 'I'll go and write it now, and then, by the time I wake up tomorrow, it will all be settled.' Fuelled by a growing bitterness, he added, 'I hope that will finally satisfy you!'

He was unprepared for the resounding slap she gave him which stung his left cheek long after she had swept out of the room.

Next morning as soon as breakfast was over, Marcus and Rose retired to the study. Marcus handed her a sheet of his paper and a pencil and she was quickly ensconced at a table by the window, composing a letter to her father in Pentonville Prison. Marcus, meanwhile, pressed ahead with his latest stage-set designs.

No longer a sketch, he had fleshed out the scene with washes of colour, trying to add something original. The shrubs were now a pale green, the tree trunks in the background a soft brown-grey, the sky a yellow streaked with red. He wanted the water in the foreground to make something of an impact because the swans would appear to dance upon it so the water was almost Prussian blue to contrast with the lighter colours and add depth.

'And, hopefully, distance,' he said aloud.

Rose glanced up. 'How do you spell your stepfather's surname?'

'F, e, i, g, a, n, t. Gerard Feigant.' He said, 'What do you think of this? Come and look.'

Flattered to be asked for her opinion on such an important issue, Rose hurried to stand beside him. To her surprise he draped what she assumed to be a casual arm around her waist while she pored over the design. 'I like it,' she told him, not quite sure whether she meant the design or his friendly gesture. A little flustered, she said quickly, 'Shall I read you my letter to Pa?'

He nodded and she fetched it from the table.

... Dear Pa, I have been to France and back to stay with Gerard and Clarice Feigant on their farm. Mrs Clarice Feigant is Marcus's mother

240

and we were taking Marie to stay with them. It was very exiting. Now we are looking forward to Letitia's wedding on Saterday. This is just to warn you that Mr Markam has murderd Connie and if they catch him he might be sent to Pentonville. If you meet him dont say you know me. So for now I am staying with Marcus's family and I have to find another job. I hope you do not find prison too awful. Keep your spirits up. Your loving dorter, Rosie. Pee Ess They might hang him instead...'

'A very nice letter, Rose.'
'Oh! D'you think so?'
'Very good.'
'I wonder where he's gone?'
'As far away as possible, I should think. South America or Timbuctoo! Poor Connie will have to be identified. I wonder who will do that?'
'Maybe Mr Coates or Mrs Jupp. They've known her a long time.'
'We said you would give them a statement about your whereabouts and they will ask you about her relationship with Markham. You'd better think it over before we reach the police station ... and they might ask you to identify her. You did share her flat. They can't make you but...' He shrugged.

Rose frowned. 'I think I could do it. What I mean is, she won't look very different, will she? Not weird or frightening. A bit quiet, probably, and pale.'

241

'Very quiet, I would imagine.'

She looked at him suspiciously but Marcus kept a straight face.

'People in their coffins usually look very nice, don't they?' she persisted hopefully. 'They wear long white nightgowns and with their hands crossed over on their chest. I wouldn't mind that.'

'She might not be in a coffin yet, Rose. She won't be at the undertakers. She will be at the mortuary on a sort of trolley, covered with a white sheet.'

She sighed. 'Well, when you have finished working we can go to the police station. I think I'd like to get it over and done with.' She took another look at his design. 'A few flowers would brighten it up. Hollyhocks, maybe. I love hollyhocks.'

'I don't think they grow around lakes.'

'That's a shame, then.' Remembering she still needed to address the envelope she returned to the table in the window.

Grudgingly considering her suggestion, Marcus added a few water lilies to the lake with surprisingly good results.

An hour later, Rose sat at a table in a small cramped room in the local police station while Marcus waited outside, patiently pacing to and fro while considering his brother's future. As the older brother, Marcus felt vaguely responsible for Steven who, hot-headed and irresponsible, had no father to guide him.

While the constable made notes in preparation for the statement he would put together for her to sign, Rose screwed up her face in an effort to remember anything she could about the relationship between Connie and Andrew Markham. She wanted the latter caught and punished and desperately hoped that her information would be of use to the police.

She said, 'She used to be fond of him ... I mean, she liked him a lot but maybe he didn't like her ... but she thought he did. It must have been a long time ago. I suppose you could say they were romantically linked.'

'Romantically linked?' He rolled his eyes. 'Blimey! This is a statement, not *The Ladies Journal*!' He wrote and then reread it as 'She was his fancy piece!'

Rose glared at him. 'I didn't say that! She wasn't. She was a dancer. She was pretty.' She snatched the paper on which he was writing the statement and began to read it. 'You're supposed to be writing what *I* say – not what you think I should have said!'

He shrugged. 'Please yourself. I'll say ... tart ... or woman. How's that?' He snatched it back. 'Anyway, she's not pretty now!' He scrutinized a list. 'You're down to identify her. Done it yet?'

'Not yet.'

'You'll see for yourself then.'

She disliked his attitude and wondered whether she was entitled to give up on the statement or whether that would count against her. They might say she'd been wasting police time or refusing to cooperate.

He tapped the pencil on the table, searching for further questions. 'So how was she when you left on this convenient trip to France? Did she say they had quarrelled? Did you think she was afraid of him? Can you think of any reason for him to kill her?'

'No. He did have a temper – everyone says so – but she believed that she could always sweet-talk him because of what they had meant to each other. He let her stay in that flat rent-free.'

He rolled his eyes and added a few words to the statement. 'I'll rewrite this in ink,' he told her, 'and then you have to read it and sign it if it's correct. Now ... do you have any tickets to prove you and Mr Bennley really were in France? You could have gone to Brighton for a few days for all we know.'

Alarmed, she was silent. He seemed to be enjoying the notion that *she* might have killed Connie. Did his question mean she was a suspect? 'I think the crew of the boat would remember us,' she said at last, 'because we had an invalid with us who had to be carried on and off.'

He whistled tunelessly as he wrote down her words, then scratched his head with the blunt end of the pencil. 'So you can't think why he might have killed her? She didn't owe rent or anything?'

'I told you – he let her have the flat rent-free and I gave Connie some money, just to help her, and she cooked a meal in the evening.'

Recalling the dreadful bacon and onion roll, Rose's eyes filled with tears. 'She didn't deserve to die.'

He regarded her impassively. 'Tears don't wash with me,' he told her, as he stood up. 'I've seen too many in my time. We'll get you down to the morgue; then when the identification's over you come back here and sign the statement.' He rang a small hand bell and Rose stumbled to her feet as a young man in a large green apron arrived moments later, and she followed him down a corridor, down some steps and along to a door which stood ajar. He kicked it open with a practised blow and Rose found herself in a grim room surrounded by trolleys bearing covered bodies. At the far end of the room a man was wielding a knife which he applied to the inert figure on his slab. Rose shut her eyes, sickened by the smell of cold blood and some kind of disinfectant.

'Over here, Miss Paton.'

Shaking inwardly, Rose walked across the room as indicated. The assistant whipped back the white sheet to reveal a pale shadow of the woman Rose remembered. Gone were the careful curls – the result of all those

245

overnight curling rags – and in their place she saw dank and lustreless hair.

The assistant said defensively, 'We had to wash her all over. It's the rules.'

Gone was the exaggerated rouge on her cheeks and carelessly applied lip colour. The often clown-like results of Connie's every-day make-up had been removed and were now replaced by dull yellowing skin and pallid lips. There was a stitch in the upper lip and a bruise had started to form. Rose look-ed at her with growing dismay. Poor Connie would hate to be seen like this, she thought, even in death.

She whispered, 'I'm so sorry, Connie. This shouldn't have happened but the police are looking for him.'

There were dark marks around the scraggy neck. The assistant pointed. 'You can see the thumb marks ... those bruises, there. He strangled her but he must have hit her first.'

Rose nodded wordlessly. She was aware of a deep sadness settling into her heart. This was something she could not undo. 'If only I had been there with you, Connie,' she said softly. 'But at least you are at peace.' Lean-ing nervously over the body, she lifted one of Connie's thin, claw-like hands and pressed it to her cheek by way of goodbye. She was ashamed that she felt unable to kiss the ravaged face and felt the tears returning.

'That's enough now, miss.' He cleared his throat. 'Is it, or is it not, the body of Miss

Constance Wainwright?'

'Yes. That's Connie.' What's left of her, Rose thought with sudden bitterness. 'I hope they find him and string him up!'

He shrugged. 'Most crimes like this go unsolved. They reckon this one's long gone. Mexico or somewhere like that!'

Replacing the sheet with a quick movement, he nodded towards the door and Rose thanked him and made her way slowly back to the front desk.

'Ah, Miss Paton!'

She nodded and the constable pushed her statement across the counter for her to read. She read it slowly, weighing every word. It seemed the last thing she could do for poor Connie. Satisfied to see that he had finally called Connie 'a woman friend of the suspect', she took the proffered pen, signed her name at the bottom, then hurried outside to rejoin Marcus.

'How did it go?' he asked.

'Horrible ... terrible ... all of it!'

Her voice shook and she began to cry and he put his arms around her and held her close until she recovered.

Saturday 5th July dawned bright and sunny which was considered by everyone to be a good omen. In Longley Manor, home of Bernard's wealthy uncle, preparations started as soon as it was light. Caterers had been booked for the lavish luncheon and money was considered no object as the whole event was the uncle's wedding present to the bride and groom.

It seemed as though an army of servants had moved in. In the ballroom, where the luncheon would be served, men were to be found on ladders set against the walls, as they hung gold ribbons and trails of green ivy at suitable intervals. Above them down the centre of the room, three elaborate chandeliers had been taken down and washed in vinegar and water and these now sparkled in the sunlight. Two women were busy arranging flowers in sparkling crystal bowls; pink, white and dark red was the chosen colour scheme interspersed with sprays of gold-painted leaves.

A trolley was pushed into the room bearing china and cutlery, to be set out when the polished table had been covered with the white, gold-edged tablecloth. Dozens of glasses waited on the top of the sideboard, alongside piles of dark red serviettes and a bowl of place names waiting to be set out.

At seven fifty-four, Henry da Silva entered the ballroom and patrolled the room with a critical frown on his face but he was quickly hustled away by his wife.

'Do please go, Henry! You make people nervous. They all know what they're doing.'

'I'm just looking, dear,' he murmured as she steered him firmly towards the door.

'That's what I mean! Now leave this side

of things to the professionals and to me. Go and see how Bernard is faring. He might appreciate a wise word or two on the joys and woes of marriage from his favourite uncle.'

'Bernard? Is he here? Should he be here?'

'Bernard. Your nephew, remember!' Her tone was exasperated. 'He slept here overnight.'

'Oh Lord! So he did. I'd quite forgotten.'

'Alicia couldn't stand any more of his dithering. She was worried about him. Thought he was feeling a mite desperate. She asked if he could come over here. Thought it might buck him up.'

Outside the door he stopped. 'He's not going to jilt her, is he? That blasted Carlotta...'

'Hush dear!' She glanced round, uncomfortably aware that his voice would carry, but thankfully everyone seemed to be engrossed in their work. 'Of course he's not going to jilt her. That little awkwardness is in the past so please don't refer to it again.' She gave him a gentle push and went back into the ballroom.

Bernard was pacing the room when the knock came. 'Come in.'

It was his uncle and Bernard forced a smile.

Henry said, 'The big day, eh? Quite an occasion, what!'

'It seems somehow unreal.' Bernard was sitting on the bed, still wearing his dressing gown, and his feet were bare.

'You don't look old enough to be getting wed.'

'I'm twenty-seven! But I admit I'll be glad when it's all over.' He sighed as he turned away and walked to the wardrobe. He pulled out his outfit, dark suit, crisp white shirt, brand new shoes.

His uncle said, 'Don't forget your buttonhole. The florist is coming at eleven, the hairdresser will be here in an hour or so for my wife, the photographer is already flitting around the grounds, planning his backgrounds.' He shook his head. 'I tried to take a look at the ballroom but your mother saw fit to chase me out.'

Bernard nodded gloomily. 'Did you go through all this fuss when you married?'

'Of course we did, old boy! In the time it took I could have organized a battle and won it! Still, never mind. Look on the bright side. You and Letitia will be off to Torquay for your honeymoon and will forget all about the hassle of the wedding. Damned nice place, Torquay. You'll like it. But take my advice and steer clear of the sea. All that nonsense about the benefits of salt water! Poppycock! I caught the devil of a cold last time I was there. A real beast, that was. Laid me low for three days. Didn't please your aunt, I can tell you that for nothing! Rather restricted her socializing.' He laughed. 'Still. Women are funny creatures. We can't live with them but can't live without them. Know what I mean, do you?'

'Yes. Of course.'

'Er ... no worries, then? Nothing I can say to set your mind at ease?' Without waiting for an answer he went on. 'That's the ticket. Good lad!'

A maid knocked on the door and came in with a large jug of hot water.

Seeing his nephew's surprise, he said, 'I'm afraid that damned geyser thingy in the bathroom isn't working again but Ellen will bring you up a second jug of hot water if you stand the first outside the door when you've emptied it into the bowl.'

'Right you are, Uncle. Thank you.' He summoned up another smile.

Henry, feeling that he had done rather well, took his chance and left his nephew to his ablutions.

Marcus and Steven eyed each other across the breakfast table. Both had finished eating but neither felt inclined to start the rest of the day. It was just before ten and the rest of the house appeared to be in a state of turmoil. The hairdresser had arrived and Letitia had retired to her room to have her hair dressed by Mrs Stimpson. At breakfast Letitia had eaten almost nothing, complaining that she felt slightly sick with nerves and could only manage half a slice of toast.

Rose had come down late, having over-slept, and was now coming to the end of her scrambled egg and bacon. When the front door bell rang they glanced at each other. Steven said, 'It might be for me,' but hesitated, making no move to enquire further.

Rose laughed. 'It certainly won't be for me,' and glanced at Marcus.

'I hope not!' he said in answer to her un-answered question. They waited for foot-steps in the hall which would indicate that Mrs Bray was on her way to answer it. There were none.

Steven said, 'If it's for me, I'm not here.'

Rose swallowed the last mouthful, dabbed at her mouth with her serviette and jumped up. 'I'll go!'

The man standing on the front step looked remarkably like Andrew Markham but she told herself that was not possible because since Connie's murder, he had not been seen. Unless he was trying to disguise himself.

'I want to speak to Steven Bennley,' the man said truculently. 'Tell him it's Bart Markham.'

'He's not here, I'm afraid.' Rose tried to look honest.

'Just tell him it's best he comes to the door. I'm in a—'

'I've just told you – he's not here, Mr Markham.' So this was the other part-own-

252

er. She regarded him curiously. He looked slightly younger and was slimmer in build.

'And I know he *is* so tell him to—'

'I could take a message. Would that help?'

'You can tell him he must settle his debts or expect serious consequences. Say next time he might not get off so lightly. He's been warned.' He turned on his heel but then had second thoughts and turned back. 'You his sister?'

'No I'm not. I'm Rose Paton. My stage name is Miss Lamore. I shared a flat with Connie.' She gave him a hard look. 'So where is your brother? The police think he killed her.'

For a moment he looked disconcerted, then his surly manner returned. 'None of your ruddy business! Just give Steven Bennley my message or he'll live to regret it – or maybe he won't!' His laugh grated in an ugly way and in spite of herself, Rose shuddered.

She watched him go, then returned to the dining room to pass on the message. Steven groaned.

Suddenly Marcus said, 'Rose, could you leave us if you've had enough to eat? I need to speak with Steven.'

She was mortified at being excluded but went without a word.

Left alone Steven said, 'I know what you're going to say and—'

'No you don't. I have a proposition for you. I wasn't fooled by your reason for the beating. I'm afraid that next time you might be killed.'

'Killed?' he blustered. 'Don't be ridiculous. Who's going to kill me?'

'Markham's thugs – I can put two and two together, Steven, so please don't treat me like a fool. Just listen. I'm prepared to borrow the money you need to pay off the debt but on one condition – that you enlist in the army.'

'Enlist in the ... Are you out of your mind?' Steven regarded him incredulously. 'Join the army? For God's sake, Marcus! I'd rather chop off my right arm!'

Marcus remained calm. 'I'm perfectly serious, Steven. You may not realize it, but you would make a very fine officer. It's a first-class career. One that...'

Steven's eyes hardened. 'You'd like that, wouldn't you, Marcus?' To get rid of me! Well, you can forget it! Nothing would persuade me to—'

'You owe a lot of money and I'll get it for you. That's the quid pro quo. I don't want an answer right now. We've got Letitia's wedding to think about and you need time to think the offer over.' He looked at his brother, his expression enigmatic. 'Please at least think about it. We know what Andrew Markham did to Connie and what his thugs did to you – oh don't bother to deny it! You're not a very good liar and I've known you all your life. Lord knows what they'll do to you next

254

time. Just think about it, Steven. A commission in the army is not a bad alternative.'

'Why can't you simply lend me the money?'

'Because I haven't got it and will have to arrange a loan – and also because we both know it won't end there, Steven. Firstly, you'll never pay me back and secondly, you'll ask me again and again. I've given this a lot of thought—'

'And why spring it on me today of all days?'

'I didn't mean to but that visit from Markham's brother brought it home to me. If he sets his bullies on to you and they half kill you ... I don't want to see that happen, Steven. I'm trying to help you. Think about it.' He stood up abruptly. 'I'll ask Rose to go up and help Letitia. I'll be glad when today is over and she is happily wed!'

'I wish Marie could have been here.'

'She's better off with Mother and Gerard. We could both go over there if you wish, after the wedding. Mother would love to see you.'

Before Steven could make an argument out of that suggestion, Marcus hurried out and went in search of Rose, wondering if life for the Bennley family would ever go smoothly.

Nine

As close friends and family, Rose, Marcus and Steven sat in the front pew. On the opposite side of the aisle were the groom's family which included the uncle and aunt. As Marcus and Rose walked to their seats, he whispered to Rose that Carlotta and her parents, Simon and Nora Todd, were close friends of the da Silvas.

The rest of the small church was filled with invited friends and at the far end, a group of local well-wishers had gathered. Outside they had passed a large group of villagers enjoying the spectacle of a wealthy wedding.

Rose was determined to enjoy the day and was wearing the clothes that Marcus had bought her to wear to France. She had pushed aside the sad thoughts about Connie, believing that she owed it to Marcus's family to prove herself a perfect guest at the wedding.

As she glanced at the polished guests in their beautiful clothes, she decided that she would not marry until she was wealthy as well as famous and could do things in a similar style. Determined to enjoy herself, she refused to think about Clarice and Gerard miles away on the other side of the Channel, who were missing such a wonderful day ... or about Marie, who would have loved to be present.

An abrupt change of music heralded the arrival of Letitia, who was being given away by her godfather, and although Rose had seen and admired Letitia earlier while she was helping with her dress, the sight of her walking down the aisle brought a glow of happiness to her face. Rose glanced up at Marcus, who was also smiling. Steven, having turned down the invitation to be an usher, was busy arranging his hassock and only looked up when his sister had passed.

The service began in earnest as they all knelt to pray and then resumed their seats for the actual service. Rose thought that Bernard da Silva looked suitably dignified and very handsome in his dark suit, and wondered who she herself would marry. Maybe another successful performer – an opera singer might be suitably dignified and sought after, she thought wistfully – but then he might outshine her and that would be a pity.

The vicar, small and thin, was somewhat swamped by his black and white vestments, but he made his way through the familiar phrases of the marriage service with a comforting air of assurance, never missing a word and speaking clearly so that no one had to strain to hear him. Steven, paying little attention, was now riffling through his book to find the appropriate hymn and Rose, forgetting her intention to be the perfect guest, nudged him with her elbow and frowned at him.

'What is it?' he demanded irritably in a loud whisper.

At that moment the vicar was heard asking if anyone knew of any reason why the couple should not be joined in Holy Matrimony. There was an anxious moment as his enquiring glance roved over the congregation and then a sudden gasp and a turning of heads.

Hearing this, Letitia turned and so did Bernard. Startled, Marcus and Rose also turned and saw a young woman standing two rows back.

'My God!' hissed Marcus. 'It's Carlotta Todd!'

Carlotta's voice rang out. 'I know just cause. Bernard da Silva is not in love with her! Ask him!'

Her parents, white-faced with shock, tried to pull her back down in her seat but she fought them off.

The vicar, taken by surprise, began to stammer and lost his poise. Letitia was staring, ashen-faced, at the cause of the interruption and Bernard, Rose saw, had sunk down on to the pew and had hidden his face in his hands.

'Marcus! Do something!' Rose urged. 'Say something to her!'

'Such as what?'

'Just stop her!'

Carlotta continued. 'Ask Bernard if he truly loves his bride-to-be. His answer, here under God's roof, will be "No!"'

The vicar took a few tentative steps forward as though to confront her. Carlotta still stood, defiantly ignoring the protests that came from all directions. Her mother swayed and almost fell. Her father, now red-faced and furious, was shaking her by the arm, begging her to sit down.

Letitia clung to her godfather who supported her as well as he could.

Suddenly Steven decided to become a player in the drama. He shook Bernard and said, 'Stand up, for God's sake, and say something!'

Letitia cried, 'Bernard! Answer her!'

'Yes, yes!' said the vicar gathering his wits. 'You will have to answer the claim or the service cannot go ahead.'

Urged on by Steven, Bernard stared at Carlotta who had now pushed her way into the aisle. 'Carlotta...' he stammered. 'You can't ... This isn't...'

The congregation fell silent as Carlotta walked slowly towards him. 'Who do you love, Bernard?' she asked, her voice low. 'Her or me? In God's name, tell the truth.'

Time seemed to stand still and a hush fell

over the congregation as all eyes focused on Bernard. When the moment lengthened and still he did not speak a low, shocked murmur ran through the congregation.

Marcus said, 'Bernard! What's the matter with you? Don't you see what the vicar is saying – that you have to answer Carlotta's question? You have to say that you love Letitia or the marriage won't go ahead!'

He stared at Marcus, the picture of misery. 'I do love her!' he said.

Steven said, 'You do love *who*? That is, which one?'

Marcus groaned. 'This is farcical!'

Around them the murmur of disapproval grew to a grumble of discontent.

Rose could stand it no longer. She stepped forward and glared at Carlotta. 'You wicked little troublemaker!' she snapped. 'Why don't you just get out of here? You've caused enough trouble already!'

Someone in the congregation called 'Hear, hear!' And there were mutterings of support.

Carlotta was not to be distracted from her purpose. She said, 'Mind your own business!' and pushed Rose so that she fell backwards.

The push took Rose by surprise and she rocked back on her heels with the force of the blow and fell against the pew behind her.

Letitia, appalled by the way her wedding day plans were disintegrating, hitched up her skirts and ran, sobbing, past them, up the aisle, past Carlotta and out of the church. While everyone stared at her departing back, Marcus helped Rose to her feet while Steven and the vicar huddled together with Letitia's godfather, wondering what to do next.

Bernard's mother joined them, pale with shock, a trembling hand pressed to her heart. She spoke to the vicar. 'I'm so sorry, vicar. What on earth possessed that wretched Carlotta? This is quite unbelievable ... My heart won't stop racing! Dear Lord!'

They guided her to a pew and she sat down heavily. 'What on earth can I say? What shall we do?' She looked at Marcus. 'Your poor sister. Shouldn't somebody be with her?'

Rose said, 'I'll go,' and hurried along the aisle which was already filled with people who had left their seats in confusion. She avoided eye contact with Carlotta, still smarting emotionally, as well as physically, from the push she had received. To Rose it appeared that nothing could now go ahead as planned, except perhaps the wedding breakfast. People had travelled long distances and would need to be fed at some time. She imagined the ballroom and the waiting caterers who as yet had no idea the wedding had descended into chaos.

Once in the churchyard she caught sight of Letitia running down the path towards the lychgate. 'Letitia! Please wait!'

The crowd outside were staring in astonishment at the runaway bride who seemed
unaware of their startled expressions. Rose
caught up with her and took hold of her
hand. 'Please stop, Letitia!' she begged, trying to stop the headlong flight. 'Where are
you going?'

Abruptly Letitia stopped, clutching her
side and breathing heavily. 'I'm going home!
What else can I do? Bernard ... he didn't
deny it! Oh God. I hate him! How could he
let her do that? How, Rose? In front of all
those people – it was so cruel of him not to
defend us ... to let her humiliate me like
that.' Clinging to the corner post of the gate,
she tried to control her tears while the
watching villagers drew back a little, mur-
muring to each other in shocked tones.

An elderly woman looked at Rose. 'What's
happening, miss? Ain't there going to be no
wedding?'

Before Rose could decide how to answer
Letitia raised her head. 'There may be a
wedding but I won't be part of it,' she cried.
She waved her hand for the carriage that
had brought her smiling and full of hope, to
the church gate, and the puzzled driver hop-
ped down and walked back to them.

Rose told him, 'There's been a change of
plan. Letitia and I would like to go straight
back to Victoria House.'

From beneath his black top hat he looked
from Rose to Letitia. 'Is that right? I mean ...

where's the bridegroom? Shouldn't we wait?'

Letitia recovered her breath. 'Miss Paton is quite right. We are returning alone to Victoria House. Mr da Silva will not be coming with me ... ever!'

Rose eyed her with a mixture of admiration and astonishment. There was no hesitation in Letitia's voice and it left no room for a change of mind. It flashed into Rose's mind that Letitia did not seem as surprised as she should have been at the unfortunate turn of events, and she wondered whether somewhere deep in Letitia's subconscious there had been a premonition of such a disaster. If so she had certainly not shown any signs of anxiety – at least, not in Rose's presence.

The driver looked bleak. 'So I'm not to go to Longley Manor?' He had imagined the wonderful spectacle they would make and the admiring glances he would receive as he drew up at the door with the smiling couple. 'The lady who made the booking said I was to pick up the bride at Victoria House but take them both to Longley Manor after the wedding.'

Rose said, 'It's been changed. Do please get a move on.' She glanced nervously over her shoulder but there was no sign of a pursuit.

After a futile glance around him in search of further enlightenment, the driver agreed and assisted both women into the carriage and whipped up the two beautiful chestnut horses. They set off in the opposite direction, his expression grim, his stiff back an indication of his disapproval.

Inside the church, the vicar had retired to the room which served as a registry to sit and stare blankly at the page on which the unhappy couple would not be placing their signatures. In all his days as a vicar he had never before been faced with such a disastrous turn of events and he blamed himself for not having taken control of the situation. Was there something he ought to have done? Was there a way he could have saved the day? He was plagued by the idea that he had failed in his duties. It would be all over the village by morning and he would go down in everyone's estimation.

He thought fleetingly of the loving attention given in the previous days by the two ladies who prepared the church – polishing the woodwork, cleaning the brass and the silver plate, and arranging small posies of flowers at the end of each pew along the centre aisle. How heartbroken the ladies would be, he thought. All that hard work for nothing. No one to appreciate their efforts – and all because of that dreadful young woman...

He recalled the feelings of anger he had experienced when she stood up to challenge him in the middle of his duties as a man of the church. She must have been sitting there, waiting for the right moment to ruin everything. He could willingly have strangled her, he thought guiltily and sighed. 'Not very Christian,' he told himself and wished his wife were still alive. She was more down to earth and might have come up with a solution.

Meanwhile Carlotta was standing face to face with Bernard, demanding an honest answer. 'You don't love her. You as good as told me so. Perhaps you would like to forget what you said that day. Well, I won't. You said you would marry me if you could but that matters had gone too far.'

Nora Todd glared at her daughter. 'You didn't tell us that! You let us go on thinking ... all that time we were preparing for the wedding ... oh, you wicked girl!'

Bernard finally glanced up and said, 'Don't blame her – blame me! It's all my fault.'

Simon Todd glared at him. 'Oh, we do blame you! Don't fret on that score. You've been leading them both on and now you've broken that poor young woman's heart! I hope to God you're thoroughly ashamed of yourself!'

Alicia da Silva suddenly stood up, her expression wild. 'We can't sit here raking over the coals. We have all the guests to think about! Some of them have come from miles away ... and there's the reception waiting at Henry's place. We can't just waste it!' She looked round desperately for someone to advise her.

All around people were discussing the predicament and some had already drifted out of the church and were standing in groups in the small churchyard.

Marcus nodded. 'I think we should announce that the reception at Longley Manor will go ahead and we will make explanations and apologies then.' He glanced at the da Silvas who nodded eagerly, relieved to have had someone else make the decision.

Marcus cleared his throat and made the announcement and then went outside to repeat it. The wedding breakfast would go ahead, but without the bride and groom.

Half an hour later, in Wissant, Clarice, Gerard and Marie were sitting round the large kitchen table, raising their glasses to the happy couple on the other side of the water. Although he made plenty of good wine for the family's use, Gerard had bought a bottle of champagne to celebrate Letitia's wedding.

Marie said, 'I hope Bernard makes her happy. It's a shame we couldn't all be there but...' She shrugged.

Clarice said quickly, 'We can't change the way things are but I'm sure Bernard will take care of our lovely daughter.' She smiled at her husband.

He nodded. 'She will look like a princess!' he boasted. 'One day per'aps they will visit us – or we shall be invited to visit them. We must be patient ... But if Bernard does not make her 'appy, he will 'ave me to deal with!'

Marie laughed. 'We must cross our fingers then, Gerard.' She opened her mouth to speak about the grandchildren but then closed it again. She had no delusions about the time remaining for her. She would never see Letitia's children but maybe her sister would call one of the girls 'Marie', after her.

Clarice had made a large cherry cake and she and Marie had decorated it with icing, and the initials L and B had been added in sugared violets.

Seeing his wife glance at the back door, Gerard said, 'No good to wait for Jean-Philippe! He's always late. He blame it on the fish! We'll start without him.'

Seeing her mother reach for the knife Marie said, 'It seems a shame to spoil it. It's such a beautiful cake! Should we send Letitia a slice, do you think?' Without waiting for an answer she said, 'Do you think she likes the tablecloth?' Marie had embroidered the wedding present with loving care and it had been sent back to England with Marcus and Rose.

'Of course she will,' Clarice told her. She

put a slice of cake on a plate and handed it to her husband, then cut a second piece and then a third. They had begun to eat when a knock on the door brought Jean-Philippe into the kitchen with a cheery greeting and an apology for being late.

Marie said, 'Let me guess! It was the fish that delayed you!'

He washed his hands at the sink. '*Les poissons!* They not 'urry!'

Gerard poured him a glass of champagne and Clarice handed him a large slice of the 'wedding cake'.

Marie said, 'Good health and happiness to the bride and groom!'

'*Exactement!*' he replied and took a large bite and then the four glasses clinked cheerfully.

An hour later Rose sat in Letitia's bedroom trying to cope with her friend's moods which swung from deep grief and shock to a great anger. Still wearing her wedding dress, she had snatched the silk roses from her hair and thrown them on to the floor. When Rose tried to pick them up, Letitia screamed and stamped on them, then snatched them up and tore them to shreds. The pink petals lay everywhere, much to Rose's dismay for she had secretly hoped to spirit them away for herself.

Now, her hair dishevelled, the abandoned bride lay face down on the bed, sobbing hysterically while Rose patted her arm and prayed for guidance which was not forthcoming.

'He isn't worth your tears, Letitia,' she told her. 'If he can treat you this way ... then he's not worth—'

'It's not him, it's her!' Letitia turned over awkwardly and sat up. Her face was blotched and her eyes red rimmed. 'It's Carlotta. She's the one to blame. That miserable little hussy! I'd like to scratch her eyes out!' She glared at Rose. 'What a spiteful, scheming creature! If Bernard marries her then I pity him – but he will deserve all he gets! Who would want a shrew for a wife? Oh Bernard, what a blind, stupid fool you are!'

Rose was exhausted by seeing so much raw emotion but she was also aware that the reception was taking place regardless of the disruption to the wedding, and she would rather have been enjoying the celebrations, however muted they might be. But she told herself that she was needed here and, in any case, she didn't know how to extricate herself. Letitia needed her.

Letitia sighed deeply, momentarily drained by her passions.

Rose asked, 'Would you forgive him if he begged for a second chance?'

Letitia pointed. 'Top drawer. Clean handkerchiefs on the left. Would you fetch me one, please?'

Rose handed two across the bed and

269

waited for Letitia's answer.

'Seriously, Rose, I don't think I could.' She dabbed at her eyes. 'Although it would put that dreadful Carlotta in her place. It would serve her right ... but then how would I ever trust him again? Oh Lord! This is a nightmare.' Her face crumpled again. 'I don't think I shall ever properly recover from it.'

Rose tried desperately to think of something positive to say. 'Look at it this way, Letitia. Suppose the wedding had gone ahead and *then* Carlotta had interfered ... and maybe tempted him away from you. Men can be such idiots.' She had no idea if this were true but she hoped it sounded like the voice of experience. 'If he is so weak that she can twist him round her little finger, maybe she has done you a favour. That might be the way to look at it.' She regarded Letitia hopefully. 'Maybe you are better off without him! There are probably dozens of men who would appreciate you more than Bernard does.'

'Maybe...' She gave another deep sigh, regarding Rose earnestly. 'I had no idea that affairs of the heart could be so complicated. I always thought that Mother had been foolish to become involved with Gerard ... Love is so difficult, Rose. You'll understand that one day. Things can go wrong so easily...' She shook her head. 'I should be Mrs Bernard da Silva by now, and look at me. Breaking my heart over a worthless man who has treated me abominably.' She sniffed and blinked and pushed her tousled hair back from her face.

'Carlotta has to take half the blame,' Rose pointed out cautiously. 'She should never have spoken up like that, of course, but all Bernard had to say was that he loved *you*. Then she would have been totally humiliated and ushered from the church and the service would have continued. He didn't say it because he's a weak man and you've discovered that just in time, Letitia.' She waved a hand towards the window. 'Somewhere out there is the right man for you just waiting for the two of you to meet. That's what you have to believe.'

Letitia dabbed at her eyes. 'Do you really think so?'

'Certainly I do. If I were in your shoes I'd write to Bernard and thank him for showing himself in his true colours. And say that you see quite clearly now that you were wrong to believe in him! That would rattle him. Don't let him think you're broken hearted or—'

A knock on the door interrupted her. It opened to reveal Mrs Bray with a tray. She, too, had been crying but she now forced a smile. 'Rose, dear, you have been marvellous but I will sit with Letitia now. Marcus is downstairs waiting for you. Letitia, I've brought you some warm barley water and some biscuits. You have had a terrible shock but you must keep your strength up.' She turned to Rose and forced another smile. 'Nothing is ever as bad as it seems, is it, Rose?'

'No, Mrs Bray, it isn't. Letitia is being very strong. I really admire her.' Rose flashed a smile at the jilted bride and, afraid that she might protest, slipped out of the bedroom and closed the door behind her with a heartfelt sigh of relief. Well done Marcus, she thought. He had ridden to the rescue.

To Rose's surprise, when they arrived at Longley Manor, the sumptuous ballroom was full of excited chatter, the wine was flowing and the hired staff were scurrying in and out with plates of food. She and Marcus found their seats and sat down and were at once bombarded with questions about how Letitia was coping with the betrayal. They answered as best they could.

The man next to Rose introduced himself as an old school friend of Bernard's and shook his head mournfully. 'Can't understand the fellow! Damned bad show. Not like him at all. Beautiful young woman like Letitia. What a bounder! What a way to treat the poor woman. Mind you, the other one was a bit of a looker, too! Two women! The sly dog! Would never have thought it of him.'

Curious, Rose asked, 'What was Bernard like at school?'

'At school? Good Lord. Now you're asking.' He paused to accept a serving of game pie and waited for the potato salad to reach him. Satisfied, he returned to the question. 'He was a year younger than me so in another dorm but we were both in the cricket team and he was a useful bat, as I recall. Steady but not exciting, if you know what I mean.'

His wife said, 'Oh darling, please don't start on about your beastly cricket!' She rolled her eyes at Rose.

Undaunted he went on. 'Not much good at fielding. We used to call him "Butter Fingers"!'

Rose suppressed a sigh of exasperation. 'I meant, as a person.'

'A person?' He looked puzzled. 'Personable, I'd say. On the skinny side. A bit precocious, though. Teacher's pet. That sort of thing, but we soon knocked that out of him!' He laughed. 'Scared of the opposite sex but then we all were then!'

His wife, a little tipsy, said, 'You still are, darling,' and smiled at Rose. 'The British boarding schools have a lot to answer for in my opinion.' She leaned across the table. 'That poor young woman. Letitia, I mean, of course. She'll never recover from this disaster. Never. Such a setback leaves a permanent scar.' She shook her head sadly. 'A friend of my sister was jilted at the altar. Years ago but I remember it as if it were yesterday. The fellow simply failed to arrive at the church. At least Bernard was there,

273

ready to make his vows ... I mean he did actually turn up but then this ghastly young woman ruined everything for them!'

With a mouthful of salmon pâté, Rose could only nod. Most of the other diners had finished the first course and were being offered game pie and salads, and she realized that she was very hungry.

The man next but one to Marcus was suggesting that someone should horsewhip Bernard 'to stiffen his spine' and another was suggesting that Letitia should find a suitable nunnery and spend a few months there in peace and contemplation.

The wife of Bernard's ex-school friend said, 'We've travelled all the way from Dorset for this wedding! And we gave them a set of silver cutlery. I suppose they will have to return all the gifts.' She raised her eyebrows. 'What a dreadful bore for them.'

At the far end of the table the vicar sat hunched in his chair, looking pink with embarrassment. He was trying to eat but was obviously suffering a severe loss of dignity. He met no one's eyes and it was painfully clear that he felt partly responsible for the collapse of the wedding service. Rose felt sorry for him. He would probably wonder for months to come what, if anything, he could have done to avert the catastrophe. She made up her mind to have a few heartening words with him later if she was given the chance. She could not see that he was in any way to blame but she imagined he, too, would take some time to recover from the ordeal.

Rose finished her pâté just as her serving of game pie arrived. For the first time she spared a thought for the humiliated da Silvas and their errant son. What was happening there, she wondered. And what of Carlotta? Were her family going to stand by her or would they send her away to a distant aunt in disgrace? Or would she and Bernard marry and quietly disappear from the local landscape?

Marcus, who had been very quiet, leaned closer to her and said, 'I don't know what this will do to Mother when she hears. Or Gerard.'

Shocked, Rose stared at him. 'Oh Marcus! How shall we tell her? They'll be terribly upset. And Marie, too!'

The ramifications of the day's events appeared endless.

The following morning was Sunday but the idea of the usual attendance at church was not even mooted as the family tried to come to terms with the recent events. While Rose sat with Letitia, who was still in bed, and Steven remained in his room pondering his brother's offer, Marcus was in the study drafting a very difficult letter.

July 6th, 1890

Dear Mother and Gerard, There is no easy way to tell you that yesterday's wedding did not take place. I hate to be the one who breaks the bad news...

He changed 'bad' to 'sad' and continued

I know how keenly you will feel this unhappy ending to Letitia's betrothal to Bernard. I daresay that Bernard is not entirely to blame but must bear most of the responsibility for what happened...

'Oh Lord! This is going to be impossible!' he cried, laying down the pen. Carlotta was certainly the trigger but if Bernard had been emphatic in his love for Letitia ... and if Letitia had stayed and faced her down ... and supported Bernard...

He sighed. Could the marriage have gone ahead? Should it have continued in the light of Carlotta's revelations ... if they truly *were* revelations and not the spiteful lies of a rejected sweetheart?

The bald facts are that when the vicar asked if anyone knew 'just cause or impediment' Carlotta Todd stood up and shouted that Bernard loved her and not Letitia. You can imagine the confusion which followed until Letitia ran from the church in distress. Rose went after her and they were driven home...

For Bernard it must have been a night-mare, thought Marcus with a glimmer of sympathy, but he should immediately have declared his love for Letitia and he did not do so. Sighing, he reread what he had written. He imagined them reading it and the grief it would cause but it had to be sent. They deserved to know the truth, however distasteful.

At this moment we have heard nothing from the da Silvas and have made no attempt to contact them. The truth is, we simply don't know what to do next although we have sent for the doctor as poor Letitia is in a state of deep shock, which you will understand. We are taking good care of her and expect the doctor within the hour. He will most likely give her a sleeping draught and something to calm her nerves.

He paused to read it through and sharpen the pencil. It sounded rather stark, he thought, but there was really no way to sugar this particular pill. However gentle the language the facts were severe and nothing would lessen the shock for them.

So please try not to worry but trust that we will do everything to help her through this terrible time. My own feeling is that if Bernard cannot defend her at their wedding then maybe he is not good enough for her and that in time she will

277

meet and marry a man who is worthy of her.
Your devoted son, Marcus.

It was far from perfect, he decided, but he wanted to be free, when the doctor arrived, to consult about Letitia. To add to his worries, Mrs Bray had been taken ill with a bout of stomach trouble which she blamed on 'all the upset'. Miss Evans was holding the fort until the housekeeper returned but although she tried her best, they missed Mrs Bray's motherly ministrations.

Reaching for the best notepaper Marcus dipped a pen into the ink and began a decent copy of the letter.

He was halfway through it when the front door bell rang and he heard Miss Evans answer it. He did not hear the door close and waited, frowning, pen in hand. As expected Miss Evans came upstairs and knocked on the study door.

'Come in!' He turned.

She looked flustered, he thought wearily. Not another problem!

'It's three men,' she told him. 'One says he's Mr Markham's brother, whatever that means, and they say they want to speak to Master Steven and he won't go down and talk to them and they say they won't go away until he does!' She looked at him helplessly. 'To be honest with you, they scare me. Two of them look like they mean trouble, if you know what I mean. Should we call

278

the police?'

Marcus stifled a groan. 'I'll deal with it, Miss Evans. Leave it to me.'

Before he could change his mind, he went along the passage and into his brother's room. Without prevarication he said, 'Listen to me! There are now three of them gunning for you downstairs and this has got to stop. Miss Evans wants to call the police and I don't blame her.'

Steven reddened. 'It's hardly my fault. I didn't ask them to come round here.'

'Obviously not but they're here because of you and you know it.'

'They'll go away. They'll give up.' It did not sound at all convincing.

'If you believe that, Steven, you're a fool!' Marcus told him angrily. 'You owe them money and they won't give up. If they don't get you now it won't be long before they do. And you might not survive it!'

Steven shrugged. 'I'll take my chances! It's none of your business.'

'I'm making it my business! Now here's what I propose – and this is your last chance, Steven. I'll write them a post-dated cheque right now for every penny of everything you owe them but only if you agree to go into the army and we go together to the recruitment centre. What do you say?'

Steven stared at him, white faced. 'The army?' He hesitated.

Marcus said, 'If you don't like it you can

279

always buy yourself out later on – that's up to you, but personally I think you'll make excellent officer material ... but it's decision time. If you don't agree right now I won't be making the offer again.'

Steven said, 'You'll pay all of it? You promise?'

'Don't insult me, Steven.'

'I'm sorry ... I just don't ... It's a big step.'

'A uniform, regular pay, travel, adventure, friendships ... prestige even!' He smiled. 'Give it a go, Steven! Get those bastards off your back and make something of yourself. I can see it now. One day you'll be an officer and a gentleman!'

'Spare me the glittering future, for God's sake!'

Marcus watched various expressions flit across his brother's face and began to pray. Let him see sense, he begged. Let him see that this is an honourable way out of his predicament. Aloud he said, 'We've got the rest of the family to think about, Steven. Haven't we got enough to worry about with the fiasco at the wedding? Poor Letitia needs all our attention right now and Lord knows what's going to happen next. You under threat from Markham's "heavies" is a burden we can do without.'

Steven's smile was a little crooked. 'You can get yourself killed in the army! Is that the plan – to get rid of me?'

'I don't need to. If you hang around here

you'll get yourself killed anyway. They'll find your body in a back alley – and sooner rather than later! London isn't healthy for you at this moment. Think carefully, Steven.'

His brother was wavering. 'How will you get the money?'

'I'll get a loan from the bank. My credit is good. And I'll pay off all the interest. You'll start a new life, Steven, with nothing to hold you back. Think yourself lucky.' He searched for anything else that might help persuade him. 'No one else need know, Steven. Just you and me. The army can be your idea entirely. I'll be as surprised as anyone.'

The silence lengthened and just when Marcus thought his gamble had failed, the men outside rang the bell again – a long, continuous ring that carried a distinct threat.

Marcus said, 'They won't give up, you know, and it's no use complaining to the police because Markham's brother is entitled to ask for what you owe. And if you run you have no money, no way of earning a living. I believe my offer is your best way out of this mess. Now make up your mind!'

Steven shuddered as the bell began again and then abruptly surrendered. 'On your head be it!' he said ungraciously.

'My shoulders are broad!' Marcus held out his hand. 'You'll make it!'

Reluctantly Steven shook hands. 'Thanks. It's a deal,' he said, his voice hoarse.

As soon as Rose heard the news her face lit up. 'But that's wonderful! We could go to Colonel Fossett and ask his advice. He'd know all about it because he's a colonel – or rather *was* – in the Royal Artillery. He's often in The White Horse and always talking about his army days.' She rolled her eyes. 'He speaks very highly of his regiment and says his army career was the highlight of his life.' She frowned. 'I think he trained at Woolwich.'

Marcus was obviously interested and she went on. 'He was decorated twice. He showed us his medals one evening. "For courage under fire" or something like that. He must have been awfully brave.'

Marcus narrowed his eyes. 'I wonder if he'd give Steven a reference. It won't be that easy getting him on to the officers' training course – if that's what they call it.'

'Why not? Steven hasn't got a criminal record or anything bad like that. He's been stupid but he's got a lot of good qualities.'

'And he's had a decent education. That will count in his favour.' Her comment finally registered with him. 'What do you mean, he's been stupid?' he asked, his tone defensive.

'Mixing with the wrong people – men like Andrew Markham.' As soon as the words were uttered Rose silently cursed her careless words.

'*You* mixed with him!' cried Marcus. 'Does that make *you* stupid?' He glared at her. 'You lived in his flat with his ex-girlfriend who was then murdered by him! It could very easily have been you, Rose. It's easy to criticize my brother but you were so determined to become a star that common sense flew out of the window as soon as you met Markham. You took a big risk! How stupid was that?'

Shocked by his tone, Rose could think of nothing to say because he was right. He had warned her about the kind of people she was mixing with and she had ignored his well-intentioned words.

Seeing that she was shaken, Marcus pressed home his advantage. 'It ought to be clear to you by now that the stage is not a suitable profession for a well brought-up woman. I'd like you to think about it, Rose – for your own good.'

Rose snapped, 'Anyone would think you were my father!'

'If I were I'd be in Pentonville!'

For a moment they glared at each other. Rose was appalled. She knew she should accept his criticism as fair, but she also knew that if she agreed with him Marcus would expect her to give up all her dreams of stardom. Her vision of the glitter of the footlights would be extinguished forever. How, she wondered, had they reached this point? They had been talking about Steven's career and now, suddenly, they were at loggerheads over hers!

'If I have a talent surely I should use it!' she said.

Marcus said nothing.

'Are you saying I don't have talent?' She regarded him with disbelief.

'If you want the truth, Rose, you do have *some* talent and you are young, pretty and precocious...'

'Precocious?' Was that good or bad? she wondered.

'...but you have to understand that girls like you are ten-a-penny and men like Markham eat girls like you for breakfast! They will flatter you for whatever they can get – and I'm sure you know what I mean by that, Rose.'

She weighed his words carefully. He thought she was *precocious* and she had *some* talent. That was hardly reassuring. Rose felt a tightening in her throat. Marcus was forcing her to face something she had tried not to accept; something she had forced to the back of her mind when Connie tried to warn her.

Looking back she realized that Markham had made it clear that her legs were too skinny and he didn't even value the songs she wrote. Her voice didn't matter either, apparently. As long as he could have his way with her – then she would be allowed to appear on stage and could try to convince herself that she was 'a star'. Markham had intended to bill her as a virgin so that the men could drool over her but that was a mixed compliment – if indeed it was meant to be a compliment.

The painful truth hit Rose like a blow in the stomach and, sick at heart, she blamed Marcus. She had tried to help him with Steven's army career and this is how he had repaid her – by destroying her confidence and ruining her future plans. For a moment she closed her eyes while she rallied her defences.

Opening them, she said coldly, 'I think Letitia might appreciate my presence more than you do!' and stalked from the room with her head held high.

She paused on the landing to prepare herself for Letitia's needs but also to begin to come to terms with the horrid truth that she had no talent and would never be a star. How could she bear it, she wondered, washed by a wave of self-pity. 'I hope they catch you!' she told the absent Markham. 'And they can string you from the nearest lamp post for all I care!'

The next two weeks dragged on and Rose's spirits plummeted. There seemed no glimmer of hope that life for the Bennley family might ever return to normal. The doctor appeared every other day and concluded that Letitia's condition was 'no better and no worse' than anyone could expect in the circumstances. Marcus was anxiously awaiting news from Wissant in answer to his letter, afraid that Letitia's disappointment would adversely affect Marie. Mrs Bray was still unwell so that Miss Evans was fast becoming a fixture at Victoria House.

Rose and Marcus had slowly reconciled with neither actually apologizing for the unfortunate argument. Rose had become aware, however, that the Bennleys had reached a low ebb and that everyone's nerves were on edge. Reminding herself that she was an outsider and lucky to have a roof over her head, she had decided her behaviour was ungrateful and she was determined not only to make allowances but to do her best to improve matters.

On Friday, thirteen days after the disaster at the church, Rose sat with Letitia, trying to raise her spirits but failing miserably. The unhappy woman, still in her nightclothes and dressing gown, sat in a chair by the window to catch the sunshine and beside her on the small table, a breakfast tray sat untouched. Rose had offered to read a short story from a ladies' magazine but Letitia had shaken her head, saying that she needed to think.

'The doctor said you mustn't be allowed to brood over what happened,' Rose reminded her gently.

Now, abruptly, Letitia leaned forward. 'I'm

286

waiting for him to come,' she said, 'or for a letter to come. Something definite. I want to think about the future but how can I when I don't know what is happening. Is he with Carlotta or not?'

'We have no idea.' Rose considered Letitia's words. 'Do you mean you expect him, even at this late stage, to refuse her? Does that mean you would give him a second chance?'

Letitia shrugged slightly. 'In my place, wouldn't you at least expect a letter from him – an explanation ... maybe an apology? Isn't it strange not to hear anything from any of them? Surely his mother would want to contact me and express regret for what happened?'

'I think we've all expected some contact from them.'

'I need to know what is happening but I'm kept entirely in the dark.' She shot Rose a keen glance. 'Is anything being hidden from me, Rose? Would you tell me if it were so? Can I trust anyone to tell me what is going on?'

Thankfully Rose could answer honestly. 'If there is any news from that direction, Letitia, they have kept it from me because I know nothing at all.'

Letitia nodded as if satisfied by her reply. 'Miss Evans knows a woman whose fiancé was killed in an accident the day before their wedding. She went to a nunnery for three months for care and spiritual support but never left it.'

Carefully Rose said, 'Poor woman. How dreadful!'

'The circumstances were different, of course, but...' She shrugged again and sighed heavily. 'I'm praying for guidance, Rose.'

Ten

That evening Rose took Marcus to meet with Colonel Fossett to learn a little more about Steven's chances of an army career and it was agreed that Steven should visit him the following morning which was Saturday 12th July. The possibility of this new development in their lives gave Letitia and Rose something to talk about besides Carlotta and Bernard. It was Letitia's view that Steven was too much of a rebel to knuckle down to army discipline and would, if he joined, soon find himself in further trouble.

'He's always been inclined to go his own way,' she told Rose next morning, as they watched the two brothers setting off for Stoke Newington. 'Even as a boy of three or four he would argue and if he failed to win the argument he would throw a tantrum. At one stage bedtimes were a nightmare. We had a nanny then for a year or two and the poor woman was often in despair over his antics. Steven hates to be criticized by anyone over anything so how will he fare in the army?'

'They will knock him into shape, I suppose,' Rose told her without much conviction. 'People can change. Anyway Marcus says Colonel Fossett sounded hopeful and said if he thought Steven was a suitable candidate for the Military Academy he would write to somebody at Woolwich and try to arrange an interview for him.'

Miss Evans had been called in again to look after them as Mrs Bray was still unwell. Now she brought a tray of tea into the garden room where the sun was already very warm and where the two young women were chatting. For the first time since the day of the disrupted wedding, Letitia had felt able to abandon her nightclothes and dressing gown and had come downstairs wearing a softly flowered dress and had tied back her long dark hair with a matching chiffon scarf. Rose had at once congratulated her on her appearance – and had been rewarded with a resigned smile.

Now Letitia said, 'I thought I heard the telephone earlier, Miss Evans. Who was it? Anyone important?' She spoke casually but Rose knew at once that she had hoped it would be Bernard even though she had insisted that she would not speak to him.

Miss Evans looked flustered. 'No. It was a foreign gentleman and I'm sorry but I couldn't make head nor tail of what he was saying so I put the telephone back on its rest.' She set out cups and saucers. 'Why do

290

foreigners speak so fast? It's impossible to catch their meaning most of the time. And there were crackles on the line, as though someone was walking on dried acorns.' She shook her head. 'If there's one thing I hate it's newfangled gadgets. I daresay the telephone has its place but it will be the end of good letter writing, you mark my words.'

'A foreigner?' Rose said. 'A wrong number, probably.'

Letitia looked anxious. 'I hope it wasn't bad news from Wissant. Could this man have been French, Miss Evans?'

'French? I daresay he might have been –' she tossed her head – 'but he might also have been German or Chinese or double Dutch!'

Rose said soothingly, 'If it was important he will certainly ring again.'

No sooner had she spoken than another ringing sound echoed through the house but this time it was the front door bell and Miss Evans snatched up the tray and hurried to answer it.

What happened next startled both women as a man erupted into the garden room without invitation. He carried a bottle of what looked like champagne which he set down on the table. No one spoke and for a long moment he stared fixedly at Letitia then held out his arms.

'At last! My beautiful daughter!'

Rose stammered, 'Gerard? But what on earth...'

Letitia had risen from her chair. 'Gerard...?' She stared at the stranger – a handsome man with olive skin and dark brown eyes; a man with hair as dark as her own and a manner that brimmed with confidence. Before she knew what was happening he stepped closer, put his arms around her and kissed her passionately.

'No! Don't!' she cried, shocked.

She struggled to free herself and he at once took a step back. Still holding her at arms length, however, he was undeterred by her reaction. 'So beautiful!' he murmured. *'Mon dieu!'*

Letitia pulled herself from his grasp. 'I don't want ... that is, you have no right to...' She cast a desperate glance in Rose's direction but received no help from that quarter.

Rose could see how delighted Gerard was to see his daughter and felt instinctively that probably this was his only chance to win her over. Letitia's self-confidence was at a low ebb after Bernard's rejection of her. Could her father save her from the despair she felt?

Gerard turned to Rose, his dark eyes shining. 'Is she not beautiful, my daughter? My lovely Letitia?'

'Yes, she is.'

Letitia was still shaking her head but words had failed her. Gerard released her but took hold of her hand, raised it to his lips and kissed it.

He said 'That man – this Bernard – 'e is an

utter fool! First I make 'im pay for 'is disrespect and then...' His stern face broke into a smile. 'And then I take my daughter 'ome to see her mother. Back to France, *ma petite*, where you belong. With Mama and Papa!'

Rose had also risen and she watched breathlessly as Letitia struggled with her confused feelings. She was obviously hugely impressed by her father's unexpected arrival and his dramatic announcement, but from lifelong habit she wanted to reject him.

Rose, the memories of the farm at Wissant still fresh in her mind, was willing Letitia to give in gracefully to her father and take the chance of a new life.

Letitia hesitated. 'Gerard, I ... that is...'

'Not Gerard!' He scolded. 'Papa! I am your father.'

Various expressions darted across Letitia's face and Rose could only guess at the struggle going on in her mind. As she searched for words her father returned her to her chair and then, determined to stay close to her, pulled another alongside for himself. He gave Rose a brief smile and she hesitated, wondering if she should retreat and leave father and daughter together, but at that moment Miss Evans appeared, red-faced.

To Letitia she said, 'I'm sorry but he pushed his way in!'

He turned to her at once. 'Forgive me, Madame...?'

'Miss Evans,' she corrected him primly.

She, too, seemed fascinated by him, thought Rose, amused. Her own hopes were rising as Letitia had so far made no effort to send Gerard away. Rose could see the strong likeness between father and daughter, now that the two of them were together. The drama of the moment was not lost on Rose and it grieved her a little that she herself was not playing the main part. She envied Letitia this dashing father who had appeared from nowhere, eager to carry her off to France. Did Letitia know how lucky she was? she wondered enviously.

Letitia said faintly, 'This is my father, Miss Evans.'

'Your father?' She stared from one to the other, grappling with the significance of the remark. Confused by her deductions she said 'Oh ... should I bring another cup and saucer then?'

He said, *'Mais non!* We 'ave champagne! Please bring us three glasses, Miss Evans – and another glass for yourself! We will all celebrate, no?'

'Oh!' Flustered, Miss Evans withdrew.

Letitia murmured, 'Champagne? Oh! Yes ... that is ... I don't know ... Rose?'

Rose said quickly 'Congratulations are in order! This is so exciting, Letitia!'

Before Letitia could change her mind and spoil the moment, Rose said, 'I'll give Miss Evans a hand.'

'Thank you, Rose.' She looked shocked by

the speed of events but her face was flushed and Rose thought she saw what might have been the beginning of hope.

After Rose had left the room, she and Miss Evans lingered outside the door and heard him say, 'You will love the farm, Letitia, and one day it will be yours. All of it. For you and your 'usband...'

As Letitia stammered her doubts he said, *'Mais oui, ma petite! Certainement.* You will find a better man in France. Frenchmen know 'ow to appreciate a woman! The English...!'

Rose imagined a Gallic shrug as he continued.

'This Bernard is weak! Pah! I spit on 'im! If I meet him, I knock him down!'

'Oh no!'

It was rather unconvincing, thought Rose.

'Mais oui! I am your father. I should do this! Who else will defend you, eh?'

Rose rolled her eyes, imagining just how soothing his words must be to Letitia's wounded pride, and she and Miss Evans exchanged delighted grins as they tiptoed further down the passage, the latter in search of four glasses.

Reaching the stairs, Rose rushed up to her room to tidy her hair and add a discreet touch of colour to her cheeks and lips.

It was Letitia's big moment, she told herself cheerfully but she, Rose, should at least look presentable.

Two days later only Marcus and Steven remained at Victoria House as Gerard had whisked his daughter away and Rose was invited to go with them. Marcus could have gone with them but he knew they were safe with Gerard and he wanted to make sure that Steven kept his side of the bargain and, if invited, turned up for the interview at the Royal Military Academy in Woolwich.

Marcus had finally completed his project for Swan Lake and made arrangements to take the designs to the theatre the following week. A letter arrived for him later in the day and he read it carefully before taking it along to Steven who was lounging on the sofa in the garden room, reading an account which Colonel Fossett had lent him, about the only Royal Artillery battery to be involved at Lucknow. Marcus was pleased to see that as the time drew nearer, Steven's interest in the army was growing and his arguments against enlisting no longer dominated their conversations.

Steven glanced up. 'You ought to read this, Marcus. All about the regiment. Widen your horizons! This chappie who won the Victoria Cross – he was only a captain. Captain F.C. Maude from the Royal Artillery. His was the only Royal Artillery battery at Lucknow. Colonel Fossett was there – all those years ago. He was a very junior officer then. It was a good show! Damned good!'

'I'll have a look through it,' Marcus told him, 'but at the moment there's some news from closer to home.' Marcus handed him the letter he had just received. 'It's from the da Silvas. I don't know what Letitia would make of it. I'd like to know what you think?' He sat down opposite his brother and watched as Steven began to read aloud.

Dear Marcus, Please forgive us for not being in contact before now but as you can imagine, life has been very difficult here...

Marcus said, 'As it has here!'

... and after the terrible business in the church we felt unable to face the rest of the world. Now, just as we hoped life might one day return to something akin to normality, we have to face another shock. Our son did not come down to breakfast this morning and we found a note on his bed. He and Carlotta have eloped without a word of warning...

He glanced up at Marcus. 'Good God! Is Bernard quite mad?'

Marcus shrugged. 'This Carlotta seems to have her claws in him. It all seems a bit hasty. Thank heavens Letitia is miles away. The details will leak out as they always do and everyone will be talking about it. Another juicy scandal!'

Steven read on.

297

We have no idea where they are and I suspect it will be some time before we hear from them. Suddenly we have lost our son and the realization is hard to bear. Our world appears to be falling apart and my husband is in a state of collapse. I am at my wits' end. I'm sure this news will not make your own difficulties any lighter but I thought you should be aware of the latest development. Sincerely and with deep regrets, Alicia da Silva...

Steven whistled with exasperation as he handed back the letter. 'I feel for them.'

Marcus nodded. For a while they were silent.

At last Marcus said, 'Do you think he really preferred her to Letitia?'

'Who knows?'

'Maybe Gerard was right and he *is* a weak man. Maybe Letitia is better off without him.'

Steven frowned. 'They may well disinherit him. It wouldn't be the first time it's happened. I wonder what Carlotta's family think about it. Damned awkward for them, too.'

'The question is, Steven, what shall we do about the letter? Letitia will have to know eventually.'

Steven frowned. 'Yes, but is this a good time? It might upset Letitia and Marie only has a few weeks left.'

'I think maybe we should save it until later – but only if you agree.'

Steven gave it some thought and nodded. 'You're right. I agree. Let's do it.'

As Marcus stuffed the letter into his pocket it dawned on him that this was the first time he had consulted with his brother on anything important to the family and that Steven had handled it well. As he turned to go he said impulsively, 'Thanks, Steven.'

'For what?'

'Oh ... you know. A problem shared...'

Steven's face lit up. 'Two heads are better than one – remember?'

'I'll remember.' Marcus grinned and was suddenly aware that a weight of responsibility had lifted from his shoulders. Steven was going to make it in the army, he decided. Somewhere, somehow, a corner had been turned.

Across the Channel, Letitia and Rose had risen early, because Jean-Philippe had decided to show them his village and this needed to done before he took his boat out for the afternoon's fishing. The village of Wissant was small but compact and centred round a large square where the fishing boats were parked between trips. Jean-Philippe did his best with very little English but Letitia had learned some French at her expensive boarding school many years earlier and somehow she now managed to translate Jean-Philippe's rapid conversation for the benefit of Rose.

'Launching the boats is difficult off this stretch of shore,' she told Rose, 'especially when there is a wind like today so the boats are wheeled into the sea on the trailers, and because there is no safe place to leave them between trips, they are wheeled back up the slope to the square and parked there until needed again.'

As she spoke, Letitia was trying, tactfully, to withdraw her hand from Jean-Philippe's. Rose didn't know whether to be amused or jealous. She was so accustomed to being the star attraction with her blonde curls, blue eyes and pretty features that it was a shock to realize that Gerard's friend had eyes for no one but Letitia. Mortified, she found herself trailing round in their wake as he hurried them through the main street which contained several small shops.

'*Boulangerie!*' Jean-Philippe pointed to it.

'Bakery,' Letitia translated for Rose's benefit.

'*Boulangerie* – bakery.' Rose nodded.

Jean-Philippe said, '*Hôtel!*'

'Hotel,' Rose echoed. 'Even I can understand that one!'

They stood by the river and stared across the millpond, listening to the rush of water as it was scooped up by the large wheel and returned, splashing and gurgling, to the river.

Letitia took a deep breath and said, *'Est-ce que c'est le moulin?'*

Jean-Philippe nodded, beaming with pleasure at her grasp of his native tongue.

Letitia rolled her eyes at Rose. 'I asked "Is that the mill?" and it is.'

'Moulin – mill.' Safe in the knowledge that their guide spoke so little English, Rose added, 'I think he has taken a fancy to you, Letitia.'

'Oh no!' She blushed. 'I am done with men. All men!'

They came to a parked boat from which the fisherman was selling his catch to a small queue of local people who, hearing an unfamiliar language, were watching the foreigners with cautious interest. They greeted Jean-Philippe with ready smiles and willingly made way for him as he bought some mussels and a crab. These he presented, roughly wrapped in a cloth, to Rose with rapid French which almost defeated Letitia.

'They are for our supper,' she said. 'At least, I think so.'

And I must carry the parcel, thought Rose, grinning, because Jean-Philippe cannot bear to release Letitia's left hand and she is holding on to her hat with her right hand!

Letitia said, 'Marie doesn't care for seafood but the rest of us like it.'

Rose nodded. She was starting to feel like the proverbial 'gooseberry' and was trying to find a way to send Jean-Philippe and Letitia off on their own. She said, 'Actually I am rather weary, Letitia. If you will forgive me, I'll buy myself a coffee and wait for you two to finish the sightseeing trip. Tell Jean-Philippe I am sorry but my heel hurts.'

To her relief Letitia made no protest. Rose watched as Letitia translated her polite lie and was a little miffed when she saw Jean-Philippe's eyes light up at the prospect of having Letitia to himself. He smiled at Rose, however, and gave her a charming bow before taking hold of Letitia's hand once more and spiriting her away.

Minutes later, sitting at a small table outside the tiny café, Rose sipped her coffee and thought about the Bennley family. Steven might well become a soldier, poor Marie would die, Letitia might stay here with her parents and Marcus would stay on at Victoria House with his design work for the theatres. She wondered how he would enjoy being alone.

Inside the cloth parcel, the crab began to fidget half-heartedly which disconcerted her and turned her thoughts from the Bennleys to the problems that she would face when she returned to England. She would have to find herself a home and a way to earn a living. She thought, with a shock, that without fully realizing it, she had decided that life on the stage was never going to be the way she had expected. Also that reading the

Bible to Mrs Granger might be her only real talent. Unless ... slowly but surely another idea was taking shape in her mind.

In Wissant that evening, the atmosphere was exciting, even though it was evident to everyone that Marie's weakness was increasing at an alarming rate, However, by tacit agreement, this was never referred to. They had eaten crab salad and followed that with a rabbit stew with rustic home-made bread, and the washing up had been done by Rose and Letitia. The latter was flushed and her eyes sparkled and Rose could see that the bitterness of the past years had been swept away by her reunion with her parents – and possibly by Jean-Philippe's very obvious admiration. Letitia, Rose thought, might well decide to stay for a while with her parents. What was there for her back in England except the reminders of heartache and the curious stares of sympathizers? Letitia and her parents had a great deal of lost time to make up for and Rose knew she would be travelling home alone, a prospect which, while it didn't enthral her, gave her no real anxiety.

On reflection, Rose was rather sorry that Gerard had been persuaded by his daughter not to confront Bernard da Silva as he had intended. Letitia had insisted that the violent confrontation, which Gerard had felt necessary, would simply supply their neighbours with more gossip and the idea had been reluctantly abandoned.

By nine o'clock they were all sitting outside in the cooler air, with the exception of Gerard who was enjoying his late night walk alone around his fields with a shotgun under his arm, checking, as usual, the safety of his animals and land.

Marie, wrapped in a blanket, had refused to go to bed and was reliving the excitement of the celebrations on Bastille Day.

'You should have been here,' she assured Rose and Letitia. 'It was a night to remember. Everyone gathered in the square in Wissant – which is more of a triangle than a square – for the little feast of bread and cheese or *moules* if you preferred them but I don't...'

Rose said, '*Moules?* Ah yes. Mussels.'

'And there were hot potatoes cooked in their jackets in the ashes of a big bonfire. Mmm!' She smiled at the memory. 'I don't like seafood but Mother had some and so did Papa. We sat under a big tent because it looked as if it might rain but it didn't. And afterwards there were fireworks and they were so brilliant and extravagant...'

Her mother said 'And noisy! It was deafening!'

Marie laughed. 'It was, wasn't it – and then that nice young man came to me and gave me a red rose! It was so romantic! And Jean-Philippe was there too and he has a

304

good singing voice and while we waited for the fireworks to begin he sang for us.'

Clarice said, 'He's going to call in again tomorrow.'

Letitia asked, 'Will he bring his wife?'

Marie laughed. 'He might if he had one but he's a bachelor. It's such a waste. Mother keeps telling him to settle down. She's becoming quite a matchmaker, aren't you Mother!'

'He's thirty-five. He should have a wife and family!'

'A shame, then,' Letitia said firmly, 'that I am quite finished with men!'

Rose cried, 'Please Letitia, don't say such a thing! Bernard's just the one bad apple in the barrel! And you're better off without him.'

An awkward silence fell because her remarks were the first mention she had made about Bernard's defection. To change the subject Rose said, 'What exactly is Bastille Day? It's to celebrate a battle, isn't it?'

Pleased to show off her knowledge of all things French, Marie said, 'The French call it the *Fête de la Fédération* and it's to celebrate the day the people stormed a prison and let out the prisoners and then the revolution started.'

Clarice smiled. 'July the fourteenth is very special to the French people.' She glanced at her youngest daughter. 'I think you should go to bed, Marie. You look tired and there will be plenty of time to talk tomorrow.'

Marie nodded unwillingly and allowed herself to be carried inside and Letitia volunteered to brush her hair before helping her into bed.

As Marie slipped down between the sheets she could hear the rest of the family making tracks for bed and closed her eyes. A little later she shared her prayers with her mother and then opened her eyes sleepily. 'I wish Marcus and Steven could have been here with us,' she said wistfully, 'but one day we shall all be together.'

'We will, my darling.' Clarice kissed her. 'Sleep now, Marie. If you need me, call me. Your bell is beside you.'

Much later Clarice woke to the sound of the bell and made her way into the small moonlit room.

'I had a strange dream, Mother,' Marie whispered. 'Will you stay a while and hold my hand?'

'Of course I will.' She leaned over and kissed her, then sat on the chair beside the bed. Taking Marie's fragile hand in hers, Clarice prepared to stay with her until she fell asleep but it was not to be. Somewhere around midnight she became aware of a slight change in Marie's breathing. Clarice's heart began to beat faster. Could she have imagined it?

'Marie?' she whispered.

'Mama, are you there?' The words were low but clear. Marie's eyes flickered open and closed again.

'I'm here, dearest.'

Having seen Clarice, Marie smiled faintly then gave a deep sigh. Her hand, already relaxed, became limp. Clarice's heart skipped a beat.

She waited. 'Oh Marie!'

As the minutes passed the warmth of life ebbed slowly from Marie's hand and Clarice pressed it to her lips.

'Goodbye, little one,' she said softly.

Shocked and grief-stricken, Clarice sat on dry-eyed through the long night until the prayed-for tears brought blessed relief.

Seven days later Marie's funeral was held in the church where she had been christened and confirmed. Clarice, Rose and Letitia had accompanied her coffin on the journey back to England but the following day Letitia and her mother returned to Wissant leaving Victoria House in the capable hands of Marcus.

After they had gone and Marie's body rested in the same grave as her grandparents, Steven and Marcus left it to Rose to see to the flowers that covered her last resting place. On Sunday July 27th Rose was kneeling beside the grave, removing any dead flowers, when the vicar found her. She stood up hastily, smiling.

'Miss Paton, isn't it?' he asked.

'Yes. Thank you for the service. Marie's mother felt she should return to the family – and the church at Wissant was Roman Catholic which would have been awkward. She and Letitia will come over to England more often now because they will want to visit the grave.'

'Marie is in God's hands now.'

Rose nodded. 'But I wish she wasn't, if you understand me, your Reverend ... No disrespect.'

'I do understand but we have to trust Him.' When she failed to agree he went on quickly. 'So there are just the two brothers left at Victoria House ... and your good self.'

He's wondering about me, thought Rose, unchaperoned with the two men. 'I'm staying there at the moment because I have nowhere else to go; where I was staying my friend was murdered but I shall find work soon and move on.' As she said it, her heart contracted a little at the thought that she would no longer be part of the Bennleys' circle but it was almost inevitable that she would have to leave. Unless ... She decided then and there to tackle Marcus later about her latest idea.

Mrs Bray was still not back at work and Miss Evans prepared them a simple supper of cold meats and salad. Later, in the study, they sat in silence, busy with their own thoughts. Marcus, slumped in his chair behind the desk, seemed preoccupied and Rose, on a chair in front of the desk, was feeling an unusual lack of self-confidence. Maybe today was not the right time, she told herself, wanting to delay the matter. She leaned forward, putting her elbows on the edge of the desk, and tried to read Marcus's expression. He looked harassed as usual.

He glanced at her. 'What's bothering you, Rose?'

'Bothering me?'

'You're not normally so quiet.' He smiled to show her that this was not an implied criticism.

'Ah!' It was now or never, she thought, and took a deep breath. 'Marcus, do you think Mrs Bray will ever come back?'

'I was wondering the same thing.' He sat back in his chair. 'The trouble is, Miss Evans told us from the start that she didn't want full-time work. She is actually a reasonably good artist and earns most of her money selling her watercolours but she isn't averse to earning a little extra now and then.'

Rose's hopes rose dramatically at his words. 'So you will need a new house-keeper?'

'It's beginning to look that way.'

'Could I do it, do you think? I could learn more recipes and there would mostly only be the two of us now that Steven is in the army. I can clean the house and do the washing ... If you gave me a room of my own you could take it out of my wages.'

There was an awkward silence.

She struggled on. 'I could do just mornings if you preferred ... or some days on and some days off. I'm quite adaptable. I would not get in your way and I would not touch your things in the study.'

His expression was unreadable. 'But Rose, what about your stage career?'

'Stage career? Oh that!' She rolled her eyes somewhat sheepishly. 'Actually I'm having second thoughts about that. Not that I couldn't make it to the top if I still wanted to,' she insisted hastily, 'but it seems you were right and it's not a very respectable way to earn a living and ... I wonder how many other Mr Markhams there are in the business, lurking about in the shadows. Poor Connie! I wouldn't want to end up like her.' She gave him an imploring look and shook her curls.

'It's a thought,' he said slowly, 'but there's another problem. You might get married and then...'

Rose felt the beginnings of panic. Somehow she had never anticipated marrying; had never imagined leaving them. Get married? Who on earth would she marry?

Marcus went on. 'If you did marry then we'd be left in the lurch, so to speak. At least, I would be left.' He picked up a pencil and began to doodle on the blotter. She watched hypnotized as he drew a row of small circles and then carefully filled them in.

Her hopes were fading. This was going to be harder than she expected. 'But I'd give you fair warning, Marcus. I mean, four weeks' notice or whatever it is you have to give. I'd never just leave you. Not all of a sudden. That wouldn't be right.'

'Hmm. Four weeks' notice. It's not much, is it?'

'Six weeks, then. Two months.'

He regarded her thoughtfully, running his fingers through his hair. 'There's another problem, Rose. *I* might marry – and then I'd have a wife and I wouldn't need a house-keeper. You'd be out of a job ... although I'd give you a good reference. I'd write a letter for you. I daresay you would soon find somewhere else.'

His words sent a cold shiver up Rose's spine. Why, she thought dazedly, had she never considered that he might marry? 'I see ... I never thought of you getting married.'

'I've never thought of you giving up your dream of the bright lights. Fame and for-tune. All those playbills saying "Starring Miss Lamore!" I can hardly believe that you're serious, Rose.'

The silence lengthened again. Rose tried to swallow but her throat was dry. She had convinced herself that he would allow her to stay on as his housekeeper. It had seemed an ideal arrangement. 'Well,' she said, with forced cheerfulness. 'It was just an idea. It wouldn't work, I can see that now. I have thought about offering myself as a permanent companion to Mrs Granger – the old lady I read to.'

She waited with bated breath for Marcus to try and dissuade her while she considered what she would do if the Grangers didn't want her. Andrew Markham had still not been traced by the police and the chances were they would give up their search. In which case there was always the possibility that he would come back at some time when Connie's death was no longer a priority for the police. Or Markham's brother might continue in his footsteps. That meant she could never set foot in Andy's Supper Room again. It had been a difficult decision but the truth was that the idea of a stage career had lost most of its glamour. There were obviously other routes to life on the stage but Rose's confidence had been badly shaken.

Marcus was studying the pencil with great intensity and she hid a smile. Only Marcus could find a pencil interesting, she thought, realizing suddenly how much she would miss his odd ways if she had to leave him. And how desperately jealous she would be of the woman he married.

Marcus took a deep breath. 'There's another possibility, of course. You might marry me and then I wouldn't need a housekeeper.'

Rose looked at him through narrowed eyes. Was he serious? Surely not.

With a quick glance at her, he went on. 'Not much of a prospect though, is it? I mean, hardly a tempting offer. The Bennleys are a rather ... How can I put it? Not exactly a successful family. So many problems. Unconventional is probably the kindest way to describe us.'

He twiddled with his pencil, stabbing the point into the blotter until it broke. After a moment he reached for a small penknife, opened it and began to sharpen the pencil.

He was avoiding her gaze and looked thoroughly ill at ease. Rose said gently, 'Don't be so hard on your family, Marcus. It's nobody's fault poor Marie died ... or that Bernard jilted Letitia.'

'Or that Steven ran up large debts and has been forced by me into joining the army!'

'You did what you thought was best for him. It will be good for him.'

'I'm wondering what will happen next.' He sighed heavily. 'Maybe we're accident-prone.'

He looked so wretched that Rose began to worry about him in earnest. 'Is it because of your mother and Gerard? They seem very happy. I know your mother left you but not until you were able to survive without her ... and she owed it to Gerard who had lived all those years without anyone to love. She had a terrible choice to make.'

'It just seems to me that being a family is fraught with difficulties. Look at your family.'

'We'll survive,' she said hopefully. 'Life's never perfect, is it? Everyone has failures and ... and disappointments. We all make mistakes.'

'I worry about Letitia. She will probably die an old maid.'

'Die an old maid?' Rose laughed. 'She will do no such thing! Your sister is going to marry Jean-Philippe. She doesn't know it yet but he took one look at her and was totally smitten. I mean it, Marcus. I have seen the writing on the wall.'

'Jean-Philippe? I don't believe it. He's a fisherman.'

'But he's a successful fisherman – and what's more he's a happy, honest man and he loves her. I saw it in his eyes, Marcus, and I was so envious. It was so ... so *romantic*! No man has ever looked at me that way. Jean-Philippe is ten times the man Bernard is!' Seeing that he looked unconvinced she said, 'Wait and see, Marcus. Before too long there'll be a letter in the post telling us the news. At the moment Letitia is still in a state of shock from the wedding disaster and still believes she is pining for Bernard but...'

To her surprise, Marcus was shaking his head. 'She will know by now that there is no hope for her there.'

'We don't know that for sure, Marcus. He might suggest they try and work through this setback. After all—'

'No, Rose. It won't have a happy ending.' Briefly he told her about the letter from Alicia da Silva which he had forwarded to Wissant.

To his surprise, when Rose had recovered from the shock, she almost cheered at the news. 'Letitia would never have been able to trust him,' she declared firmly, 'and Bernard might always have had lingering regrets. Not to mention Carlotta who might have done her best to drive a wedge between them. Letitia will be much happier with Jean-Philippe.' She smiled. 'It was *meant*, Marcus. Do you see? Sometimes Fate steps in and turns everything upside down!'

He looked doubtful. 'So ... if you're right, Letitia will never live here again?'

'I doubt it. She will live in Wissant near your mother and Gerard ... and one day, no doubt, the farm will be hers.'

'Oh dear! Then I shall live here all on my own!' He looked shaken. 'What a bleak prospect.'

'You'll have the housekeeper,' she said innocently.

Rose saw that his hands were shaking. Without looking up he said, 'If you married me, Rose, you could stay here and keep me company ... You'd have to be a little mad to even think of such a thing. I can't compete

315

with the romantic Jean-Philippes of this world but...'

Rose stood up, leaned across the desk and gently took the penknife and the pencil from him and laid them down. 'I think I've always been a little mad,' she said softly. 'You may have noticed.'

Marcus looked up at last. 'Rose, this is serious. I'm asking you to marry me. Are you saying "Yes"?'

'I don't know ... I need some time to think about it...' She closed her eyes, then immediately opened them. 'There. I've thought about it long and hard and the answer's "Yes". Is that serious enough for you?'

'And you won't change your mind?'

'How could I? I seem to have fallen in love with you.'

He gave a deep sigh of relief, pushed back his chair and came round the desk, a tentative smile on his face. 'I'm afraid Mrs Marcus Bennley doesn't have the same ring as "Miss Rosie Lamore" but—'

'No, it doesn't but –' Rose threw her arms around him – 'I may be able to live with the disappointment!'

A year later almost to the day, there had been some changes in all their lives. Mrs Bray had returned for a final six weeks in order to give Rose cookery lessons, before retiring.

Rose, a harassed expression on her face,

was creating a game pie when Steven came into the kitchen. He kept well away from the table as he turned round to show off his uniform. On leave for the weekend, he was keen to impress the few members of the household who remained in Victoria House.

Mrs Bray, her hands on her hips, said, 'Well, you do look smart! Have you shown yourself off to your brother yet?'

Steven grinned, nodding. 'He managed to tear himself away from his latest design to give me a quick glance.'

'And said what?' Rose abandoned her pastry while she inspected him.

'Marcus thinks a few medals would do wonders for the outfit!'

'Medals?' Mrs Bray tossed her head. 'You have to earn them first!'

'Give me a chance, Mrs Bray. I haven't seen any action yet.'

Rose said, 'Well, I think you look very good, Steven. Lord help the enemy when you go into battle.'

'But it suits you,' Mrs Bray told him. 'Army life is a world of its own. I always thought you'd make a splendid officer. I shall tell my mother when I get home this evening. I've told her about you and she's very interested. Both her brothers were soldiers.'

Rose lifted a floury hand to point to the dresser. 'There's a letter from Letitia on the dresser. She's still taking French lessons and—'

He frowned. 'Is she still converting to the Roman Catholic church? It seems very dramatic – oh yes, I know. It's to please Jean-Philippe and her father but is it right for her?'

Rose shrugged. 'She promised him before they were married that she would consider it and now she's very willing. It matters more now because of the baby they're expecting. His family are all Catholics and Letitia wants to blend in. Mother doesn't seem worried. She says Letitia's very wholehearted and is embracing all things French.'

Mrs Bray said, 'A friend of mine converted at the age of nine when she was adopted by a Catholic family and she says it didn't make much difference. As long as you believe in something – that's what I say.'

Steven looked at Rose's creation. 'You'd better get on with that pie, Rose. I shall be starving by the time it's ready. Life in the army does that to you. It's all the exercise and rushing to and fro.' He glanced at the clock on the wall. 'I'll read Letitia's letter later. I thought I'd go along to Marie's grave now. Shall I take some fresh flowers?'

Rose said, 'Oh yes please! If you wait I'll cut some roses.'

She looked appealingly at Mrs Bray who said, 'You run along. I'll finish the pie.'

'Bless you!' Rose hurried out into the garden.

318

Steven watched as the housekeeper brushed the pie with egg and milk.

Mrs Bray looked up at him. 'Is she going to wed your brother or isn't she? I can't bear the suspense!'

He grinned. 'Of course she is but they're in no hurry. They're taking time to get to know each other ... and you, Mrs Bray, will receive an invitation to the wedding. That goes without saying.'

'That's all right then!' Mrs Bray's smile broadened. She opened the oven door. 'Lunch at one, remember. I hope the army has taught you to be punctual! You don't want to be late for Rose's first game pie!'

'I wouldn't dare!' he laughed.

NK 11/15 .

β087